TEARS OF ABRAHAM

SEAN T. SMITH

A POST HILL PRESS BOOK

ISBN (trade paperback): 978-1-61868-819-4
ISBN (eBook): 978-1-61868-818-7

TEARS OF ABRAHAM
© 2016 by Sean T. Smith
All Rights Reserved

Cover Design by Christian Bentulan

Post Hill Press
275 Madison Avenue, 14th Floor
New York, NY 10016
posthillpress.com

Often, that which is done cannot be undone. Sometimes a pebble unleashes a landslide; a small object becomes unstoppable, smashing and sliding and gathering momentum until chaos pulverizes everything. When the dust settles, there is a new landscape, crushed and snapped and desolate, which surely the pebble did not intend. The illusion of control can be more destructive than nature itself, when hubris convinces men to believe the lies they tell themselves.

It began with a few powerful men, tinkering and arrogant, manipulating and prodding. Wealth and power, unfettered by wisdom and conscience, smashed the United States of America. History now remembers the conflict as the second American Civil War, although there were many citizens who then fervently believed they were fighting a revolution.

The first Civil War cost the lives of more than 600,000 people, and was the bloodiest conflict in our country's history. The second war was worse.

CHAPTER ONE

The Major Malfunction

GREAT FALLS, MONTANA

December 5, 2024

Henry hunched over the wooden bar and took a pull of draft beer. Country music blasted from the jukebox in the corner and three air force pilots at the other end of the bar ordered shots of tequila. The dive was smoky and dark and the air stank of bar rot. Outside, the wind moaned while a blizzard dumped snow on the Montana town.

The divorce papers under Henry's parka were heavy and seemed to burn. Maybe he should have seen it coming, but he didn't and now he felt betrayed and desolate. The papers were dated three weeks earlier, but he'd just gotten them because it took time to track him down. He'd read the document three times, staring and barely comprehending while the weight of the words penetrated his brain. His wife was demanding full custody of Taylor, giving him only limited visits with his baby girl. The complaint, on stark black and white letterhead, listed verbal abuse and PTSD to justify the inevitable *irreconcilable differences*.

1

What is wrong with me? Something is broken, misfiring. Not just one thing, maybe.

A darkness had crawled into Henry, an alien, invasive thing, and he'd never faced the truth of it until now, realizing he'd lost the love of his life. He was not sure how long the darkness had been there lurking around the nooks and crannies of his soul. Years. It had been eating away at him and he hadn't wanted to admit it. Destroying him from within while he fought for his country; it was insidious and cruel, a killing poison.

"Hey, soldier," one of the pilots shouted. "Have a shot on me.

"No thanks, man," Henry replied.

"Just drink it. We're celebrating."

"No," Henry said.

He needed to be left alone to think. Was there any way he could win Suzanne back? Were they that far gone now? There had to be something he could do. He could change. He could leave the Wolves. Settle down in Key West with her and Taylor and leave his uniform for good. Banish that darkness inside with sunshine. He loved her with a fierceness that surprised him sometimes, and he was certain, for all the distance and strife between them, that she loved him too. She'd given up on him, and he could understand why. He was convinced, though, that she wanted to believe again. He had to give her a good reason.

The pilots swaggered down the bar and plopped onto stools next to him.

"You're a southern boy," one of them said. "What do you think about this secession business?"

Henry clenched his jaw. It was all over the news.

"I'd rather not talk about it, guys. Just minding my own business."

"I'll bet you're all for it, huh?"

"You're drunk, and I'm out," Henry said. He stood up, left a twenty on the bar, and attempted to walk away.

"What's the matter," the oldest of the pilots said, in Henry's face now, eyes bloodshot and eager. "You some kind of lefty? You *like* these fascists?"

The pilot shoved Henry on the shoulder.

Henry Wilkins was not the kind of man to start a fight, but he'd ended a few. He tried to step around the pilots.

The young guy wound up for a swing. So be it.

Henry punched him in the throat and smashed the older guy in the face with an elbow. The third pilot tried to crack Henry over the head with a bottle of Budweiser. Henry stepped forward into the blow. The glass bottle smacked Henry in the eye, and he staggered backwards, Roman candles exploding his skull.

"Now you're gonna hurt," the pilot said, eyes raging as he coiled for another attack.

Henry lashed out with his knee, catching the man in the crotch. The pilot doubled over in pain and he howled when Henry pounded him on both ears.

The three pilots were on the ground, writhing and groaning, when Henry walked out of the bar and into the snow. The sheriff picked him up before he made it to the street. The bartender must have called before the fight began. Maybe she knew those boys on the floor.

*

Henry Wilkins opened his right eye at the sound of keys jangling against the metal bars of the cell. His other eye seemed glued shut, encrusted with blood and swollen. His back ached from sleeping on a metal slab.

Uh-oh.

Colonel Bragg, wearing combat fatigues and a murderous scowl, towered just outside the cell. Beside the colonel, a full-bellied, red-faced local sheriff fumbled with a key ring.

Henry pushed himself to his feet, had to catch his balance on the concrete wall, before managing a salute.

"Sir," he said. Henry's voice was raw.

"What is your major malfunction?" the colonel growled. He was not screaming. That was not his way. He was straight backed and quiet now.

"Sir, I do apologize, I know I—"

"You apologize? You're sorry? "

The sheriff slid the steel door open. Henry remained standing, staring into the face of disappointment, anger, and disgust, the colonel boring into him with these things in no particular order.

"He's all yours," the sheriff said. The colonel and the sheriff turned heel.

Henry followed Colonel Bragg through the hallway, a booking room, and then out the front door into the snow. The wind whipped his face, but that was nothing compared to the lashing he knew he was about to receive. A navy-blue Crown Vic waited in the parking lot; a uniformed driver kept the engine idling. The colonel stepped into the front seat, and Henry slid into the back.

The colonel swiveled, training baleful eyes upon Henry. "With all that's going on in the country right now, you decide to get into a fight off base? I don't care that your team wasn't on deck; you know better."

"Sir—"

"Stow it, Wilkins. To say I'm deeply disappointed in you doesn't begin to get it. The last thing this unit needs right now is any kind of scrutiny. If I didn't need every man right now, I'd boot you. I still might."

"Yes, sir."

"I don't care what you've got going on in your personal life. You are elite. Act like it."

"Copy that, sir."

"You will be confined to quarters until further notice." The voice of seething wrath was barely contained.

"Yes sir." Henry took it. He accepted this because it was fair.

The sedan wound through gray streets and the tires made a hissing sound on the wet Montana road. Henry's head pounded in rhythm to the windshield wipers slapping back and forth while big flakes swirled in the pale morning light. The main gate to Malmstrom Air Force Base was just ahead. O-six-hundred. He'd been in jail since about midnight.

Henry wanted to explain that while he knew there were no excuses, there were reasons, and that's not quite the same thing. There was context, at least. He wanted to tell Colonel Bragg that Suzanne had served him with divorce papers the morning before, that she was trying to take his child from him. Tell the colonel the last op they'd gone on was wrong. That he was sick and tired of following orders that came down from desk warriors and politicians who seemed bent on getting people killed for no reason. That those pilots he'd left on the barroom floor had it coming, and he hadn't gone looking for a fight. That he was hurting, and it was more than his marriage inflicting the pain.

Suzanne was in Key West, writing her romance novels and basking in the sun while Henry had been hunting down terrorists from Kabul to Rio to Cheyenne. When he thought about that, the serpentine thing coiled around his heart seemed to convulse, and his vision narrowed, tinged with red and violence.

They'd been married for eleven years, and most of them were good ones. They were a team, the two of them against the world. She endured the frequent moves and long deployments. She used to wait on the tarmac for him with a sign saying "Welcome Home!" and then wrap her arms around him with fervent kisses and then they'd stay in bed for a week. She'd lie on his chest and listen to his stories and jokes and he'd run his fingers through her long honey hair and she would make him feel whole again. They talked about her writing and built castles in the clouds together, the vacations they would take, the boat on davits at a dock they would build where the water was warm, and she was beautiful and he was good.

When he'd separated from the 75th and joined the Wolf Pack, she'd been happy for him. When she wanted to purchase a home in Key West to be closer to her father, he acquiesced, even though it meant most of the time he was alone in Tennessee in a dismal one-bedroom flat. When Taylor had been born, Henry was terrified and overjoyed; something seemed to shift or tear in Suzanne. Resentment began to creep in to her eyes and she started using words like "incompatible," and when he came home from an operation, sometimes the house was dark. They argued about politics. They fought over money. When they had no money, they hadn't cared about it. Now that she was earning six-figure advances, it was an issue. Henry recognized that while they argued over money, the real issue was his job. Money seemed to be a way of fighting about it without actually addressing the underlying problem.

He planned on getting out of the Pack, working the dive and fishing charter business with his old friend Bart, but then the country started to slide into hell, and Henry couldn't justify quitting. He felt needed. He loved his country in a way that transcended duty, and he loved his brothers-in-arms. The domestic terror attacks, the hate groups, images of slain children kept him awake at night. He could not walk away. He was a warrior.

Now he was paying for it.

The last time he'd seen Suzanne, back in October, he'd seen hardness in her eyes, a resolution.

"Are you having an affair?" he'd said.

They were lounging at the pier in Key West, watching a glorious sunset, drinking frozen margaritas. A band was massacring a Jimmy Buffet song, and the air smelled like conch fritters and coconut oil. She was lithe and tan in a sundress. She knew he hated tourists and crowds, but she had wriggled and cajoled and made it clear she was ready for a date night.

He had to ask. "So?"

"Don't be ridiculous," she said.

"Well, there's something."

"I'm just busy with my book tour."

"You sure?"

"I'm sure. Let's dance."

"If you're not happy, tell me, for God's sake. There's something."

"No. You're just jumpy. Realizing you don't deserve me." She giggled and kissed him on the mouth, and she tasted like tequila and lust and hope.

Over the last year, he'd felt her eyes, though, flat with veiled disdain when she thought he wasn't looking, smelled the condescension at wine tastings and book releases and art galleries. He'd heard the snickers and she'd heard the screaming in the middle of the night. And he'd endured because that's what you do. Soldier on; find your balls, never quit.

The first question from one of these clowns was always, "So what do you do in the army?"

"Logistics and support," was the pat answer. He couldn't tell the truth. Interest would fade, the condescension would begin, and Henry would watch it happen, predictable and infuriating and full of pretentious merlot and cheese. He did not care what those fools thought about him, but it *did* matter what the love of his life believed. She knew he was involved in special operations of some sort, but she resented it.

And then, there with the Key West sunset and the music and margaritas and long blonde hair, she'd seemed to be all right and not so distant. She'd pressed herself against him and the sky was painted pink and purple and there was a baby at home he wanted to get to know better. He'd pushed his doubts back behind carefully constructed walls, subdued the darkness.

*

The sedan deposited Henry in front of the barracks he shared with thirty other members of the Wolves for the moment. Colonel Bragg had no more harsh words, probably because he was engaged in a heated conversation with some egghead at NSA over his comm. The chain of command was getting complicated, but that was beyond Henry's pay grade.

Henry staggered into the spartan building, found his rack, and collapsed into it. The long room held two rows of bunks, and the soldiers slept and tossed and snored and cursed in their sleep.

He closed his eyes. His head throbbed from the blow he'd gotten from the bottle. He had regrets, and there was no way for him to escape the consequences.

If only . . . Two of the sorriest, whiniest, most pathetic words in the English language. If only what? If Texas hadn't decided to secede from the United States . . . If that last op here in Montana had gone differently . . . If I hadn't joined the Wolves . . . If Momma hadn't been a worthless pill head who ran out on her family . . . If Dad had been around more instead of banging nails to keep a roof over my head.

If only, then what? The world is tough, and there's nothing that's supposed to be easy about it. You pick yourself up and you soldier on and suck it up.

Henry despised self-pity. He preferred self-denial, self-control, and self-confidence. His father had instilled this in him from the time Henry could walk. His chosen family, the United States Army, had reinforced it. His experience in war taught him the virtues of following his personal creed: *"You may destroy me but you will not defeat me."* He'd stolen that from Hemingway, *The Old Man and the Sea*. It captured how he looked at life. Santiago fighting a perfect fish and sharks and time, and even at the end, not giving in to any of it. Undefeated because that's how he *chose* to see it. Prepare for the next fight. Get up and grab your nuts and get ready for the next battle until you can't do it anymore because you're dead. Somewhere in there, if you're lucky and strong and disciplined, there would be some glory in living. But you damn sure don't sit around feeling sorry for yourself, because when the moment comes for a perfect sunset, you miss the light and color. You miss it because you're too busy embracing the darkness inside.

Colonel Bragg made a valid point. Henry seemed to have a major malfunction, and he needed to fix it.

The country he loved had a major malfunction, too, but Henry was too exhausted to contemplate choices and consequences on that scale and he slept.

*

Henry dreamed about Operation Snowshoe. His dream was factual, for the most part, although some things did not happen exactly the way he dreamed.

The Montana ground was flat and covered with snow and the world was shades of green and white. The heads-up display on his contact lenses was equipped with microchips connected wirelessly to a relay implanted in his neck. The HUD relayed a constant stream of information. He could switch from his own field of sight to views from any of the hundred drones in the area, and cycle through infrared and heat signatures with no more than a thought. The Integrated Infantry Combat System, or ICS, allowed him to communicate with his fellow soldiers on the ground, command, and any other assets involved in the assault. The HUD revealed more than three hundred people in the compound ahead. There were guards in towers, and four on a perimeter patrol. Most of the people were sleeping.

In Montana, as always, there were few assets because the operation was not actually taking place in the eyes of the military or the government. Plausible deniability was the reason the Pack had been formed. More clandestine than the Navy SEALs or even Delta, the Wolves existed to solve problems within the United States, the kinds of problems that could not be dealt with by courts, local police, or the media. They crushed violent threats to the United States of America by any means necessary. Intelligence from the FBI, Homeland Security, the CIA, and the NSA filtered into the small, nondescript headquarters of the force, located in Nashville, Tennessee. They were ostensibly attached to the Tennessee Air National Guard. Aerial operations were often supported by the Night Stalkers out of Fort Campbell. They usually traveled via commercial aircraft, sitting beside unsuspecting civilians on the way from Nashville to Phoenix or New York or Billings. In two years with the Wolves, Henry had inserted by submarine, ultralight, and parachute into places where men tried to kill him when he got there. In Montana, he and the other members of the Wolf Pack had fast-roped from stealthy Blackhawks modified with ceramic tiles and quiet engines.

They'd humped it for a few miles over rolling hills and deep snow until the compound came into sight, then set up a perimeter for the assault.

The drones, each roughly the size of a bumblebee, flitted throughout the compound, relaying precise, real-time information on the position of targets. Some of the drones flew down the air-filtration system into the labyrinth underground, where the group of rebels had converted an ICBM missile complex into a fortress. The government had been selling those off for years to civilian bidders.

In this particular complex, there were houses aboveground, and there were children sleeping in those houses.

"Bugs in position," came the voice in his head. The ICS allowed wireless signals to be interpreted as sound, thanks to the embedded chip connected to Henry's brain. "Confirmation acquired. Radioactive materials, firearms, and munitions stockpiles."

"Range, one hundred meters," Henry said, although he did not actually speak. He thought, and the thought was converted to speech. It had taken practice and training; eventually he'd gotten used to it and no longer felt uncomfortable utilizing the system. His life depended upon it.

"Wolf One, clear to engage," came the reply.

Henry crossed the open ground, the world still and silent in crisp shades of green and white. His snowshoes impeded his progress only slightly, and his steps were deliberate and sure. Two targets in a guard tower went down. The suppressed weapons carried by the soldiers muted both sound and muzzle flashes. The Wolves closed in for the kill. People in the buildings were up and moving around. They had been alerted to the attack, through motion sensors, pressure detectors, or drones of their own.

Two men came from the door of the nearest squat building, assault rifles in their hands. Henry fired as he came forward. A short burst for each man. The suppressor making a metallic cough in the green night, the submachine gun bucking against his shoulder. Henry kept moving ahead, switching his vision so that he could see the heat signatures behind the walls ahead. Bodies, some tall and some small, milling about. More heading for the door. Henry dropped to one knee. Thirty meters.

A knot of men emerged from the building, firing automatic weapons into the darkness. Henry heard the rounds zipping over his head like angry hornets. His weapon bucked and clacked, and his fellow soldiers fired and kept moving forward the way they had been trained to do. The men emerging from the building died before they took three paces.

"Bugs are hot," said the voice in Henry's head.

"Negative! Negative!" he screamed back with a scream that was not vocalized but was searing thought. They could clear the buildings aboveground themselves. No reason to use the bugs. Mission objectives were to neutralize the threat posed by the group and gather intel on related militia groups. There weren't supposed to be kids here.

The drones did what they did best. They killed. Some of them were armed with high explosives, some with a single charge. All were locked on to targets, some big and some small.

There was screaming and burning, and sometimes it was Henry and sometimes it wasn't, but in his dream, it was all one.

KEY WEST, FLORIDA

Suzanne's air was low and she was deeper than she should have been. *Hold still, damn you! I've followed you all over this reef and you refuse to act like a grouper. Turn, there you go. Look at me, nice and slow.* The large fish hovered above a bleached-out mound of coral, turning with effortless grace, presenting his head to her.

She had chased the fish down the sloping reef from a depth of sixty feet to more than one hundred forty. The sea fans, all shades of blue, did not care, nor did the snapper, or the moray eel poking its head from a hole. Death was part of life in the ocean, and the reef was a constant riot of killing and fleeing.

The school of barracuda hovering to the right, torpedoes with teeth, waited. They knew an easy meal when they saw one, and there was nothing easier than picking off a speared fish. She'd seen it enough to know. They flashed quick and silver and strong, predators, scavengers, hunters. She hoped they would lose interest, but they'd hung around. She could not shoot the grouper, hang around at two safety stops, and then bring the fish back onto the boat. The fish would be gone. Just the head left, if she was lucky.

She checked her air one last time, looked at the waiting barracuda, and bade farewell to her grouper. She began to kick toward the surface, letting air bleed into her BC to increase buoyancy. Not in any hurry, watching her bubbles rise around her at the same pace, and listening to the crackling of the reef as parrotfish ate at it and motors plowed over it. She found the anchor line, added more air from her tank as she floated up toward the surface. At the first safety stop, she noticed her air was below 400 psi. She slowed her breathing and looked down at the reef below while she hung in the water, floated with the marvelous sense of weightlessness that came with neutral buoyancy. And she thought about Henry.

She loved him; that had never changed. But she couldn't be married to him. When he was home he was brooding, prone to violent outbursts. He had changed. When he'd come home from a long deployment, back when he was still an Army Ranger, she knew he would be moody while he decompressed. He would adjust, and she was patient with him, and every time, the old Henry would emerge, a slow transformation, the sun burning through fog until it was full light.

Since he'd joined the Wolf Pack, there was less and less sunlight. Perhaps he took issue with what he was doing, but if so, he could never tell her. They no longer spoke about what it was he did for a living. There were occasional stories about fellow teammates, and how they'd seen this or that thing, but he couldn't even tell her where he'd been. Communication was reduced to small talk. It was killing both of them.

She'd been trying to make it work, fighting for Henry, but she was sure he did not see it. He perceived threats. He accused her of having an affair, not realizing the real threat came from him.

The Pack had become a mistress, cruel and demanding and all consuming. There was nothing left of Henry to give her when he was home. She'd filed for divorce because she saw this would never change. Hope was gone. He would never leave his brothers. There would always be a crisis somewhere that kept pieces of him, stole parts of his soul.

And now, with talk of open war within the country, she knew it would be even worse. Whatever it was he did, he would be gone. She would be alone with Taylor. She decided it would be for the best to formalize the end. He would feel betrayed, blindsided. She didn't see any other way.

Suzanne drifted up to fifteen feet for the last safety stop, checked her watch and her air. It was going to be close. The surface was light and the water gentle and she could hear the waves slap the hull of the boat. The school of barracuda had risen from the depths with her, and they eyed her with toothy curiosity as they floated through the clear ocean.

CHAPTER TWO

Irreconcilable Differences

MALMSTROM AIR FORCE BASE, MONTANA

Henry sat up in his rack, the familiar sound of packing, clinking, and rustling in the barracks. He opened the footlocker at the base of the bed and took out a fresh uniform. His fatigues bore no insignia of rank, unit, or even branch. Nothing had come over the comm, but something was happening. The men were preparing for a fight. He'd find out soon enough.

He strapped a holster to his right thigh along with a Beretta 9mm pistol with extended magazine. His Tac V assault vest contained additional magazines for the nine mil, and also longer mags for the Heckler & Koch MP7/10A4 submachine gun. His black Nomex coveralls were lightweight yet resistant to wind, water, and cold. He bloused them into his assault boots.

His head was clear and he moved with focus and practiced efficiency. Gadget bags on his vest contained flashlights, lighters, maps, a med kit, suppressors for his sidearm, and the submachine gun. He also had advanced optics for the HK. He carried flash bangs and three frags in pouches on his left hip. He hadn't heard anything over the comm, but the tension in the barracks buzzed and throbbed.

His rucksack contained a lightweight tent, duct tape, emergency SATCOM, gloves, MREs, a full water bladder, and more magazines.

Despite the amount of gear he carried, it was still less than what he'd grown accustomed to as a Ranger. It came to slightly over sixty pounds, much of it in the extra magazines.

"Whoa, Sleeping Beauty, nice of you to join the living," Carlos said, lacing up his boots. Carlos was the largest man in the unit, a towering black man with thickly corded muscles at his neck, shoulders, chest, and, it seemed, eyelids. Muscle layered upon muscle. Henry was smaller, leaner, at only six feet tall and less than two hundred pounds. The men in the unit tended to be of middle height and weight. The really big guys couldn't usually handle the endless humping and running the training entailed. Carlos could, though.

"What's happening?"

"Dunno. Base is swarming with activity. Nothing on the comm. Can't reach Big Dog." Big Dog, or Alpha Dog, was what the men called Colonel Bragg. It was mostly a term of endearment. Mostly.

"What's got everybody so spooked?" The Wolves never kitted up at a military installation unless they were about to go on an operation, and they never went on an op without hours of briefings beforehand and usually at least a week of mission-specific training and rehearsal. "It's all over the net," Carlos said, looking up at Henry from his boots. "There's gonna be war for sure now. The entire southern block of senators and representatives just walked out of emergency meetings in Congress. A lot of the western states are with them."

"Good God," Henry said. He'd really thought Congress would figure this out, despite all the rhetoric plaguing the country.

"Exactly. In case you hadn't noticed, we're *in* a western state. Montana doesn't care much for Washington these days."

"But on base?"

"Hey, soldiers are from everywhere. If the base commander is sympathetic to the separatists, well, that ain't good, now is it?"

Henry thought about what that might mean. Carlos spelled it out for him.

"They might be rounding people up; trying to make us choose sides. You're a good ole boy from Georgia, so you might be all right. They might not take kindly to me, being from New York. Then again, being that none of us are even *in* the army or air force, we may have a problem. They'll figure out we work for DC."

"I thought we all did."

"You know what I mean."

Henry walked to the bank of windows and looked out at the base. There wasn't much to see. The buildings were low and gray, and snow covered the ground. His breath fogged the window, and he stepped back, noting the pair of helicopters sweeping overhead.

*

Secession had been discussed openly for more than a decade, at first only by politicians on the fringes of sanity. Henry, along with the rest of the country, assumed clear heads would prevail. But as the middle class shrank, the idea of secession began to seem possible, if still insane. The schism within the Republican Party left the party vulnerable and floundering. Democrats had been in control of the White House for almost twenty years. The influx of immigrants into the country, combined with a lack of clear purpose from Republicans, enabled the Democrats to maintain control of the executive branch, and the country was mired in mudslinging and angry discourse while few laws of use were passed.

Liberals pointed fingers at conservatives, claiming the Republicans were obstructionist, favored the wealthy, and were motivated by religious zeal. Conservatives howled that the ivory tower liberals were socialists bent upon destroying the country, stripping individuals and states of rights. In Henry's opinion, both sides made some valid points. The ban on handguns, an executive order that went into effect on December 1, two weeks ago, seemed to be the final straw.

Much of the country felt that the federal government no longer existed to serve the will of the people and viewed the continued intrusions of the government into their lives with hatred. The media on both sides elevated the rhetoric, pandering to paranoia, inflaming passions, creating the illusion of a world of black and white.

The divisions within the country were not reduced to geography; the racial divides between Anglos and everyone else were a great part of the unrest. In much of the nation, white people were now in the minority, and they didn't care for that. The growing disparity of wealth was a part of it, too, and the richest segments of society continued to pull away from the rest, retreating into gated enclaves with private security and cameras.

Militia groups popped up in every part of the country; most of them were vocal but nonviolent and consisted of doomsday preppers and gun-rights folks. They were loyal citizens who loved America, and were stressed and worried about the future of the country. But as time passed, a few groups began to take action. White Pride organizations saw their membership rolls swell. There were bombings and sniper sprees and assassinations. The federal government responded by increasing domestic surveillance and tightening restrictions on firearms. By 2016, more than 30,000 unmanned drones proliferated over US airspace. Now, in the last month of 2024, the number had tripled. Big Brother was indeed watching.

Henry had no problem taking down a terrorist cell bent upon destruction. He'd seen the stockpiles of ammunition, the heavy machine guns, mustard gas, dirty bombs, and even some biological weapons like anthrax in the hands of extremist groups. He believed he was saving lives.

Until the last op in the hills to the north, children had never been harmed. He believed in the preservation of the Union, but now he was questioning his role. The unit was unconstitutional, and while he'd justified it in his mind in the past, he was increasingly uncomfortable. He knew he was not alone in his thinking.

The comm implanted in his head came to life.

"Big Dog en route. Prepare to extract."

There was a kind of clicking sound in his head Henry had never heard before.

"ICS no longer secure." That explained the sound. An un-hackable system had been hacked.

Henry shouldered his ruck and weapon.

Somewhere outside, the sound of gunfire echoed from buildings. At first, just a few rounds. Then it became more urgent, the rolling chaos of a full-blown firefight.

Henry helped overturn bunks to make some cover. The Wolves were skittish, communicating with hand signals. Some of the men took up positions near the rows of windows, back far enough so they would be harder to see, but placed so that they could cover the snow-covered grounds outside.

Henry took position just inside the doorway, off to the side, his submachine gun slung over his neck with a strap.

The firefight subsided outside the barracks and there was the sound of shouting and the rumble of helicopters and the scream of jets. The idea of American troops firing on one another was unthinkable. Shattering.

Sergeant Major Alex Martinez, from his position near one of the windows said, "Two birds inbound. They're ours."

Henry recognized the distinct sound of the stealth helicopters. He leaned around the door frame. The rotor wash from the birds blew snow into the air as they touched down. He could not see any other soldiers outside.

"Move out!" Sergeant Major Martinez ordered.

Henry jogged toward the LZ and then halted, crouched on one knee, weapon at ready, providing cover for his fellow operators. The men who had been on his heels out the door did the same.

Less than a mile away, something exploded. Maybe a bomb, perhaps an ordinance dump. The Wolves bounded forward and climbed into the waiting helicopters.

An armored personnel carrier lumbered around one of the nearby buildings off to Henry's right flank, close enough that he could see the gunner on top. A gunner behind a .50-cal, the long barrel swiveling.

Henry was out in the open courtyard, no cover to hide behind. The helicopters were on the ground and vulnerable. The APC had them dead to rights.

Henry ran, that naked feeling in him, the sense of being a target, being hunted and waiting for hot metal to cut him in half. The APC never opened up. Henry jumped into the nearest Blackhawk, strong hands pulling him onto the flight deck as the bird lifted. He turned once he was fully aboard, looking over the door gunner's shoulder as the base swept past below. Smoke roiled over the airstrips in the distance, oily and dark, and some of the buildings on the base were burning.

In less than a minute, the helicopter was over wilderness, white and green and eternal, and the chaos of the base was behind them. The pilot flew nap of the earth, skimming the treetops and hugging the terrain. Henry held on to a strap mounted to the ceiling as the bird banked and dipped and his stomach lurched.

After half an hour, the pilot seemed to relax, and the flight became less white-knuckled. Sergeant Major Martinez grinned at him.

"You all right, Wilkins? Ya look a little green around the gills."

"Good to go, sir," Henry said. "What the hell is going on?"

"Dunno," Martinez said. "You know as much as I do. Big Dog is in the other bird. I guess he'll fill us in."

Carlos leaned over and smacked Henry on the back of the head. "That was close."

"Where are we heading to?"

"I don't know. Calgary, maybe. We're flying north. Calgary then maybe Seattle or San Fran," Martinez said.

Henry wished he had a tablet, but personal electronic devices were not permitted during operations. He had no way to access the net without using his ICS, which was out of the question. He needed to know what was happening in the rest of the country. He was cut off from the rest of the world.

A civil war in America. It didn't seem real. *Talk is one thing. But bases going up in smoke?* If that was happening here in Montana, then what did the rest of the country look like? Soldiers were killing each other. The cities would be burning as the conflict spilled out onto Main Street, from suburbia to downtown urban areas.

Suzanne and Taylor were in grave danger. Henry wondered what was transpiring at the naval air station in Key West. If Florida went with Texas and the rest of the South and West, what would Florida be like? From West Palm Beach south all the way to Key West, it's like a different state. Sweet Jesus. South Florida wouldn't want to leave the Union. *I've got to get home to my wife and child. Her old man might be able to protect her, but then again, if there is open war, the base might look like Malmstrom or worse.*

Henry had been in combat more times than he could count. He was calm and steady under fire. He was not a man given to panic. Yet thinking about Suzanne and Taylor alone in Key West, he felt a deep cold fear in him. There would be food shortages, water shortages, and potentially general breakdown of society. He needed to get home, and there were thousands of miles separating him from his family.

KEY WEST, FLORIDA

Suzanne surfaced at the stern and removed the regulator from her mouth, breathing the warm ocean air and blinking against the bright sunlight. As she slipped out of her BC she saw Bart, his hands on the stern, peering down at her. He was sun bronzed and blond, and sometimes when they walked around town people assumed he and Suzanne were brother and sister. Bart's wife, Mary, appeared at his shoulder. She looked worried.

"You gotta stop doing that," Bart said.

"What?" Suzanne handed Bart the long speargun.

"Leaving your dive buddy, then chasing fish to the bottom of the damn ocean. You have to be about out of air."

"Well, I'm safe and sound," Suzanne said. Bart gripped her tank along with her BC and hauled it into the boat. She removed her weight belt and pushed her mask onto the top of her head.

"He was about to go in after you," Mary said.

"Okay, jeeze," Suzanne said. Bart offered his hand but she ignored it and pulled herself onto the dive platform, removed her fins.

"It's dangerous, is all I'm saying," Bart said. Mary produced a towel while Suzanne stripped out of her wetsuit.

Suzanne dried off and put on sweatpants and a fleece over her bikini. She shivered, feeling a sense of accomplishment and tingling with life. After a dive, especially a deep one where she cut it close, she always felt that way. Something about the proximity to danger made her feel the most alive. She recognized this about herself and found it to be somewhat incongruous with the way she generally lived. She was essentially careful and conservative in the way she conducted herself. She always wore a seat belt, she did not like to drink heavily, and she didn't do drugs, jump out of airplanes, or engage in risky sexual behavior. *But put me down at a hundred twenty feet with a great hammerhead circling around, and I'm in heaven.*

She munched on some sushi they'd picked up that morning, ate some cut oranges, and washed it down with bottled water while Bart busied himself with the anchor. They were about ten miles offshore, and the sky was clear and blue. The *Blue Mistress III* rose and fell with the gentle waves and there was the burble of the bilge pump. She sat on the cooler behind the cockpit and stretched her legs out, facing the stern. Mary plunked down next to her.

"Have you heard back from him?" Mary said.

"No."

"It's been what? Three weeks?"

"Yeah." *You're messing with my calm, woman. Leave me be.*

"Have you told Taylor yet?"

"No. Not yet. I will when I need to. She's too young to understand, anyway." *Yeah, I'm dreading that talk. Mother-of-the-year material, that's me.*

"You know if you need to talk, I'm here for you." Mary squeezed Suzanne's shoulder. "Sometimes you kind of keep things bottled up. But you've got friends."

"I know, Mary." Suzanne sighed. "I know. And I appreciate the invite today. I needed it."

"Well, I'm not going to pry," Mary said. "I'm just . . . worried, I guess, and want to let you know me and Bart are here for whatever."

"Thanks."

"Hello, ladies," Bart said with an atrocious fake English accent from behind the steering wheel. "Are we ready to make way?" The engine rumbled and the boat began to move forward.

A sharp tearing sound split the sky, faint at first but growing to a crescendo. Sonic booms shook Suzanne's insides and made the boat vibrate. Specs on the horizon resolved into more than twenty fighter jets flying just above the deck, hurtling south at supersonic speed.

"Holy shit!" Bart said from behind.

Suzanne stood and shielded her eyes against the sun with her hand, watching the jets. They were in two separate formations, one low and one slightly higher. She was accustomed to aircraft performing training exercises, but she'd never seen that many fighters in the air at once. Not even close.

The planes flew by at blinding speed, less than a mile away.

"Hang on!" Bart hollered. The boat leaped forward and the bow dipped and slammed between the troths, and then they were beyond the reef and up on a plane and the ride was not quite so bumpy.

Suzanne did not know what the jets meant. Maybe nothing. Then again, she'd watched enough of the news lately to be afraid. Her father had said a few ominous things about stockpiling water and food. She hadn't seen much of him for the last few months, but he wasn't one to be alarmist. He was, after all, an admiral in the United States Navy, and not prone to exaggeration.

A few miles away, Suzanne could see other pleasure craft beginning to run back to harbors in the kind of mass exodus that preceded a severe ocean storm. She heard Bart on his radio, but could not hear what he was saying over the roar of the engines and the slapping of the hull. Cool water splashed her face and she tasted the salt. Adrenaline was pumping through her veins, and in spite of herself, she grinned, looking at the rooster tail and the foaming wake.

She faced Mary, who looked terrified, hanging on with both hands to the front of the cooler. Her long curly hair was plastered to the sides of her face and her eyes were scrunched almost shut. Mary's pendulous breasts jumped and jiggled and her heavy arms quivered.

The boat abruptly slowed, causing Suzanne and Mary to lurch.

"Sorry," Bart said, leaving the wheel and stepping around to face them.

"What's happening? Did you find out anything?" Mary asked.

"It's started. War."

"You mean—"

"I mean *war*. Civil war. I'm gonna haul ass back to port. When we get there, we need to head for the base. Suzanne, you can get us all on to the base, right?"

"I don't know. Probably. It depends on what's going on, I guess. I don't even know if Dad is in Key West right now."

"Well, we should try that first," Bart said. His face was pinched, tense. Suzanne had never seen him look like that. *Not the relaxed beach-bum charter captain just now. The Army Ranger in him coming out.*

"Taylor is at your place, right?" Bart said.

"Yeah. With Ginnie."

"We'll go there first, get Taylor, and head for the base in your car. Do you know the code for Henry's weapons safe?"

"Yeah."

"All right, then. Hold onto your butts."

Bart stepped up to the console and put the boat into gear and the twin Mercury 250s roared.

Suzanne thought about Henry and wondered where he was just then and what he was doing. She prayed he was safe, and she felt a longing for his arms around her, the steadfast reassurance of his touch. Guilt descended upon her like a coat filled with lead. *Irreconcilable differences. I attested to that. God forgive me, and keep my husband safe.*

CHAPTER THREE

Second Suns

WASHINGTON, DC

Stephanie James stared at the gridlock, sputtering curses. Her vehicle hadn't moved more than ten feet in the last hour, and Independence Avenue was a parking lot. Some people had abandoned their vehicles. DC was not a good place to be at the moment.

"Net search," she said out loud. "News feeds, top stories."

"Net unavailable at this time," the car replied in a matter-of-fact female voice.

"Search radio," Stephanie said.

"Unable to acquire signal," said the car.

"Call home," Stephanie ordered.

"Calling. Unable to place call. Please try again later."

"Arrragh! What *can* you do, bitch?"

Stephanie loved her car, a super-compact electric that folded up vertically when she had to park. She could plug it in for a recharge at stations all over the downtown area. The car had cost her more than she could afford, but the buttery leather seats and burnished mahogany dashboard still made her smile when she slipped into it after a long day on the Hill.

Just now, though, she felt helpless in her car, and leather seats were no comfort. She'd gone to undergraduate school at Vanderbilt, then law school at Harvard. She banked on the assumption that her time as a congressional aide would serve her well later on when she decided to run for office herself. She had done everything right. She had studied long into the night during college, forgoing spring breaks and parties. She was going places. And now she was stuck in traffic in the middle of Washington, DC, and the country was at war with itself.

Senator Bartram, her boss, had abandoned her with not even a handshake. She'd worked with him for two years, pulling all-nighters fueled by buckets of coffee and Red Bull and faith; she'd believed in him. He was a great man, she had told herself, a visionary and a patriot.

The senator had poked his head into her tiny office before he fled Washington. "Get out of town, Steph," he'd said. And then he'd literally run from his own office.

"Wait! Senator!"

"No time," he'd shouted over his shoulder, his suit coat flapping and his shoes echoing on the tile floor. Gone just like that while she stood outside her office feeling foolish.

Senator Bartram represented the great state of Tennessee, and there had been talk of him running for president. He was genteel and dignified, and Stephanie had once been convinced the man was incapable of even sweating. He was that tough and calm. But she'd watched him run out of his own office, probably to hop on a private jet, leaving her and the rest of his staff to fend for themselves. Congressmen and women had scurried from the Hill like rats abandoning a ship.

Now she was stuck in a traffic jam of epic proportion, wondering what she had been thinking when she decided to drive. Most of her fellow staffers had elected to walk. But she couldn't leave the damn car. Just couldn't do it.

Helicopters buzzed overhead. She saw drones hovering above the streets. In front of the Lincoln Memorial, soldiers or police, or FEMA, she couldn't tell from her vantage point, were working to disperse the crowd of protestors that had been camped there for the last few months. The troops were mounted on horses, and it looked like they'd fired tear gas into the crowd. She thought she heard some firecrackers. She gave both middle fingers to the traffic cams mounted on the curb.

She'd helped draft the resolution Senator Bartram had signed. To Stephanie, the process was an intellectual exercise, a series of elegant arguments crafted to make the other side take things seriously. She'd been pulling quotes from *The Federalist Papers*, Lincoln's letters, Reagan's press conferences, Supreme Court opinions, anything to bolster her arguments. She did not have time to surf the net, listen to the news, or even socialize with her colleagues. She had been holed up in her office. She'd expected some back-and-forth negotiations, concessions if not outright capitulation from the Democrats. Senator Bartram was reasonable, measured. He wouldn't actually press for secession; it was philosophical. A political maneuver.

There were more firecracker pops, and she could hear car alarms blaring. And then there was a louder sound, a blaring klaxon sound. The city itself under attack, a sound she hadn't heard since her childhood in Oklahoma. It was a tornado warning. But the sky was clear, and DC didn't have a tornado warning system.

"Emergency Threat Network activated," said the car.

The eight speakers came to life with the grating beeping of the ETN. "This is the Emergency Threat Network." A man's voice, authoritative and terse. "This is the Emergency Threat Network. This is not a test." Another voice came on then.

"Take shelter immediately. If you are able to reach a fallout shelter, do so at this time. There are shelters throughout the downtown area. If you cannot reach a shelter, seek cover underground. The president has declared a state of martial law. Remain indoors."

"What the hell?" Stephanie said.

"This is the Emergency Threat Network . . ." the speakers proceeded to repeat the same message, and Stephanie shut off her radio. People were running from cars, streaming down the street. Outside the safety of her car there was chaos. She couldn't leave her car, just couldn't do it.

She waited inside while people ran screaming down the street. And when a second sun appeared in the sky she was blinded, but not long enough to think about it because she and her car were melting and all she had time to do was think, *Damn*.

SAN FRANCISCO, CALIFORNIA

Ai Wong walked uphill toward the flat she shared with her family, feeling afraid and confused. The teachers had herded the children into a classroom and explained school would be out early today. Go home. Teachers never said that. And father would be angry.

San Francisco was cold and gray and there was fog, even this late in the morning. The teachers had offered no explanations, but they'd seemed frightened, eager to be someplace else. Ai had been looking forward to practice after school; she had a cello recital in two weeks and she felt unprepared.

Her father had sacrificed to put her into the best private school, and he would not be pleased to learn she was home early. But maybe he wouldn't find out, maybe Grandmother would not tell him. But she knew differently. She knew she would face her father when he got home from work, tired and beaten, and that he would be distant and cold. She could already feel his disapproval. He was constantly disappointed in her, often, it seemed, simply because she was a girl. He'd wanted another son, and she believed he'd never forgiven her for being female.

Ai didn't know what was happening, and she did not really care beyond what awaited her when she got home. She caught snippets of conversations from the other students. She heard something about Washington being attacked, about a war. But Ai had never paid attention to the news or to politics and she listened to the music in her head instead, floating apart from the other students and teachers in the way she always had.

Ai was seventeen years old, overflowing with potential. Next year Juilliard and freedom. Emancipation. She would be surrounded by students as serious and gifted as she, and then she wouldn't have to float and feel apart from others and she could embrace the constant concerto in her soul, creating a masterpiece that would make her father proud. She would touch people, make them *feel*. She found it vaguely ironic that her name meant "love," yet she had never even kissed a boy. Her love was music. She would have time for relationships when she was older, after she'd done what she needed to do.

She did not hear the inbound missile traveling faster than a bullet. Even if she had, the symphony in her soul would have drowned it out. One second she was walking uphill, floating apart from the other children around her, a heavy backpack laden with books and black shoes and a blue checkered skirt, and then the next second she was flying into the air, burning, floating, and the music stopped and there was just the silence.

NASHVILLE, TENNESSEE

Leon Smith decided it was time to take a break. He'd been on the chain saw all morning, trimming the old trees that lined the driveway of some rich white people. His arms were shaking and his face was raw from the wind. He was busting his ass working six days a week and could barely feed his kids and keep the lights on. And here were these folks on Belle Meade Boulevard, old-money people whose families probably used to own slaves and probably thought of him that way still, with their maids and house staff and mansions with white columns. He'd never felt real racism until he moved to Nashville and started to work around wealthy white people.

Growing up in Harlem, he'd been around other black folks all the time. Church on Sunday, public school, store owners, coaches: all black people. He'd served four years in the army, but hadn't felt . . . looked down upon. That's what it was, this feeling that people believed he was somehow *less*. That he wasn't good enough no matter what he did.

He'd seen the news, watched shows streaming over the net, and he'd talked about it with his friends and fellow soldiers. In the army, he'd been around whites, blacks, Hispanics, Asians; it didn't really seem to matter. He knew for a fact that racism existed, but he'd never been subjected to it the way that some of his friends had, never known the deep-down hurting rage. He did now.

Part of it was his boss, Harry Wilson. A redneck from Knoxville who tried to ingratiate himself with his clients by putting down his own workers.

"Them boys can be lazy," Harry would say. "Sometimes ya gotta crack the whip." And a woman with frosted hair and painted nails and fake boobs and a sleek Mercedes would smile and ask him if he wanted some sweet ice tea. Harry didn't actually do any work. He left that for "them *boys*."

When Leon protested the crummy pay and poor treatment, Harry would shrug and say, "Ain't nobody stopping you. Hit the road. Good luck with finding another job."

Leon felt trapped. There weren't other jobs. He'd been applying every week, in person and over the net, for a year. Harry was a terrible boss, a little tyrant, but at least he paid in cash and he paid a bit over minimum wage. Leon raged against it, but he showed up for work every day on time. He swallowed his pride and his anger and in the summertime he was soaked with sweat and in the winter his hands were stiff and cold. He was a young man still, only thirty, but he felt old and stooped beyond his years. He'd fall into bed at night after a quick shower, and his wife would tell him what a good man he was, how proud she was of him, and his boys looked up to him and he would lie there feeling like a failure and then get up in the morning and do it all again.

He climbed down from the tree and unhooked the harness. Up the gentle hill and beyond the acres of manicured lawn, the homeowners appeared to be packing their SUV for a vacation. They were moving quicker than rich white folks tended to move. He saw Jesus and Dominic coming down from trees, too. *A mutual break, then. All right.*

Leon walked toward the pickup truck full of lawn equipment to grab a drink of hot coffee from his thermos. Mary made sure, no matter what, when he went out the door he had a full thermos to take with him in the winter.

He saw Harry sitting in the cab of the truck. No surprise there. Harry would sit there and look at porn all day long, then shake hands with homeowners. *I'll never shake your hand, you nasty bastard.* Behind him, up the long stately driveway, Leon heard a woman sobbing and a man shouting. He looked over his shoulder. The guy, wearing a suit and tie, was shouting at his wife. There was luggage piled up next to their car. Leon couldn't hear what they were saying and he didn't care. A couple of assholes getting a divorce, maybe. The chain saw was heavy and he put it down. Police sirens were wailing somewhere close, an unusual occurrence in Belle Meade. He was aware of the sirens in the way of a black man in Belle Meade. Potential danger. He wasn't driving, though, so he figured the sirens weren't for him.

Harry stepped out of his truck. He looked jumpy. More squirrely than usual, his eyes darting around like he couldn't make up his mind what to focus on. Leon prepared to bite his tongue.

"Ah, Leo. Glad you came down."

"What's up?"

"Looks like we're going to call it an early day." Those words had never dripped from Harry's mouth before. Not once.

"Do what? We're not even close to being done."

"Well, yeah," Harry said, wringing his hands, "but the, uh, the homeowners have decided we've taken enough off. They don't want any more limbs cut."

"Uh-huh," Leon said. "What's with the piece?" Harry had an enormous holster strapped to his hip. Leon stood a few paces away from him. Harry looked at the ground, then the trees, then somewhere beyond Leon's shoulder. His right hand was hovering close to the brown leather holster at his hip.

"Well, you know, I just heard there was a bank robbery over on West End. Cops are looking for suspects around here. Some armed bank robbers. Can't be too careful."

"So you're packing?"

"Well, yeah. Look, can you get a lift home? I need to go. I can't drop you off back at the shop."

"Come on, Harry. That's bullshit." Leon was aware that his fellow workers had come up behind him. Harry looked like he wanted to bolt. He looked terrified. *What the hell?*

"I just gotta go," Harry said, backing away. Twitchy.

The silver Mercedes blew past them, tires squealing, as it turned onto Belle Meade Boulevard. Leon had to jump out of the way to avoid being hit.

"What the hell, ming? Jesus said. "You can't leave us stranded here."

"Just stay back," Harry said, edging back around his truck.

"Hell no!" Dominic shouted, stepping forward to get in Harry's face. "You not leaving—"

Harry pulled the revolver from the holster, his face red and mean.

Leon took one step forward, reacting, not thinking. Training coming back to him, at least some of it. He should have gone for the throat, groin, the soft parts, but he didn't. His fist smashed into Harry's nose, a year's worth of fury and muscle and endurance behind it, the momentum of poverty, retribution, and justice in an angry fist. Harry flew backwards, feet off the ground, and his head smacked the front bumper of his truck.

Leon stepped up to Harry and took the nickel-plated .357 from his hand, then held the weapon at his side, looking down at his former boss. Harry wasn't moving and his eyes were open, surprised and vacant.

"Aw, shit, he dead. You killed him," said Dominic.

Leon looked down at Harry Wilson; Dominic was right. Maybe it was the chrome bumper that did it. Maybe it was a heart attack. Maybe he'd hit him so hard and just right that he snapped the man's neck. Leon was panting and he wanted to throw up. He felt hot even though he could see his breath. The sirens kept on going and going.

"That's one dead redneck," Jesus said. "You showed him." Jesus then said some things in Spanish Leon did not understand, yet still managed to comprehend.

Leon wanted to double over and puke. He hated Harry Wilson, but he hadn't meant to kill him. He'd never taken a life.

"He was about to shoot you," Leon said. "He was reaching. Why was he strapped? What the hell?"

"I donno, ming, but we gotta go," Jesus said. "Cops everywhere. They not liking you killing some white boy on Belle Meade Boulevard. String your black ass up."

"Yeah," Leon said, staring down at Harry Wilson's dead eyes. Leon was shaking. Anger, remorse, fear, and uncertainty kept him rooted on the lawn in front of the red pickup truck with the chrome and the dead Harry Wilson lying in front of it. He had to do something, but he didn't know what it was. Not just stand there looking dumb and waiting for the police to put him in prison for the rest of his life.

"I mean *now*, man!" Dominic said, rounding the truck. "If you wanna stick around and go to prison, go for it. I ain't waiting."

Jesus and Dominic stepped around Leon, opening the doors on the quad cab truck. Leon stood over the man he'd killed. No white witnesses, nothing he could say that would sway authorities. He'd be in jail for a long time before a trial ever happened. Meanwhile his wife and kids would be starving. Even once he got his day in court, he was far from confident that he'd be set free. He'd be convicted of manslaughter. Ten years in prison, at least.

"We leaving, man!"

"Okay," Leon said. The sirens kept wailing. He stooped down to Harry Wilson's dead body and undid the man's belt. He removed the belt and holster, put them on his own hip, and placed the nickel-plated .357 snugly in its place. He pulled his coat over the weapon, and it felt heavy. He was not entirely sure why he felt the need to take the gun. He wouldn't shoot a cop. No way.

He got into the truck, walking like a wooden soldier, stiff and strange even to himself, and he climbed into the driver's seat and put the truck into gear. *Y'all were about to leave, huh? But you damn sure wanted me to drive. Okay, then. I'm driving home to my wife and my boys, and nobody better try to stop me.*

NASHVILLE, TENNESSEE

Marshall, whose real name was Jessie although he insisted people call him Marshall, was excited. The war was finally happening, the war between the invaders and the real Americans. A fight between the givers and the takers, producers and freeloaders. Words like that. Jessie was ready for the war because he'd been preparing and wishing for it his entire life. They were taking over the country, and he felt like he was under attack from the day he was born. They'd taken over the schools, the government, and even his neighborhood.

His home was skirted by tin, the blocks and wheels beneath it not showing. His yard didn't have broken-down cars and weeds and toys from 1999 and toilets and couches on his porch. He was raised better than that. There was none of that yammering they did when they decided to argue. He had himself a respectable home, a double-wide that he'd paid off on land he rented only because his granddaddy hadn't had the sense to hang on to it. He'd been watching the news and waiting, knowing what would happen. He'd told everybody within bar-shot how it would play out. Watching it stream live, he let out a rebel yell for himself.

"HEEEEEL YAUGHA," he howled at the screen. The announcers were grave, but Marshall, whose real name was Jessie, was not grave.

"Tennesseeeee!" said Jessie. He stomped through a field of empty beer cans on the way to the gun cabinet. The glass case contained a 12-gauge shotgun, and that was it. He'd sold or pawned the rest of his 'daddy's guns. But he had that one left.

He'd watched the news all morning long at the Antioch Social Club, a dark, shabby bar where he could drink until he passed out and no one would try to steal his Marlboro Reds. Salt of the earth folk just like him. They even let him run a monthly tab, and then allowed him to use his food stamps and disability check to pay for his beer. The regulars there were his family. The battered pickup trucks in the gravel parking lot held gun racks in every rear window. Many of the trucks were adorned with bumper stickers of rebel flags and "Secession Now!" logos.

He'd known this was coming, and the only thing that took away from his triumphant mood was the fact that his daddy couldn't be here to see it too. Daddy had known.

Was a high school football player with college prospects. Fast and mean, like the old man said. Shake and bake. Taliban took my knee and a Mexican took my job and now it's war.

This was a lie he'd repeated so often that he actually believed it. He'd tried to join the army, but they'd refused to let him in. He'd been a benchwarmer in high school, with no prospects. But the stories were good for free beer, and he'd built a life and friends around these stories until he was convinced he was a different man than he actually was. *Okay, you motherfuckers. My turn!*

Marshall took the shotgun from the case, staggering, seething, and finding a fight in the way that people named Jessie who want to be called Marshall always do.

CHAPTER FOUR

The Enemy Is Us

SOUTHERN ALBERTA, CANADA

The helicopter touched down in a pristine valley surrounded by mountains, and Henry hopped off the bird into the snow in front of a squat log cabin. Smoke coiled from a stone chimney. The other Blackhawk landed behind him as he walked toward the cabin. The flight crews and several team members pulled cammie netting over the birds.

Henry waited on the wide front porch while his teammates sauntered forward. Carlos grinned at him and said, "Guess this is a safe house the colonel had up his sleeve."

The sky was clear and blue and the temperature was in the teens. Henry stomped his boots on the wooden porch. His face was numb from the ride in the helicopter, but he was not concerned with the cold; he wanted to know what was happening.

Colonel Bragg nodded at the expectant faces of his men as he strode onto the porch and knocked on the door.

A woman opened the door at the first knock. She wore her dark hair in a long braid, and her face was the color of tanned leather. There was the smell of fresh bread wafting in the warm air. Her expression was flat, gazing at the thirty armed soldiers gathered around the front of her cabin. She looked neither surprised nor afraid.

"Hello, Colonel," she said.

"Hello, May," replied Colonel Bragg. "Sorry to intrude. But, you know the deal."

"Yup. I was really hoping you were off somewhere else. Come on in. Not that you need me to tell you that."

"We won't all be here long," said the colonel. "Just need to regroup and figure out what the next move is."

"Well, come on, boys, don't just stand there in the cold," she said, moving away from the door.

Henry followed the colonel into the cabin. A friendly fire blazed in the stone fireplace. The sound system played Mozart. Henry was befuddled.

"Boys, this is my cousin's wife, May. She's good people. Try not to track snow inside."

"Not his wife anymore."

"Well, no. May God rest his soul." The colonel led the way down a hallway. He pulled a sconce on the wall, and part of the wall slid back, revealing a stairway.

"I'll bring you men some coffee and bread. Got some venison stew for supper if you're going to be staying."

"That'd be great, May," said Colonel Bragg.

Henry and the Wolves followed the colonel down a series of metal stairs, and Henry guessed they descended about four stories below ground.

The colonel entered a code onto a keyboard mounted on metal blast doors; the doors opened with a hiss, revealing a cavernous room, three or four thousand square feet, with a row of bunks along one wall. Inert computer screens surrounded what looked like a command center. Metal racks contained assault rifles and ammunition. The colonel walked to the op center and began turning on the computers, which sprang to life. He turned heel, hands behind his back, to face the men. His gray eyes were the color of the ocean before a storm, sober and sad.

"Take a knee," he said. The men gathered around him like a football team around the coach after practice.

"I know you all have questions; I'll try to answer them as best I can. I'm gonna ask you to trust me. We don't have much time, and there's a lot that needs to be done. Here it is in a nutshell." His gaze swept the room, locking eyes with each man for a moment.

"This place belonged to a group of guys the Mounties took down about ten years ago. I acquired it quietly, using shell companies. May has been keeping up appearances here, just in case we ever needed a rabbit hole in this neck of the woods. I've stashed diamonds, gold, passports, weapons, food, and just about everything we could need to survive a damn apocalypse. I never really thought I'd wind up here."

"Washington, DC, was attacked this morning. It is unclear whether it was a missile launched by military assets or if it was a bomb detonated by terrorist separatists. San Francisco was subsequently attacked, and I'm pretty sure, based on the eyewitness reports, they did get struck with a missile, maybe something launched from a submarine."

Henry closed his eyes. Several of the men had families in San Francisco.

"The United States is at war with itself. At installations around the world, there has been fighting. On a lot of bases, there has been no bloodshed. Some base commanders are allowing troops to leave if they choose, trying to maintain order without anyone getting killed. Throughout the separatist states, troops are being given the option to join, disband, or depart, and in most places it's orderly. But the chain of command is completely broken. Now, every one of us signed an oath to uphold the Constitution, to defend our country against all enemies, foreign and domestic. Frankly I'm not sure what that means right now."

"Sir," Carlos said, "shouldn't we be trying to stop the rebels? I'm confused. Why are things unclear?"

"We *could* do that," Colonel Bragg said. He looked tired, depleted. "We have zero assets beyond what you see here and our two birds. We could try to make it to federal territory. We'd run the risk of being shot down."

Several of the men began to speak at once, but the colonel held up his hand. The men shut up.

"I *bleed* red, white, and blue, you men know that. I have been a loyal soldier, and I've followed orders I disagreed with because that's what we do. For the last six months, I've been making discreet inquiries through some contacts I trust. Men and women I've known for decades. I fear our unit has been manipulated and compromised. We have operated outside of the chain of command of even SOCOM." US Special Operations Command coordinated the joint efforts of the various special ops units the United States deployed around the world. The Navy SEALs, Delta Force, Green Berets, and Marine Raider Regiment all fell under the purview of SOCOM. "We've worked *with* them, but not *for* them. This much I knew when I signed on; it made sense in terms of operational security and the fact that what we've been doing falls into a constitutional gray area."

"I had a contact within the NSA follow the money trail. The Wolves are funded through a series of offshore shell companies. No real surprise there. But after untangling some of the web, my friend found that most of the money flows from odd places. There is a conglomerate of multinational corporations. Names you know. Defense firms, banks, big pharmaceuticals. The money has been funneled through a private security firm, bounced through various cutouts. These guys have strong ties to the media. People that purchase elections. I haven't had time to analyze the data, and I don't know exactly who is involved. It's a shell game these guys are playing."

The colonel paused to let this sink in.

Henry's head was spinning. *A conspiracy? So powerful and pervasive that a group could use the Wolves as attack dogs? Why?*

"Now I don't have definitive proof of any of this, and I'm glad of it. My friend in the NSA had a fatal car accident last week. Something stinks, that much I am certain of. I don't trust anyone. And I'm not going to be a puppet on a string, not anymore, that's for damn sure."

"So now what?" Henry asked.

"Right. First of all, the Wolves are no more. If you choose to leave, you are free to do so. If you decide to stay, you are welcome. I intend to hole up here until the shooting stops."

Henry was shocked. Colonel Bragg was a warrior and a patriot. Henry assumed they'd be headed into the fray, one way or another.

"You boys know I'm from Texas. I swore an oath to my country, but my country has let me down. It let you down, too, whether y'all can see it yet or not. I'm not going to fight my fellow Americans. I'm just not going to do it. I don't care if the order comes from the president of the United States or from the governor of Texas. I'm done."

"Um," Sergeant Major Martinez said, "where exactly are we?"

The colonel chuckled. "Alberta," he said. "Just north of the US border. Now the first thing we need to do is remove the ICS relays. I don't know who might be tracking us. We *probably* don't matter anymore, but just to be on the safe side, we need to cut those out. Next, those of you who are leaving need to take whatever gear you can carry and get those birds the hell out of this valley. I don't want to be spotted by a drone or a satellite."

May came downstairs with a tray of mugs and several metal pitchers of coffee. She put the tray on the floor and went back upstairs without saying a word.

The computer screens displayed continuous images of Washington and San Francisco burning. Reporters pointed and gestured and looked grave. Other screens showed rioting in New York City, Atlanta, LA, and places Henry could not identify.

The Wolves formed a line and Doc Alex, the unit's medic, performed minor surgery on each man. The ICS relay was about the size of a mosquito, embedded in each man's neck. The device contained a microchip, power supply, and wireless Internet portal. The relay was not physically attached to the chips embedded in each soldier's brain, so the operation was simple and mostly painless. Without the relay, the men could still utilize the night vision equipped in their contacts, but would be unable to interface with drones or one another.

The men gathered around to decide who was going where, and how they planned to get there. A third of the men were from the Northeast, another third from the Southeast, and the rest were from the Midwest and West. The flight crews for the Blackhawks were Night Stalkers.

Ultimately, the men compromised. The birds had already expended a considerable amount of fuel and would only be able to travel about three hundred miles. They would stay together and try to refuel at one of several small airports in Canada. From there, some of the men would fly west. The other bird would head south, flying low. They would abandon the aircraft and disband on foot once they reached civilization.

They were loading weapons and food into crates, when a piercing beeping sound erupted from the computer center.

Henry paused and looked over toward Colonel Bragg.

"We're too late," he said. The colonel toggled a switch on the console in front of him. "May, get down here," he said, turning to the busy soldiers.

"We've got company. UAVs are circling our position. We may have some infantry on our asses within minutes. That ass-hat commander at Malmstrom couldn't let it go."

The computer monitors, some of which had cycled through news broadcasts, and some of which relayed images from security cameras positioned throughout the valley, went fuzzy. *They're jamming us*, Henry realized.

Colonel Bragg called Martinez over to the command center and spoke to him for a few seconds in hushed tones. Henry stuffed extra magazines into the webbing in his vest, feeling the rush of adrenaline and heightened awareness that he always did before a firefight.

Colonel Bragg talked as he inserted a magazine into an M4 from a rack on the wall. "We'll exit through the back of the bunker; there's a tunnel that comes out at the base of a ridge about two hundred meters west of the cabin. Haul ass up that hill and spread out. I've got a concealed machine gun emplacement up there with a fifty. There's good cover and high ground. *Get some.*"

Sergeant Major Martinez led the way; Henry grabbed his now hundred-pound ruck and followed Martinez down a long concrete corridor lit by naked light bulbs. There was the sound of boots slapping on the floor and gear rustling and breathing. The walls were close and the men jogged in single file. They bunched up while they waited for Martinez to open the final steel door. When it swung open, sunlight—different, brighter and more real than the anemic light cast from the bulbs—streamed into the cement tomb, a portal of white with the men silhouetted against it.

Henry was the sixth man back from the door. *No gunfire, that's good. No explosions. Yet.*

The men broke left, then right, in pairs. The feeling in him was reminiscent of how he felt the first time he jumped out of a plane more than ten years ago. Following a line of men into the unknown from a safe, dark place into chaos and wind and light. Watching his brothers ahead move without hesitation, wondering whether he'd have the sack for it when his time came, yet knowing he did and dreading it and loving it at the same time, proving something vital to himself with each step . . . and then he was in the light and the wind and cold. Pride, fear, and loyalty and . . . *Oh shit, here it comes!*

He broke left.

There was a hum in the air, a vibration of wrongness and tension, a crawling thing Henry could feel on his skin as he slogged uphill through snow up to his knees. He followed in the footsteps of the previous team members, noted where the path broke off behind a boulder, fixed his attention on making it to a stand of birch trees twenty meters upslope. He made it to the trees and slid down behind cover, the HK in his hands like an extension of his body. Not five feet to his right, Carlos moved into position, facing away from the cabin covering the approach from upslope.

Henry felt conspicuous. He'd worn what he had available; his fatigues were designed for a nighttime assault, albeit in cold weather. But in his dark gear he presented a target against the blindingly white snow. He burrowed into the snow. He heard the crunching of combat boots and the clicking of gear as the next team ranged past him.

The cabin, with the smoke trailing from the stone chimney and the snow on the rooftop, might have adorned a Christmas card.

One second, the cabin was a warm tranquil refuge, and the next it was a fireball. The inbound missiles struck almost simultaneously, and the cabin was erased in flame and fury and a rolling boom Henry felt in his bones and soul and teeth. A yellow-orange flash, then roiling smoke and pieces of cabin flying through the air and spiraling down. The helicopters exploded next, before Henry took a breath. He flinched with rage and the feeling of being violated.

Before the last pieces of the helicopters rained back to the earth, the crack of small arms fire echoed through the valley.

Henry leaned into the scope and scanned the opposite hillside. Figures clad in white darted between trees.

"Movement," Henry said, keeping his voice just above a whisper. Controlled.

"Taking contact," Carlos said. "Who the fuck is shooting?"

"Muzzle flashes. Two o'clock, opposite slope. Not our guys."

The enemy. But the enemy is us this time. Our own troops, guys I might have passed by on base or shot a game of pool with. Men better trained and equipped than any enemy he'd faced.

*

In Afghanistan, Henry had learned to put certain things from his mind in the midst of combat. When someone is trying to kill you, you shoot back. On his first deployment he'd found that combat is chaos and death and there is no room for philosophy when the rounds are smacking the dirt. Afterward, yes. But in the moment, you try to survive and you do what you have to do. The first time his team got hit with a Taliban ambush, he'd been riding in an open-top Humvee, one vehicle back from the lead, when an IED rocked the vehicle thirty yards ahead. Henry was riding shotgun, his SAW, or squad assault weapon, pointed out the window.

"Ambush!" shouted the driver.

Another explosion, this one behind them, tore through the air. The narrow street was lined by two-story homes, and from the alleys and windows, small arms fire erupted. An RPG fired from a rooftop narrowly missed the Humvee Henry was exiting. He hunkered down next to the right front tire, firing at the muzzle flashes and shadows. The five-vehicle convoy was pinned down in a kill zone, a carefully orchestrated attack. From the backseat, Corporal Christie was on the radio calling for air support.

Private Birch, a pimple-faced kid from West Virginia, hammered at the rooftops with the .50-caliber machine gun mounted on the Humvee. The lead vehicle was burning, and Henry saw two Rangers dragging wounded men out of the inferno.

Under their current rules of engagement (ROE), the Rangers were only allowed to fire if fired upon and were not permitted to engage civilians. In theory, this made sense, but in practice, the lines were blurry. Henry would discover throughout his experience in Afghanistan that the Taliban and al-Qaeda did not follow any rules.

Henry ran toward the burning Humvee to help his fellow Rangers. Rounds smacked into the yellow-brown wall to his left as he ran. One of the Rangers ahead, Sergeant Pratt, fell as he was dragging another man by his armpits. The .50 kept pounding the enemy positions and the thirty-yard dash was the longest run Henry had ever experienced as time seemed to stretch out and make no sense. He was aware of the smell of propellant and smoke and fuel.

He was about ten yards from the wounded men when a woman in a bright blue robe, face covered with a burka, stepped from the shadows. She was only thirty or forty feet away, and beside her was a child dressed in rags, maybe ten or eleven years old; she held the boy's wrist.

Later, Henry would try to recall the exact sequence of events, putting them together in his mind like puzzle pieces strewn over a floor, jumbled and nonsensical. He was pretty sure he had seen the trigger device in her hand.

He turned, slowing his pace, acting on muscle memory and reflex. The SAW bucked, peppering the woman in blue and knocking her from her feet. Somehow, the boy was unharmed, and he disappeared into the shadows.

Henry made it to the Humvee, and then Cobra attack helicopters swept in, strafing the rooftops and buildings with 20mm cannons and missiles. The cannon fire made a deep, vibrating feeling in Henry's chest, a terrible and wonderful thing. The enemy fighters ceased the attack, many of them killed, and others melting into the town.

Henry learned the woman he had killed was wearing a vest armed with explosives and ball bearings. He was fairly certain the trigger in her hand made him shoot her. He still dreamed about it, and sometimes there was a gray cord with a red button in her hand and sometimes there wasn't and in the worst of the nightmares, the kid got knocked off his feet too.

His actions earned him a medal and the respect of his fellow Rangers. If he had not shot that woman, the blast and shrapnel would have wiped out every one of the soldiers from the lead Humvee, along with him. Sometimes the enemy doesn't look like the enemy.

*

The soldiers coming down the slope now didn't look like the enemy, either. But there was no time to debate ethics and morality. They were here to kill Henry and his fellow Wolves, and Henry was going to shoot back.

KEY WEST, FLORIDA

Suzanne Wilkins shivered with the wind, although it was not cold. The bow slapped the water and salt spray splashed her face and rivulets of ocean streamed down her cheeks. Bart eased back on the throttle as he came to the line of boats waiting to enter the channel. Shallow flats stretched off for miles where the water was only inches deep, covering sandbars and turtle grass. The cold came from inside her, not from the wind or the ocean.

Hundreds of pleasure craft streamed into the channel, creating a snaking traffic jam. Cell phone service was down, and they had no means of communication other than the radio. Bart cycled through the channels. On the emergency station, a Coast Guard message informed boaters to clear the waterways. Martial law was in effect. On other channels, captains chattered, voices raw and tight. There were wild stories of boats attacked by military vessels, pirates, and bombs going off in Miami. More fighter jets screamed off the coast, low to the deck.

Suzanne was afraid. *Is Taylor all right? Are roving groups of criminals kicking in doors and burning houses? Did the nanny abandon Taylor to go be with her family in Miami?* Suzanne's fear was the primal terror of the mother huddled by a fire in the wilderness, with the rustling of bears and wolves skulking in the night, circling and hungry, heard but not seen. Her fear was worse, perhaps, because she was not with her child. She could not protect her. The trepidation of the abyss, dark and uncertain, pressed against her soul.

"Take the helm," Bart said. He reached beneath the console, removed a Glock from its hard-shell, foam-lined case. He stuffed the 9mm into the elastic waist of his swim trunks and pulled his Hawaiian shirt over the weapon. He moved up to the bow, scanning back and forth, hands on his hips.

Suzanne stepped behind the center console. The *Blue Mistress III* chugged along at idle speed. The no-wake zones ahead were there for a reason, and apparently the captains were obeying the posted signs. Suzanne fought the urge to zip around the other boats, but she knew she would only run aground on the flats. The wait was maddening.

They were behind a sixty-foot yacht, and at the stern a group of gray-haired men surrounded by young women were drinking and laughing. "Margaritaville" blared from the speakers for the tenth time. The men seemed oblivious, having a party and unwilling to allow the world to impinge upon their fun.

Behind the *Mistress*, a sleek red cigarette boat rumbled dangerously close to the stern. A pair of coeds lounged topless on the bow. Behind the cockpit, Suzanne saw a hairy guy with gold chains, beefy and tanned and radiating arrogance and impatience. The clown in a BMW who tailgates and cuts in and out of traffic, speeding ahead only to stop at the next red light, and then gets angry because you pull up ahead of him in the next lane.

Suzanne gestured at the guy to back off. He responded by flipping her off with both hands. She turned back to the wheel in disgust.

*

Bart's wife, Mary, lay on the cooler with a towel over her head. Suzanne thought Mary was making whimpering sounds, but she could not be sure. She wished Bart would sit beside the woman and offer some reassurance, put his arm around her. But Bart probably wouldn't do that because he despised his wife. Everyone knew it, including Mary. So she lay on the cooler with a yellow towel over her face, confronting her fears alone. Suzanne felt sorry for her, but she couldn't step away from the wheel, and at that point, she had little in her to give, no words of consolation or hope.

Mary and Bart were one of those couples who made no sense. Ten years ago, they had been solid and well matched, but they both changed dramatically. Bart separated from the Rangers with a shrapnel wound in his knee. He and Mary moved down to the Keys to begin a charter business. Mary wanted more than anything to be a mother, but after several painful pregnancies and miscarriages, something vital in her soul had died. She'd given up on living, and put on a tremendous amount of weight. She stayed in bed most of the time, watching reality TV and popping painkillers with the blinds drawn.

Bart, who had been Henry's best friend and Ranger Buddy going through Ranger School at Fort Benning, went from being a happy-go-lucky young man to becoming a prematurely old young man who carried a seething bitterness in his soul. Bart and Henry were still close friends, but the relationship was strained. Suzanne sympathized with Bart. He'd tried to be a good husband, tried to get Mary help, but he'd fought a losing battle.

Bart's fierce loyalty and sense of duty prevented him from seeking a divorce, which Suzanne admired without fully understanding. Bart spent his days on the water and his nights at the bar, and the couple existed in parallel. Separate, lonely, passing one another in the halls, eating the occasional meal together in quiet loathing and brittle silence.

Suzanne sensed that Bart was a bit in love with her, a fact she did her best to ignore. She didn't think he would ever act upon it now, but she'd caught him gazing thoughtfully at her, felt his eyes on her back, seen a kind of longing in his eyes, a sad, wistful expression bereft of real hope. She found Bart to be attractive, but there was no part of her that reciprocated his feelings. She'd made a mistake once, many years ago. He was a friend, and that's all he could ever be.

Suzanne and Mary were no longer close, although Suzanne did her best to pretend they were still great friends. Mary seemed to have an impenetrable cloud about her, a sucking thing that left Suzanne exhausted after spending an afternoon in her presence. Suzanne was ashamed to admit that she despised Mary sometimes for her weakness. There had been times, particularly when Taylor was a newborn, that Suzanne saw naked envy on Mary's face, almost hatred. Suzanne never forgot that.

*

"Bart! Do something about this idiot behind us," Suzanne shouted.

Bart turned from his perch on the bow, nodded and walked to the stern, gestured with both hands.

"Hey, asshole! Back off!"

The hairy guy flipped Bart off, then pulled out a nickel-plated revolver, something big, a .44 maybe, and waved it around.

"You gonna to shoot me for telling you to back off?" Bart yelled. "Really?" The girls on the bow of the cigarette boat sat up on their elbows, smiling. Bart stood with his hands on his hips.

"Screw you!" said the fur-back from behind the cockpit of the cigarette boat. He pushed the throttle and his boat growled and surged forward to within a couple feet of the *Mistress*.

"You've got to be kidding," Suzanne mumbled.

Bart shook his head and joined her behind the wheel, took a seat on one of the captain's stools. "I can shoot him if you want," he said, chuckling.

"No, let *me*," Suzanne said. It felt good to laugh. "But I want to use my speargun."

"Well, if he rams my boat, I wouldn't rule it out," Bart said.

Bart tried the radio again, and this time he was able to raise one of his buddies on land, old Bobby Ray, a retired captain and part-time bartender at one of the dives Bart lived in. Bobby agreed to swing by Suzanne's home to stay with Taylor and Ginnie, the nanny, for as long as it took. Suzanne was relieved.

When Bobby Ray called back an hour later to let her know Taylor was safe and sound, she felt even better. Key West was not burning, Bobby reported, and there were no thugs looting and pillaging, at least not yet. In fact, he said, there was a carnival atmosphere throughout the small town. Civil war parties had sprung up all over, and the bars and restaurants were packed with locals and tourists alike. Duval Street was one giant festival. *Gotta love Conchs. But how long will that last? When the water runs out and the power is off and there is no more gasoline, how are people going to get along then? When the freezers are full of rotting meat and bellies full of empty, what then?*

CHAPTER FIVE

God Help Us

ALBERTA, CANADA

Soldiers in white winter-warfare fatigues descended into the valley. Henry and the rest of his unit remained silent and concealed, weapons ready while the soldiers below picked over the wreckage of the cabin and the smoking helicopters. The small arms fire ceased; apparently some of the men below had itchy trigger fingers.

Henry had no idea where Colonel Bragg was, whether he'd even made it out of the bunker, and he could make out only two positions where his teammates lay beneath snow and branches. Henry hoped the troops below would decide the airstrikes had done the job, leave without further bloodshed. He remained prone in the thick snow, motionless, alert, and cold.

Moments later he heard the faint sound of an unmanned drone. The drone, like a distant mosquito buzzing high in the air, would find the Wolves, no matter how well hidden. Thermal imaging would light the Wolves up, their bodies bright in the screens of the drone pilot who might be three thousand miles away sitting in an office beside a steaming cup of coffee. The operator would communicate with the men on the ground, and that would be that.

The .50-caliber opened up, red tracer rounds tearing into the clustered soldiers below. All along the ridges, the Wolves attacked, firing into the men in the kill zone. A second or two later, the first Hellfire missile slammed into the ridge, destroying the .50, then another smashed into the rear entrance to the bunker.

Henry controlled his breathing, firing slowly and deliberately. The soldiers below dove for cover and began to return fire from behind smoldering wreckage and trees.

Behind Henry, Carlos was firing continuously, swearing, shouting. Clouds of snow erupted near Henry's head as rounds fired from across the valley sought his flesh. Henry wiggled backwards. The sound of battle was angry and close, thousands of rounds zipping through the winter air, a wind of metal.

Someone laid down a barrage of M203 fire, grenades launched from under the barrel of one of the M4 carbines favored by some of the Wolves. The grenades were small, rounded canisters with a kill radius of five meters, and sprayed hot shrapnel in all directions, wounding out to twenty or thirty meters. Smoke hung in the valley.

Even from a distance of more than two hundred meters, Henry could see blood staining the snow below, shockingly red against the white. There was no time to ponder the significance, but Henry felt it in his guts, nevertheless. The sense that what was happening was a great sin. Tragic, avoidable, and in the end, evil.

A part of him yearned to stand up and wave his arms, shouting "Go home! We're all Americans!" But the metal tearing through the air made this idea ludicrous.

Henry switched magazines, his third. "Reloading!"

"They're trying to flank us," Carlos said. "Reinforcements coming along the ridge at three o'clock. Firing." Carlos switched his sector of fire to target the incoming troops.

"Wilkins, suppress that ridge line!"

Henry turned and saw men darting from tree to tree, rock to rock. There were too many.

"We're gonna have to pull back," Henry said.

"No shit. To where?"

Henry fired at a muzzle flash. A heavy round smacked into the tree above him, and Henry could smell the sap from the tree. He scooted backwards, using his elbows. Snow had gotten inside his smock and thermals and was wet against his belly.

"Moving," Carlos said. He got up and edged backwards while Henry continued to fire, shifting his aim to the troops moving along the ridgeline.

Henry scooted back further, then risked coming to a crouch and made for a boulder a few meters up slope. The small arms fire was less intense now, as the Wolves conserved ammunition and the attacking troops sought targets from behind cover.

This might just be the day I die. I've been in some fixes before, but none as bad as this. Outnumbered, drones hunting me, and my own guys trying to kill me. His ears were ringing and his heart hammering and his mouth tasted like a copper penny. *Why do they have such a hard-on for us? We shouldn't matter. We're just a few guys who bugged out of the base. They hunted us all the way into Canada. Who the hell are we up against?*

Henry scanned the area. Carlos was making his way toward the top of the ridge, and Henry decided that was the right idea. If they could make it over the ridge, they'd be out of the line of direct fire. The drones would still be a threat. But, so far, there had just been the initial attack. The drones probably spent their ordinance, still circling overhead, but unable to engage. But they might have friends.

Henry was cresting the ridge, struggling with deep snow and a steep slope, when the world rocked him sideways. His hearing was gone and his bones and organs and brain seemed to convulse and all of the oxygen in the valley disappeared. He pitched face-first into the snow with the shock wave as the second bomb hit.

There was smoke and fire. Trees burned and the wreckage where the cabin had been was a roiling crater, a perfect mushroom cloud forming in the valley. Henry was aware of Carlos, grabbing him by the collar and dragging him back from the slope. Henry looked at his friend, saw his mouth moving, but there was just the high-pitched ringing. From the expression on Carlos's face, he was shouting and speaking slowly. Henry felt sluggish and punch-drunk in the way he'd felt after stepping into the ring with his first hand-to-hand combat instructor at Ranger School. He'd been wearing headgear, but after a flurry of fists and chops and one particularly nasty kick, he was swaying on his knees, gasping for breath, not entirely sure what his name was. He felt that way now.

Carlos gave up on trying to talk to him and hauled Henry to his feet. Carlos wasted no time, moving out. Henry staggered behind him, taking one last look at the wrecked valley.

The sun had slipped behind the mountains and the valley was tinged in blue, dying light, tainted by smoke and blood. The bombs, probably JDAMs, laser-guided bunker busters fired from an aircraft, had killed many of the attacking troops. Henry could make no sense of it.

He knew he probably owed Carlos his life, though. If he'd been on the other side of the ridge, the bombs would have turned his insides to jelly. If Carlos hadn't decided to make a run for it, that would have been the end of Henry Wilkins. As it was, he knew most of his fellow teammates lay dead in the snow. He grieved as he ran and slid through the twilight and powder.

While the Wolves, like other elements of the special ops community, were trained and indeed selected for their individual ability to make decisions and act independent from the chain of command, every operation was carefully planned and rehearsed ahead of time. Before any given direct action, the men invariably went into the mission armed with contingency plans, fallback rendezvous points, and clear mission objectives. Henry had become accustomed to this structure. Even if things went sideways on an op, which they often did, there was always another move, a planned step in the face of chaos. There was at least the hope of extraction. Henry felt lost now.

*

He'd been cut off in enemy territory before, back when he was a Ranger humping it over the hopeless mountains of Afghanistan, waiting on a medevac that took days to come because the Rangers were actually operating in Pakistan and the politicians and brass couldn't get their shit together. They'd pursued a high-value al-Qaeda target across a border without markers, an alien world of thin air and hate and snipers and mortars fired from hillsides miles away. No matter where you were in Afghanistan, there was always someplace higher, and the mujahideen were always there, sniping from cover. It seemed no matter how high he climbed, there were loftier peaks and crags and rocks and the enemy was there. He'd watched guided munitions smash enemy positions, seen the Spectre gunships pound hillsides, shouted with his fist in the air as a squadron of Cobra attack helicopters hammered hillsides with Hellfire missiles. But the enemy always came back. Millions of dollars in munitions up in smoke to kill a five-dollar camel that seemed to never die.

Lieutenant Michael Cox, a soft-spoken young man from Lexington, Kentucky, had taken a round to the thigh high on some unnamed mountain in Pakistan. Lieutenant Cox was the kind of man who inspired others without seeming to try. He was not given to fiery speeches and angry exhortation. He cared about his men, unwilling to take foolish risks with their lives, and he was more likely to quote Jesus or Kipling than utter a harsh word. Henry, along with the rest of his platoon, loved Lieutenant Cox. Henry was only twenty years old then, and although Cox was maybe only twenty-five, he seemed wise and calm and just. Lieutenant Cox was a venerated warrior, and Henry trusted him with his life without question.

"You are the MOST OUTSTANDING FUCKING Rangers in the battalion," he'd tell his men. "The baddest men on the planet. Take a knee.

Oh, Lord, protect my Rangers this day and watch over them. Protect them with Jesus fire and the Sword of Righteousness. Amen."

And then Lieutenant Cox would lead them into battle. Henry had watched the lieutenant hunkered down beside a boulder, calling in fire missions from artillery units or radioing for air support while rounds peppered whatever it was he was using for cover that day, the rounds missing him as if God himself turned them aside. One of the men had dubbed Cox "Meshach" for the Old Testament man who had endured a furnace in the name of God and emerged unscathed. The name stuck.

On January 2, 2014, Lieutenant Cox, aka Meshach, bled out on a mountainside in Pakistan that God, command, and the rest of the country did not seem to care about. Lieutenant Cox went hard, fighting it to the end, issuing orders while his lips were turning blue and his face turned gray. The medic had done what he could, but it wasn't enough. Lieutenant Cox's eyes seemed to sink into themselves.

"Wilkins," the lieutenant said. His voice was strained, but calm, not the voice of a dying man. He couldn't die. But his eyes were fluttering and he was in shock because a .50-caliber round had torn through his leg and severed his femoral artery. Doc Wilson was swearing and trying to staunch the bleeding. Lieutenant Cox gripped Henry's wrist and pulled him close, face twitching with pain and visions of whatever it was he could see in that awful moment, something urgent on his lips.

Maybe he was about to order Henry to take the men to higher ground, or to leave him until they could come back for his body, or tell his wife or momma that he loved them, or reveal the secret of the universe.

Henry would always wonder what Lieutenant Cox meant to say on January 2, but he would never know. The man died in his arms. No ring of Jesus fire that day, no hedge of protection. The last thing he'd said was "Wilkins."

America had long since lost its fascination with that particular war. Henry and the rest of his platoon were stranded, and repeated requests for evacuation were denied. The Rangers had to climb twenty miles of hard ground back into Afghanistan before they were extracted. Throughout the trek, they were harried by enemy sniper and mortar fire. On those jagged, windy mountains, Bart lost his knee, Henry became a leader, and Jesus Christ abandoned the Rangers and Henry and especially Lieutenant Cox.

Later, Henry would admit that the lieutenant would have disagreed with Henry's assessment of life and even his own death on that forlorn mountain. The only people he would share those thoughts with were fellow Rangers. Lieutenant Cox probably would have told Henry to keep the faith, to trust in God even though God *appeared* absent.

Stateside, after a long ride in a cargo plane, Henry stood with some of his fellow Rangers in a field of stone. Arlington was somber and gray, and the rows of markers stretched off into the distance over rolling hills. The grounds were manicured and somber, and many of the graves were from the first Civil War.

A preacher from Kentucky spoke kind words and a widow received a folded-up flag, and Lieutenant Cox's eight-year-old son cried quiet tears while Henry sat next to Suzanne. Henry did not cry that day, although he wailed inside. His face was a mask, a hard shell, clean-shaved and false and strong-jawed. The honor guard fired shots with crisp efficiency and pressed uniforms and the rain drizzled cold and bleak.

Henry sent Mrs. Cox money over the next ten years. Budget cuts had reduced veterans' benefits, making it hard for a surviving widow to get by. When Suzanne got her first big check, she graciously agreed to make an anonymous donation to Lieutenant Cox's son's college fund. Whatever it was, it was not enough, and could never be.

*

With a thought, Henry activated his night vision lenses. The twilight became clear and crisp following a moment of vertigo. The wind was a blade with a keen edge cutting his face, and the snow was up to his waist in places. Ahead, Carlos blazed a trail like an elemental force of nature. Over the ridges behind them, the sound of sporadic gunfire still echoed through the deep forest.

Henry could only hope some of his fellow Wolves made it.

KEY WEST, FLORIDA

The night appeared normal as Suzanne swept Taylor up into her arms at the dock. Bart helped Mary step off the boat, then secured the lines. Taylor wrapped her tiny arms around Suzanne's neck, and for a moment there was peace and relief. The canal behind her home was quiet; the Christmas lights along some of the windows at homes up and down the waterway cast friendly reflections onto the dark water, and a group of teenagers in a skiff went past, waving, the sound of their engine like a lawnmower.

Ginnie stood hugging herself several feet back. "The net is down," she said.

"I know," Suzanne replied. "Do you want to leave? You can, if you need to. Or you can stay, whatever you like. You're welcome here for as long as you want. Your call."

"I don't know," Ginnie said, her face in the shadows and her voice full of worry. "I tried calling my folks in Miami, but there's just a beeping sound. One of the neighbors came over earlier to check on us. And of course, there's Bobby. He's taking a nap on your couch."

Suzanne led the way down the coral path lined with palms and orchids. The pool lights were on, and, it seemed, every light in the house as well, as if Ginnie had tried to banish the war with wattage.

Ginnie had been with Suzanne for about two years. The only child of affluent parents in Coral Gables, Ginnie had an artistic bent, and was taking a few years off before going back to college. She helped Suzanne take care of the home and watched Taylor for four hours every morning so that Suzanne could write. Ginnie was good-hearted, but with a sadness on her Suzanne felt she understood. The girl's childhood had been lonely and full of great expectations.

On the leather sofa, old Bobby Ray snored. Bart padded into the great room and took a seat in the easy chair while Taylor sat on Suzanne's lap.

Ginnie sat down beside Suzanne, and Mary squeezed in beside Bobby. Mary looked vacant, a shambling, shocked woman.

"I guess for now, we should wait here," Bart said. "We'll go into full hurricane mode. Fill up the bathtubs with water. Start stockpiling our food. We'll make a run into town in the morning and see what we can find out."

"You don't want to try for the base tonight?"

"No. Too risky. It sounds like everything is pretty calm here. But I'll feel a whole lot better going out in the daytime."

"All right."

"Tonight we'll alternate watches. I'm gonna need the code to Henry's gun safe. You all get showered and fed, then try to catch some sleep. I'll take the first watch, then wake you up at about four."

"Ugh."

"Yeah, I know. But you've got a lotta windows. Somebody could throw a brick through and be on top of us before we knew it. We' need to stay vigilant. One of us will remain awake at all times."

"Right."

"Um," Mary said. Everyone turned to look at her. She was sunburned, and her hair was a riot of curls.

"What is it, dear?" Bart said. The exasperation just below the surface.

"I was just wondering if you had anything?" Mary's voice was small and thin. "Anything to help me sleep maybe?"

"I'll see what I can scrounge up," Suzanne said. "I've probably got something."

"It's just . . . My nerves, you know."

"I know, hon. It's all right."

Great. Mary is in full-blown helpless mode. What have I got? Maybe some Lortab from the last time Henry was home. He had a prescription, but he never takes anything. Worst comes to worst, I bet Ginnie has some weed.

Suzanne went into the bathroom and searched for a bottle, ultimately found one beneath the sink. She handed it to Mary.

"You might want to save them," Suzanne said. "That's all there is."

"Thanks," Mary mumbled, looking at the floor.

Suzanne went back into her bathroom and stripped out of her clothing. Her bathing suit was dry, but the residue of salt made her itchy. Steaming water blasted the salt and stress from her. She washed her hair and luxuriated beneath the jets, knowing that this shower might well be her last for a long time.

She was grateful Taylor was safe, but as she thought about what might be happening around the country, a chill came into her bones in spite of the hot shower and she turned up the heat.

Hopefully, this will be over quickly. Hopefully, it's not as bad as people are saying. Yeah, the country is divided, but America is stronger than that. We're not some third-world hellhole where people are used to slaughter in the streets.

Even as she attempted to push away desolation with hope, ugly thoughts and images sprung unbidden to her mind. A senator banging his fist on the podium, face red and angry. A militia group with white hoods and swastikas and guns spewing hatred for the cameras. Inner city war zones after hurricanes, looting, shootings, beatings, gangs, and riots. Black-and-white images of the first Civil War with trenches filled with dead American boys, bloated, uniformed, and clutching guns fitted with bayonets.

The country, she decided, had forgotten what war is. To them, war was something to watch on the net, entertainment. A video game that didn't affect them in the real world. War happened someplace else. She thought about generations of soft, angry people who were convinced they wanted a fight; they would bleed and regret and then die. *Because soldiers are not soft. And if they are unleashed on our own soil, pitted against one another, they'll do what they have been trained to do. They will kill.*

God help us.

CHAPTER SIX

Good Neighbors

HOUSTON, TEXAS

Reince Blackaby galloped his fingers on a burnished mahogany desk with one hand and pushed the metal balls, a desk toy given to him by his wife, with the other, taking comfort in the predictable clicking sound and the laws of physics. He was having a bad day.

Reince, sleek as an otter in his $10,000 black suit and slicked-back hair, was afraid. Things had gotten out of control, and he was forced to realize that his life as he knew it was over. Beyond the broad window, Houston looked mostly calm. A few military helicopters in the distance, but nothing burning, no rioting here. Not yet.

He had spent his life telling himself that he was the embodiment of the American Dream. His father had been a boilermaker in upstate New York, hardworking, blue-collar, honest. Reince wanted more for his life, and had joined the army with a plan when he was seventeen. Six years, then college at SUNY with the help of the GI bill. Law school at Columbia, then a job with a hedge fund firm. He'd been approached by the Directors to head up a "security firm," as they had put it. The million-dollar signing bonus made the decision a no-brainer. He was now fifty years old, and worth more in millions. Life had been good. Country clubs, yachts, vacations all over the world in private jets. He was proud of himself for what he had accomplished.

"Pulled myself up by my own bootstraps," he'd lecture his children when they were acting spoiled, which was often. "You don't have any idea how good you have it."

As a hedge fund manager, he'd learned to see patterns beneath the chaos, manipulate it even. There were constant fluctuations in the market, but there was always a way to make more money.

The Directors were going to blame him for this debacle, though, and he knew firsthand what that meant. They were not people in the forgiveness business. As far as he knew, he had met only one of them, a withered, unassuming raisin of a man with intense blue eyes and a chilling smile. The man, who identified himself as "Mr. Smith," was the one who had recruited Reince years ago. Since then, communication was via encrypted phone and self-destroying e-mail. The Directors were ghosts.

While Reince liked to consider himself a "Master of the Universe," really, he was no more than a glorified middleman, a cog in the wheel, and now he feared for the lives of his wife and children. He'd already called Amy to tell her to get the hell out of town, empty the bank accounts, and go off the grid. It was a backup plan he'd rehearsed with her and had in place for several years.

Until this morning, everything had gone according to a plan years in the making. The right palms were greased, elections bought. The media played along, and Reince would chuckle as he watched the two sides having it out, feeling like a puppet master. A nudge here, a poke there, a bit of blackmail sprinkled in, and he was amazed sometimes how easy it was. He wasn't privy to the Directors' larger objectives. He followed orders.

The threat of secession was supposed to be only a means to make more money. It was never about actual war, only making dollars. More defense contracts, more gun manufacturing, more favorable tax laws, relaxed environmental regulations. Somehow, Reince had lost control. Washington, DC, was never supposed to be attacked. San Fran should not have been nuked. People had lost their minds.

Reince stared at the phone on his desk, waiting.

NASHVILLE, TENNESSEE

Leon Smith pulled the pickup truck onto West End Avenue. Traffic was snarled. The radio was talking about a war, and Leon was confused. Some of the stations had only static.

He tried the cell phone: no signal. The computer screen on the dash displayed Washington, DC, burning, and the scrolling headlines reported casualty counts, crazy numbers. "One hundred thousand people believed dead in the nation's capital . . . Rioting in cities around the US."

"You believe this shit?" Dominic said. "This some kind of joke?"

"I don't think so," Leon said, looking at the line of brake lights stretching for as far as he could see. People were honking horns.

The sky was low and gray with the promise of rain or sleet.

"The traffic lights stopped working," Leon said.

"Yeah," Jesus said. "No light in the stores either."

"Oh man!" Dominic shouted, gesturing out the passenger window. "Look!"

Leon leaned over and down so he could see what Dominic was yelling about. Across the street, people were running out of a Wells Fargo bank. A pair of cops were walking toward the door with scatterguns.

Shots rang out, dull booms. Leon could hear people screaming.

Leon saw a woman fall down. The window on the passenger side of the truck shattered, spraying glass onto Leon's lap, and a round slammed into the door next to him. He looked down at his chest, half expecting to find a gaping wound, but he was unharmed. Dominic and Jesus were shouting.

"There's a bank robbery going on right next to us," Dominic was saying. "Dog, you almost got shot."

"Yeah."

There were more gunshots then, and Leon slid low in his seat. The truck was hopelessly mired in the traffic jam. The sound of a wailing woman hung on the chill gray afternoon.

"I'm outta here," Dominic said, opening the door.

"Adios," Jesus said, jumping out behind Dominic.

The gunfire ceased, and a crowd of people formed around the cops with the shotguns. Apparently, they had shot the bank robbers. People were crouched around a middle-aged woman, and Leon could see a pool of blood on the parking lot. He decided it was time to go on foot.

He abandoned the vehicle, ignoring the malevolent stares from fellow motorists. Other people were already doing the same. With so many empty vehicles on the road, traffic would be snarled for hours even if the power grid was restored.

Leon did some quick math. He was about ten miles from home. If he jogged, and if he didn't encounter any problems, he could make it home to Antioch in a few hours, even with the hills.

He felt pretty good for the first mile, but then his feet began to ache. Work boots were less than ideal for running on pavement. By the time he made it to Nolensville Road, he was in agony. He could feel the burning blisters on his soles, and his feet felt tortured.

Police officers directed traffic at intersections, and traffic moved along only slightly faster than his steady jog.

"Hey, man," said a bearded guy stopped before an intersection. The man had rolled the passenger window down and was leaning across the seat. His blue Ford F-150 was dusty and the truck bed was filled with lumber and construction tools. Leon stopped.

"You need a lift, brother?" the guy said. "Where ya headed?"

"Lower Antioch," Leon said, panting.

"C'mon, hop in," the guy said. "I'm goin' your way. I live down off Harding. You look like you're about to drop." He reached over and opened the door.

Leon hesitated. His feet hurt, and the rain had started.

"Okay. Thanks a lot, man," Leon said, getting into the truck. There was a battered brown leather Bible on the dashboard and country music coming from the speakers.

"Name's Burt," said the man with the beard and friendly eyes. His hair was short and the color of snow, face weathered and strong. Maybe sixty years old, with some hard miles in there. Leon shook Burt's hand, a firm grip. Honest, but without challenge. "It's gonna take us a while, but it's better than walking in that cold rain."

"I'm Leon. I really appreciate it," Leon said, still breathing hard. "Trying to get home to my wife and my boys." *And I just killed a man and I'm wearing his gun. Good Lord.*

"The country's gone insane," Burt said. His voice was southern and rocky. "Don't mean we gotta join it. They say there's war."

"I don't get it."

"Well, join the club. Buncha assholes in Washington doing what they do."

"No shortage of those," Leon agreed.

"I thought it was all just talk. I guess not. I don't know what things have come to." He chuckled. "Whoa there, we're doing twenty-five. Get my smellin' salts. What line of work you in, Leon?"

"Landscaping."

"Ah, yeah. That's an honest trade." Burt nodded as though Leon had uttered something profound. "You served? If you don't mind me askin'?"

"Yeah. Army."

"Me too," Burt said. "Six years stateside. Got out before the first Gulf War."

"I hope this doesn't last."

"Naw, it'll be over quick. People ain't as dumb as Washington thinks. We got problems, but nothing worth killing everybody over. Folks'll see that pretty soon. It'll take some time to set things right again. But maybe we'll be better off in the end. Maybe. Then again, if what they're saying on the radio is true, maybe not. My wife always said I wore rose-colored glasses."

"There's a whole world full of hate out there, Burt."

"I know it. But the nasty folks have always been the loudest. Sooner or later, they get drowned out by the rest of us, the ones not so full of venom."

"Well, I hope you're right."

"Uh-huh." Burt hunched over the wheel, squinting into the misting rain. A half mile away, blue lights flashed on both sides of the road. The truck had not moved in twenty minutes.

More than anything, Leon wanted to put his arms around his wife and his boys. He wanted to pretend today had never happened.

NASHVILLE, TENNESSEE

Jessie Johnson, a man who had lied to himself so many times he could no longer distinguish fact from fiction, racked the 12-gauge, put it on his shoulder, and strode down his muddy driveway. He was feeling bulletproof, and it wasn't just the case of Old Milwaukee he'd consumed. This day was like Super Bowl Sunday and the first day of deer season all rolled into one.

His bulky cammo coat was threadbare but warm. The sun had gone down fast and it felt like the rain might turn to snow overnight. He stood next to his dilapidated mailbox, swaying slightly, realizing he did not know exactly what he wanted to do. *Let it out. That's it. Just explode like a bomb.*

He noticed that the lights inside the trailers had gone out while he was walking. The street had gone dark. All except for the trailer directly across the street. Somehow, their power kicked back on. He could see the huge flat-screen through the window. One of those fancy new 3-D jobs. The family who lived there were Mexicans. *Probably ten of 'em piled up on top of each other. They got a television they probably stole. Probably stole the power too.*

He raised the shotgun, aware that he was lurching and his aim was unsteady even though he was not moving. He wanted to shoot out the window and kill that big TV. The front door opened.

"Hey, Marshall!" the man said. *What was his name? Alejandro or Hondo or some spic shit. I could shoot him right now.*

"Hey, man," said Santiago. "Hey, I've got a generator. You need to store any food or anything, let me know."

"Do what?" Jessie said, faintly pleased the man had referred to him correctly. Jessie lowered his weapon.

"Just trying to be a good neighbor, man," Santiago said. "Spread the word. If we're still without power tomorrow, we gonna have us a neighborhood cookout."

"All right," Jessie said. He felt strange, unfulfilled. *Maybe I should go home and sleep this one off. I can kill his TV tomorrow.*

CHAPTER SEVEN

Incoming

ALBERTA, CANADA

Henry crawled out of the snow shelter he'd spent the night in. Dawn was gray and frozen. He and Carlos had dug burrows into a drift in the dead of the night because the snow would help to conceal their heat signatures from drones, satellites, and anything else with bad intentions that might be hunting them. They hoped the attackers would decide their mission was complete.

Carlos was already up and looking around. "I was really hoping some of our guys might cut our trail and show up. Some of them might have made it."

"Maybe we should go back?" Henry already knew the answer, but felt compelled to put the question out there. He needed confirmation.

"No. You know the drill. They'll do what we did. Evade the enemy. If there were wounded back there, the guys sent to kill us got to them already."

Henry tore into an MRE and ate a cold burrito. He'd lost friends before, but never so many. He was still numb. He needed a plan. He needed explanations. He had neither, just a sense of desolation.

He pulled out a snapshot of Taylor and Suzanne he kept with him in one of his chest pockets, right next to field dressings, tape, and painkillers. The photograph, unposed and natural, was one he'd taken a year ago of a perfect moment. Suzanne and Taylor playing in the pool, laughing in the sun. He stared at it for a time in silence. It was like a door to yesterday, a tiny portal with warmth and light and hope filtering between worlds, and more than anything, he yearned to slip through and become a part of that other world, to go back in time and place. He gazed at the picture with longing, like if he stared long enough, the door would open and he could step through.

"You okay?" Carlos said.

"Good to go."

"Let's get moving, brother. We've got a lot of hard miles to cover."

"Copy that." Henry put his rucksack over his shoulders with a leaden feeling in his legs. They moved out into the wilderness, trudging south.

The woods were lonely and silent, as if the snow sucked the sound from the world and hid it beneath a blanket of white. The branches on the trees were naked of leaves and coated with an armor of snow and ice, and the pine and spruce stands were heavy laden, branches weeping to the powder. There was an air of quiet expectation, as if the mountain held its breath, waiting to exhale.

They took a brief stop at around noon. Henry sat on an exposed boulder and gobbled down an energy bar.

"So who were those troopers?" Henry said. "And who dropped the bombs?"

"Yeah. My wheels are turning," Carlos said. He had his big hands wrapped around the mouthpiece of his CamelBak drinking tube to thaw some ice buildup there.

"I think the first guys, the ones on the ground, probably were air force commandos out of Malmstrom. Now, why they got dispatched, I have no idea. I think maybe the colonel stirred up a hornet's nest with his inquiries."

"And the bombs? The UAVs?"

"You got me, Henry. Somebody wanted to be damn sure the Wolves were dead. Dropped ordnance on their own guys. In Canada, no less."

"One of the things that's got me concerned," Henry said, "is that they know who *we* are, whoever *they* are. If they figure out we made it, they may keep coming."

"I've got no family," Carlos said, his voice flat. "I'll get you home, Henry. I swear."

"I appreciate that, my friend. Maybe we're just paranoid." But he knew otherwise. *Would they go after my family to get to me? If they think I know something I shouldn't, then, yes.*

"Just because you're paranoid doesn't mean they're not out to get you. Let's move out. We ought to run into a road before too long. If we're lucky we'll find an empty cabin. Maybe grab a car. Change into civvies."

They walked for another four or five hours, saying little. Henry was awed by the stark beauty of the winter Rocky Mountains. They slipped past frozen waterfalls, terraced and glittering like crystal. Henry's feet were blocks of ice and his hands felt clumsy. His face burned with the subzero temperatures and the lashing wind. He thought about the Keys and sunshine and warm water; he walked in a kind of trance, physically alert, but mentally absent as his mind took him to friendlier times.

*

Henry marveled at the way seemingly inconsequential decisions changed lives. He'd seen it in combat, and he'd experienced it in relationships. One guy breaks right and falls, another guy goes left and makes it.

He and Bart were twenty-two years old and on leave for two weeks with a pocketful of combat pay. They'd started out in Daytona with a rented red convertible Mustang that just begged to be driven. After the first night, they got a wild hair and decided to drive down to the Keys. They'd stopped at Holiday Isle. Bart had just completed rehab on his knee, and Henry was about to be deployed again. But they had two weeks to be young and dumb.

Holiday Isle was an oceanside resort in Islamorada, and spring break was in full swing. College kids from all over the country flocked to the Keys to get hammered and laid in the sunshine. Bart was driving when they pulled into the gravel parking area across the street from the sprawling hotels and bars. They both had their shirts off, sunglasses on, and were highly alert for contact with the opposite sex.

Bart was driving through the parking lot with a sense of urgency. A bikini-clad pair of girls stepped out from behind a van, directly in front of the fast-moving Mustang. Bart slammed on the brakes and the car slid on the loose gravel.

The girls squealed and tried to leap out of the way, but not before the Mustang knocked the brunette down. "Assholes!" screamed the blonde. "You could have killed us! Mary, are you okay?"

Henry and Bart jumped out of the car and ran around to the front of the vehicle. Henry was appalled and terrified they'd really hurt the girl on the ground.

"Oh, man," Bart said. "I'm *so* sorry. My bad." Bart knelt down next to Mary, who was bleeding a little from one of her knees, a scratch.

"He just learned how to drive," Henry said, deadpan. "But we'll make it up to you. Drinks all day on me."

"Fuck off," said the blonde who would end up marrying Henry.

"Well, if you put it that way," Henry said with a broad grin. The blonde cut her eyes at him, shaking her head, still pissed.

Bart helped Mary to her feet, and she smiled at him. "Well," Mary said, still gazing at Bart. "You gotta admit they're cute."

They danced and drank frozen daiquiris and rum runners and lounged in the sun for a week. The night before the girls were scheduled to return to college at the University of Florida, Henry made a pitch to Suzanne.

"Look," he said, "what really matters in life?" They were sitting alone on a rock looking out at the moonlit ocean. In the distance, a band played old eighties rock, and there were hoots and howls and the sound of fevered mating rituals. But Henry was serious. He reached out and held Suzanne's hand.

"Ten years from now, when you look back on next week, what will you recall? What will matter then? Will you remember the test you took or the paper you wrote? Will you care about the boring-ass lecture you sat through on Shakespeare's sexuality?"

"I like the Bard. He wasn't gay, by the way."

"Well there you go. You don't need to go to *that* class. What I'm saying is, you should take an extended break. Give it another week, and we'll make memories that will last a lifetime." He leaned in and kissed the softest part of her neck. "And one of my favorite lines in literature is 'Barkis is willing.' I'm not saying all that, but I'm *willing* for seven more days. No promises, no regrets. One hell of a week."

"You're sweet, Henry. That's not going to happen. And Dickens is overrated."

"I want you to really think about it. Justify it. If you go back to school this week instead of the following week, what's that going to change? How does that make a difference in your life? Whereas if you stay down here for another week, you can look back later on and explain to your kids you lived life to the fullest. You took every moment and—"

"Do you really believe this shit? You seriously should leave the army and become a car salesman."

". . . and sucked the marrow from life," he continued, as if she had not spoken. "You didn't leave anything to wonder about later on. No promises, no regrets, but let's make this week *something*."

"And why would I do that?" she said. And he knew he had her.

"Because I've got great abs, can quote Hamlet, and because we're going to rent the suite for a whole week. Take out a boat every day. We'll fish, dive, eat like royalty, live like kings."

"That'll cost a fortune. That suite is probably close to a grand a night."

"Well, you know what? I don't care, because I want to make this week something special. I might die in a month. A year. You know where I'm going . . ."

"You're laying it on a little thick, soldier boy. And what about Mary? What if she wants to go back?"

"I trust Bart to handle that," Henry said.

And that week made all the difference.

*

"You boys are slow and deaf," Henry heard over his shoulder. He jumped, spinning, even as recognition penetrated his reverie. Sergeant Major Martinez strode through the snow, smoke coming from his mouth in the arctic air, bloodstains on his chest and arms.

"Are you hit?" Carlos asked.

"No. Not my blood. I cut your trail this morning."

"Anybody else?" Henry said.

".Just me. All my boys. Gone. The colonel, too. Never made it out of the bunker."

"How do you know for sure?"

"Against my better judgment, I hung around. Got a few more of the bastards that hit us. They were SF. No insignias, no dog tags. One of the men I killed was a guy I went through SERE school with. He was a good fucking soldier."

"What the hell?" Carlos said.

"Colonel Bragg gave me this." Martinez reached into a pocket and held up a black square the size of a match, a case for a micro-drive. "He didn't have time to tell me much. But he said if anything happened to him to get this out on the net worldwide. I'm guessing it's the proof he claimed he didn't have. Proof we've been usurped by something, someone, some *whatever the fuck they are.* The guy behind the guy, the puppet master all the gringos in tinfoil hats have been yammering about. He's real, that guy. And he's evil."

"And on our ass," Carlos said.

"Yeah, that too," Martinez replied. "But we've got one thing going for us."

"What's that?" Henry said.

"The *guy* thinks we're all dead."

KEY WEST, FLORIDA

Suzanne was up with the sun. She padded across tiled floors, brewed a cup of coffee in the kitchen, and sat down at her desk. Her office was in the master bedroom, and afforded her a nice view of the pool and foliage and the waterway behind her home. She looked at her computer with a bit of disdain. *Why bother?*

She was under a deadline to complete a novel she had procrastinated on. She forced herself to write every morning, but she had not made much headway on her latest book, a romance novel set in Renaissance Florence. It was hard to come up with flowery prose and erotic double entendre when divorce was looming in the real world. *And now, my publisher might not even exist.*

The house was silent and the sunlight had a kind of promise in it, a special light that happens in the Keys in December when the rest of the country is shrouded in snow. She looked out at the blue pool and the dark water and boats up on davits. The people who owned the house on the other side of the canal were only there a few weeks a year, and this was one of them. She had met them a couple of times over the last two years, and she and Henry had attended one of their parties, a catered event with tuxedoes and evening gowns and strings of pearls. Henry had been miserable, and they'd left after only an hour. Suzanne smiled with the memory.

*

A string quartet played *The Four Seasons* by Vivaldi and the balmy night shimmered with class and diamonds. The guests moved with measured grace and held their champagne flutes *just so* and smiled and lied and talked about yachts and skiing and how bad the help was. An ice sculpture of a mermaid was the centerpiece by the pool.

"You know," Henry had whispered, "I've got PTSD. I might not get convicted if I killed these people."

"Shut up," she'd said, giggling. "They're awful, I'll give you that."

"So let's get outta here." He'd kissed her neck the way he did when he really wanted to convince her, in the way he knew she couldn't refuse.

"Okay. Another half hour. Then I'm all yours."

"All right then."

A couple was approaching, locked on. There was nowhere to hide.

"Incoming," Henry said. "I say number four."

"Three," she'd said. "Usual bet?"

"Done."

Then, "Hello, I'm Suzanne, it's so nice to meet you . . ."

Yes, I wrote that. No, it wasn't a movie. Yes, my husband is in the army. No he doesn't have any exciting blood and guts stories for you.

A couple of hours later, lying in the bed with a satisfied sheen of sweat covering both of them, he caressed her back with feather fingers.

"You're purring again," he'd said.

"You know you love me."

"Yeah. And you know that I know that you know it."

"I guess that worked out well for both of us."

"No arguments there," Henry said in that husky voice he had when he was half-asleep and content. The old Henry, the one she'd fallen in love with so hard. Not the one who'd been showing up lately.

She'd rolled over then and touched his cheek. "How do they do it? Why?"

"I have no idea." He'd done some interesting things, then.

An hour later, she'd said, "Seriously, why? How can one man decide to marry four different women? I mean, wouldn't you at some point decide that enough is enough?"

"Well . . . you did *see* her, right. I get that."

"Pigs."

"That we are. But those tits were real. I can sort of understand."

"Ugh."

"I'm just sayin'."

"Well, so are these . . ."

The sun was coming up, with that golden, sweet light filtering into the room. Henry turned on his side to face her and there was a sadness on his face she did not expect.

"Tell me," he'd said, his voice soft. "Do you plan to trade *me* in on a new model?"

"Never."

"Money seems to breed restlessness and stupidity. You're rich now."

"Give me a break."

"How is that not true?"

"*We're* rich, yeah. I guess we are. We should swing from the chandeliers. You're a little beat up, but I happen to like the model. You're a classic. You've got character."

"You're too good at it."

"What do you mean?"

"The game. The dance. The wealthy charade. You're like a fish in the water. You blend in without trying to blend in because you're in your element. You're not faking it."

"Bullshit. You know that's bullshit. There is no element. It's called life. I sold a book. Be glad. Don't try to—"

"Suzanne, you love the attention. You crave it because you never got it from your mother or your father because they never gave a damn about you and now you have this urge to fit in. You're changing. Maybe you don't see it, but I do."

"Don't *you* talk about *my* parents. Just because your momma was a worthless piece of white trash and your daddy was poor doesn't give you the right. Money is just a tool. It doesn't make you evil. It sure as hell doesn't make *me* evil. And it seems like that's what you think lately. Are you that insecure? You're supposed to be a *Ranger!*"

He'd bolted from the bed then. Banging drawers and pulling on clothes. "Yeah," he'd said. "You grew up with money. Good for you. Your old man is an asshole, and your mother was worse, and those are your own words. We're done here."

"Come back and fight like a man, damn it! Don't run away!"

But he'd gone out the door and hadn't come home until late that night and she couldn't figure out what had gone wrong, what had poisoned the morning.

*

The memory of a good evening gone bad soured as Suzanne sat in the same room with the same kind of golden light and she put her head in her hands over a computer she hadn't flipped open and a book she'd never finish.

"Momma!" Taylor said at the doorway, rubbing her eyes and wrapped in a fuzzy blanket. "I'm hungry. Can you make me some oatmeal?"

"Yes, honey," Suzanne said. "Give Momma a minute, okay?"

"O-kay." Taylor's voice was a singsong of morning exuberance. "I had a dream about a big wolf last night. But he was a good wolf. A big black wolf. And he was helping people. He was nice."

"Go watch some *Sesame Street*, Love. I'll get you some breakfast in a minute."

"O-kay," Taylor sang. "Kisses first." She ran up and put her arms around Suzanne's neck and kissed her on the cheek.

Suzanne watched her daughter run away, cloaked in her softie-soft, little feet pattering on the floor and blonde curls bouncing.

Suzanne had not cried in fifteen years, not since her cat Missy had died when she was in high school. "Buck up and get your ass off your shoulders," her father would say to her when she was young and in need of a good cry. Just a little kid.

"Tears are unattractive, dear," her mother would admonish. "They make you look weak."

The tears came now, anguished and angry, a deep chested howl born of pent-up emotions and regrets and the recognition of the kind of mistakes that shatter lives. She punched the desk with her fist, not caring about the pain. She cried for her past, for the little girl that had been told to *buck up*. She pounded that desk because she had screwed up her life. She had not been paying attention to the things that mattered. A perpetually happy four-year-old cloaked in a softie-soft blanket. The husky voice and earnest love of *her man*. The light over the water on a warm December morning imbued with promise. *Those* things mattered. She yearned for a life of purpose, yet seemed bent upon unraveling everything important.

It was over quickly. A brief outburst, a volcano of the soul, an immediate relief of pressure. She wiped her face.

She felt renewed clarity and purpose. The storm windows needed to be pulled down. She had to talk to her father, on the off chance that he was in town and that he could get them on base and that he gave a damn. Hit the stores now. Food, fishing gear, antibiotics, water.

She needed to contact Henry somehow, and tell him she had made a promise she intended to keep. She had regrets. She wanted to make it right.

CHAPTER EIGHT

Semper Fi

NORTHERN MONTANA

Henry Wilkins was willing to give his life for his country, but at the moment, his country seemed intent on killing him. This did not sit well in the jagged corners of his soul, humping through the Canadian Rockies with drones hunting him. His ideas of God, country, and honor had been defined long before he became an Army Ranger. His father had been the architect. Now, the pillars, walls, and supports that should have been true were askew. His entire belief system was under attack, the very things he knew to be true not because he had been told to but because he believed.

There are bad guys and good guys, and there will be a fight. It is inevitable. Whether it's a playground, a city, a country, or the globe. There will be conflict between good and evil, the bully and the bullied.

*

"Stand up for yourself," his father had said when Henry walked home with a bloody nose again. 'His old man, Tim Wilkins, peered down at Henry. A tall, rangy man with a straight back, pale blue eyes, and a face worn out by life, Tim Wilkins was not prone to overt displays of affection or sympathy. But he was the center of Henry's universe.

In Henry's eyes then, his father was granite, solid rock, unbreakable, unchangeable, and strong in the way of a proud mountain. The lens of hope and faith filtered out the cracks and fissures, the broken blood vessels on Papa's windburned face, and the hurting eyes of a man eroded, but not yet completely worn smooth. Blasted by hard years, bad luck, and the love for the wrong woman, Papa remained undefeated then.

"Be a man. You're gonna have to learn this some point or other. It's tough and it ain't fair, and nobody said it was. And if they said that, they lied to you. Now I could go up to the schoolhouse, and I could argue with them about how my boy is getting his ass kicked. But what does that teach you, son? What do you learn from that? A better lesson is *life*. Life will knock you down if you let it, so you'd better damn sure figure out how to punch life right in the mouth. You don't—"

"But I got suspended!"

"Well, did you hit the other guy?"

"Well, yeah. That's why I got kicked out of school."

"Good."

"But he gave me a bloody nose, and the teacher believed the other kid. Not me. But the asshole hit me first."

"All right. Look here. And don't say that word, Henry. You know better than that."

"But Dad—"

"Don't 'but Dad' me. You got into a fight. Your nose is bleeding and I'm not gonna wipe it for you. I'm sorry, son. You're learning, see. You get punched, and then you hit back."

"I *did*. That's what I'm saying. It's not fair. I—"

"I know it, son. Get used to that. Life won't be fair. You outta know it by now, but you probably don't, because it takes a bit for it to sink in.

The thing is, you don't just sit and take it when it ain't fair. You figure out what you have to do to make it *less unfair*. Sometimes that means you shut up for a minute. But you're thinking about what happens later on, and even though it looks like you're taking it, you're really biding your time. You're thinking about the next time you catch that son of a bitch alone without his friends. And other times, you have to just stand up and punch somebody in the nose. What happens, happens. You might get beat, but that's all right because you'll know something. You'll learn a thing about yourself."

"What's that?"

"You'll learn you can take more than you think you can. You learn self-respect. You learn you can take a punch. And later on, when you look in the mirror, you might remember that when you need to."

"But I'm going to miss a whole week of school."

"That's all right. You learned more with this thing than you would have in a classroom. Sometimes you gotta stand and fight. Sometimes when you do, you get punished even when you're *right*. That's how the world works. You put your faith in the good Lord and you back it up with your actions. With your deeds and fists if you have to. Now let's have some ice cream."

That was one of the proudest and happiest days of Henry Wilkins' life. He sat with his father and had an ice cream cone. The kitchen was abandoned, unused to laughter and conversation, and the house was still and the ice cream ran down his arm and spilled onto the floor and no one cared. His father had tousled Henry's hair with a gruff, loving kind of pride. Henry felt that pride growing inside himself, and he felt it from the old man. Henry felt like he'd passed a test, even though he'd actually been kicked out of school. Henry Wilkins was becoming a Wolf, although neither he nor his father knew it.

*

Now, thirty-three years old and half frozen, Henry *knew* he could take a lot. He could embrace the suck when he had to. He could bide his time. With his family threatened by bullies, he felt the strong urge to punch someone in the throat. And not only were his wife and child under threat, America was being bullied as a whole. He did not feel like biding his time. For the moment, though, all he could do was try to survive. Embrace the suck.

Late in the afternoon, the Wolves came across a logging road. They followed the road, piled with heavy snow, until it came out on a paved, plowed, and salted road. It was dark by the time they hit the blacktop road, but Henry, Carlos, and Martinez were unaffected by this because of the night vision contacts they wore. It felt like they'd humped more than a hundred miles. Henry hoped they'd at least made it back to the States.

The crust of ice and snow on the road crunched beneath his boots. They were leaving the mountains, traveling east and south. No cars passed them that night, and they stopped for a few minutes only twice. There was a sense of urgency in all of the men.

They had decided to stick together until they got down to Texas, where Martinez's family lived. They hoped to be able to upload the stick drive to the net from there, using one of the servers at the University of Houston to spread whatever information Colonel Bragg had accumulated far and wide. From Houston, Henry and Carlos would travel together to Florida.

Shortly after sunrise, a logging truck stopped. The driver, a scruffy looking guy who reeked of cigarettes and coffee, offered the Wolves a lift. He didn't seem inclined to talk, and if he had questions about the soldiers walking through the wilderness kitted up in full battle rattle, he kept his questions to himself. He turned up his radio and played old country music. Henry crawled into the back of the cab, a coffin-sized space where the trucker apparently slept, and was out in seconds.

The sun was already going down when Henry woke to the hiss of air brakes and the blare of a truck horn.

"Okay, boys," the driver said. "There's a motel and a diner up ahead. You can take a couple of my coats if you want. You're still going to stick out, but it's better than nothing. If you want, I can see if I can raise another driver who's headed further south. Might be able to find you a lift."

"That'd be great, brother," Martinez said from the front seat.

"All right, then," said the trucker. He picked up the CB radio and put out a call.

"Anybody north of Great Falls got your ears on?" There was static.

"Bubba Red, here. Holler."

"Bubba, go to the Harley," said the driver. He looked over at Martinez. "Bubba's good people."

"That you Mountain Man? Come back."

"Roger, Bubba. Got a couple of Road Rats headed south. Come back."

"Can do, good neighbor. Got me some suds and mud."

"See you in ten, Bubba Red." Mountain Man put the handset into the clip. "There's a half-assed store at the truck stop up here. I don't suppose you've got any money?"

"No," said Martinez. "How about a nine mil?"

"Well, then," said Mountain Man. "That's better than money. I'll fix you up with some cash. I'll get you some clothes in the store, if they've got anything that fits you oversized bastards."

An hour later, Henry sat down at a corner booth with Martinez, Carlos, and Mountain Man, who said his real name was Joe. There were few patrons in the diner, all men, and they were hunkered down over coffee and food watching the news. There was no conversation, as if everyone there put up invisible walls around themselves. There were some hard looks at Martinez and Carlos from the truckers.

Henry and his companions ordered some hot coffee and fried chicken from a flirty, bleached-out waitress who'd smoked a few too many Camels. When Henry ordered his second dinner, she raised her eyebrows and laughed.

"You boys are going for a record," she said.

After Henry pushed his plate away, he felt almost human again. Bubba Red came to the table and joked with Mountain Man for a few seconds about lot lizards, then squeezed into the booth, the table pressing against his ample belly. Martinez briefly explained that they were trying to get to Houston, and stay off the grid.

"You men picked a fine time to go sightseeing," Bubba said. "National Guard's got checkpoints set up all over the place. We should be able to make it down to Colorado without too much trouble. Then it's gonna get dicey for you."

"Why is that?" Martinez asked.

"Colorado is a war zone right now," Mountain Man said. "Where the hell have you been?" He gestured with his thumb at the muted bank of television monitors on a wall. Images of burning cities filled the screens. "The interstates are shut down. Nobody in or out. Now you could swing east and cut through Nebraska and avoid Colorado altogether. Trouble is, I'm headed home to Albuquerque. I'm not trying to cut all across Texas. No sir. Bottom line, I can get you down close to the Colorado border, then you're on your own."

"We'll be in your debt," Martinez said.

Bubba and Mountain Man discussed the news that was available. The news was not good.

*

The national cable networks were reporting that the war was over, that reports of bloodshed were overblown. But reports from the Internet and the BBC painted a very different picture.

The United States was convulsing. People streamed across state borders, trying to go home. Trying to return to wherever they came from and the roots were the deepest. The highways and state roads were clogged. In many parts of the country, the power grid was down. Curfews were in effect, travel restricted, and interstate commerce was at a standstill. Each state had activated its own National Guard troops, while the larger bases and installations were on lockdown. Some of the bases disintegrated into chaos, like Malmstrom did.

The country had fractured into five distinct sections, and there were divisions within those areas. The Northeast down to Washington, DC, remained loyal to the federal government. The South, from Virginia to Florida and west to Texas, had declared independence under the name the Jefferson Republic. The West Coast had declared allegiance to the federal government, from California up to the Northwest. The Midwestern states were trying to stay neutral, restricting federal troop movement, threatening to shoot down all aircraft that violated their airspace.

The western states were leaning toward joining the Jeffersonians, but thus far had declared neutrality. The state governors seemed to be calling the shots; most of the United States Congress was dead.

Wall Street was closed, and the economy was in free fall. The United Nations had offered assistance, as had China, Russia, Australia, and the UK. The president of the United States was at an undisclosed location, calling for peace and unity. The US Navy set up a blockade along the east and west coasts to keep foreign powers at bay. For now, at least, the navy was staying out of the fighting spreading around the broken country like wildfire.

In large southern cities like Atlanta, racial tensions exploded onto the streets. Minorities clashed with police and National Guard units, protesting the secession. Entire city blocks were engulfed in flames and looting was rampant. One of the networks showed images of a gang shooting up a police cruiser, then burning it with a Molotov cocktail while the officers inside thrashed about and then collapsed onto the street, charred.

Trash and raw sewage covered city streets in big cities, as waste treatment plants shut down. There were water shortages, and killings over food.

On the outskirts of San Francisco and Washington, DC, thousands of people suffering from radiation burns camped outside overwhelmed hospitals and FEMA tents.

*

It was worse than Henry had imagined, and he had expected the worst.

"It's all coming apart," Bubba Red said. "They're tearing the whole country to pieces. Burning it down to nothing so that the damn Chinese can come in and pick up the pieces. Won't be anyplace safe. Things aren't ever going back to normal, not after this."

"I'm going back to Canada," Mountain Man said. "I knew it was bad, but not *this* bad. No offense, but if I'd known, I'm not so sure I would've stopped for you." The man stood and bade a brisk farewell. Henry shouted a thank-you as the man walked out the door into the cold.

"We'd best be getting on the road, too," Bubba said. "I'm all filled up."

Henry stood, feeling uncomfortable in the itchy new civilian clothes. His parka was bulky and the flannel shirt made him feel faintly ridiculous. His gear was stowed into two oversized black duffel bags. Martinez and Carlos wore similar attire, and the three men could almost pass for truckers themselves. Martinez wore a bright green John Deere cap, which Henry found amusing.

"Aw, shit," Bubba said, looking through the blinds into the parking area outside. Flashing red and blue lights reflected off of the wet pavement.

"Buncha county mounties," he said.

Henry followed Martinez and Carlos out the back door while Bubba went through the front entrance. They stayed in the shadows and moved around the side of the building. Two local police vehicles had pulled up beside Mountain Man's rig, and it looked like the cops were giving him a hard time. Mountain Man stood gesturing wildly at his truck. One of the cops had his weapon drawn. Henry noticed it was a revolver.

"What do you think?" Carlos said. The Wolves were concealed about thirty yards from the truck.

"Wait and see," Martinez answered. "They might click him up for crossing the border into the States. Or maybe they'll let him go."

Henry watched Bubba walk up to the police officers. One of the cops started shouting at Bubba.

"Get down!" the cop yelled. "Hands on the back of your head." Bubba complied, on his knees. One of the police officers pulled out handcuffs.

"Aw, hell no," Carlos muttered.

Another cruiser pulled into the parking lot. Two more cops stepped out.

"Wilkins, stay put," Martinez said. "Carlos, flank right." Both men stepped from the shadows, weapons drawn, advancing on the police officers.

The cop with the nickel-plated revolver was young. The fact that he preferred the showy weapon to a more practical sidearm worried Henry. The man was clearly afraid and uncertain, and this made him deadly.

Henry dropped to one knee and quickly rifled through the duffel bag containing his submachine gun. He withdrew the HK and snapped a magazine into place.

Martinez and the local sheriffs were shouting at each other.

"STAND DOWN!" Martinez was yelling.

The one cop who had already drawn his weapon was now pointing it directly at Martinez. His partner had his hands in the air. The other two policemen, the new arrivals, were edging back toward their patrol car.

"Drop your weapon!" said the cop with the revolver. "I will fire. Drop it now. Who the fuck are you?"

Henry put his sights on the sheriff on the near side of the cruiser. The man was moving sideways with his arms at his sides like he was pretending to fly.

The cop with the nickel-plated revolver was young. Early twenties. He was clearly afraid and uncertain, and this made him deadly.

"Don't do it, son," one of the other cops said. His voice was barely a whisper, but Henry heard him. Or maybe he just wanted the older cop to say that, a brief vision of Operation Snowshoe flashing through his mind.

Henry focused on the other cops because Martinez and Carlos would be targeting the immediate armed threat. *Don't make me do it. Lord, forgive me. I don't want to shoot a cop.* Finger on the trigger.

"We're soldiers," Martinez said. "We're on your side. These guys are helping us get home, that's all."

"You have drawn a firearm on an officer of the law," the young cop yelled. "Put your gun down. You're under arrest."

"Look," Martinez said. "That's not happening. You're outnumbered. No one needs to die here today, but *you* most definitely *will* unless you put down that fucking popgun. Wilkins?"

Henry peppered the cruiser door with a burst from the HK. The cop with the revolver jumped at the crack of the shots and the slap of the rounds into the metal car door. The other officers dove for the ground.

Martinez closed on the young cop while Carlos remained twenty feet away in a shooter's stance. The cop handed his revolver over.

Henry stepped from the shadows, and then helped Martinez and Carlos disarm the cops.

"I don't know what to do with them," Martinez said, giving the policemen a hard look. The cops, wearing dark brown uniforms under bulky black leather coats, remained silent. The oldest of the four stepped forward and offered his hand to Martinez.

"I'm Sheriff Bradshaw," the man said. He sported a thick beard with more than a little gray in it and his eyes were not unkind. "I know things are crazy right now. We'll let you boys pass. Never saw you, if you catch my meaning."

"But—!" the young cop who had waved around the revolver said.

"Shut up, Josh," Sheriff Bradshaw interjected. "These guys are military. Special Forces, I'm guessing?" He raised his eyebrows at the question. "Ah, well, you won't tell me anyway." Bradshaw raised the sleeve on his coat and shirt, revealing a tattoo on his inner forearm of a skull and the words "Semper Fi."

Martinez grinned at the sheriff. "A jarhead. Well, all right then."

"Yes, sir," said Sheriff Bradshaw. "Marine Recon. Two tours in Iraq. Home to this sleepy little shithole."

"You give your word you won't pick up a radio?"

"No reason to do that. Haven't seen a damn thing but truckers and moose."

"Good enough for me," Martinez said.

"You mind telling us what is going on?" Bradshaw asked.

"You probably know a lot more than we do," Martinez said.

"I doubt that. Steer clear of the interstate if you're trying to get far away from here, and I'm sure you are, because there's nothing happening here. Don't go near major cities. From what I understand, it's gotten ugly quick-like."

Henry, Carlos, and Martinez said good-bye to Bradshaw and the truck stop and piled into Bubba Red's Peterbilt truck. The interior was more spacious than the last truck. Henry sat up front on a bench seat with Carlos while Martinez got some sleep in the rear.

Bubba Red regaled them with stories of the open highway and drove nonstop through the night over back roads and state highways. Progress was slow because the roads had not been plowed since the last snowfall. Bubba Red's truck contained two computer screens, one for media and one for navigation. The GPS system was down, but maps on the hard drive proved accurate and up to date. From time to time, Bubba chatted with other truckers over the CB radio in a jargon incomprehensible to Henry. About all Henry was able to discern was that truckers did not care for police, and there were a whole lot of "bears" out and about.

Henry entered what the men called "field sleep," and allowed his body and mind to rest while staying in a state of semi-alertness. He had long since learned to sleep when he could, storing up on moments of repose like a bear stocking up on body fat before a long winter, because he knew there would be times when he wouldn't be able to rest for days at a time.

Colorado lurked in the darkness over the horizon.

CHAPTER NINE

Bad Neighbors

KEY WEST, FLORIDA

Suzanne finished loading her convertible Mercedes, wishing at that moment she'd chosen a more practical vehicle. There wasn't enough space. The trunk was loaded down with yellow five-gallon water jugs, canned food, and boxes of Little Debbie snacks, which had a shelf life of about a thousand years. The shelves at the stores were picked clean. She was lucky to get what she had. The front seat was crammed with bags of dog food for Beowulf and as much medicine as she could get from the local Walgreens pharmacy. She had antibiotics, painkillers, dressings, and a variety of topical ointments. She felt grossly underprepared.

She pulled onto US 1, waiting for the US Navy sailor who was directing traffic to give her the go-ahead. Sailors and marines had emerged from the base, armed with assault rifles and wearing body armor, to provide security for Key West. There were soldiers and police officers at the stores to stop looters and try to prevent price gouging.

Suzanne turned on the radio, hoping to catch some news, but instead "Born in the USA" came on, and that was all right with her. It took her more than an hour to make it home, and by the time she pulled into the crushed coral driveway, the sun had gone down. She saw that Bart had been busy. The metal hurricane shutters were bolted over the windows on the front of the house.

Mary, Bart, Ginnie, and old Bobby Ray helped to unload the car.

"We're in good shape for now," Bart said. "We've got enough water to last us a couple of weeks, probably, if we're careful. I've filled the boat with fuel, and I've got some extra tanks filled up. The house is fairly secure. I'm thinking we should stick together here, if that's all right with you."

"Sure, Bart. I was kind of assuming that."

For one thing, Bart had old wooden hurricane shutters in his hundred-year-old home. And from Suzanne's they could utilize the boat to catch fish or get away if they had to. Bart and Mary had purchased their historic home with the idea that Mary would run a bed and breakfast. That never happened.

They were all eating steaks hot off the grill at the dining room table when the power went out. Suzanne and Bart lit candles, and they resumed the communal meal.

"This is fun," Taylor said. "It's like a party."

"Yeah," Suzanne said. "A birthday party."

They laughed and joked, but beneath the levity, Suzanne was afraid. No more running water, no more toilets that flushed. With the windows shut, the house became hot and the air was stale and sweaty before the night was over. They heard cracks outside that might have been fireworks or gunshots. They couldn't be sure.

After dinner, Bart called for a group meeting.

"From here on out, we need to set watches," Bart said. "Twenty-four seven. That's how it's got to be. We'll rotate in four-hour shifts. No one goes anywhere alone. We'll split the watches between Suzanne, Bobby, and me, for now. Ginnie, I'm going to teach you to shoot tomorrow so you can help."

"Okay," Ginnie said. She looked afraid.

"The base would have been better," Mary said.

"I know," Suzanne replied. "I tried. Like I said, they would let me and Taylor on base, but no one else. My father isn't there, I guess. I left word for him."

"Suzanne," Bart said, cutting his eyes at Mary, "we're grateful you decided to stick together. Really."

"No worries," Suzanne said.

"Now look," Bart went on, "I've got a bug-out bag set up by the back door. There's food and water, one .38 revolver with extra rounds. If we have to leave by boat, we take that and go. When I say it's time to bug out, nobody better argue. Got it?"

None replied, but Suzanne nodded along with the others, faces dancing with warm candle light and dark shadows.

"I think we should all sleep in the living room. We can pull mattresses from the beds and use the sofa and love seat. If the house gets breached, head for the laundry room. There's a loaded 12-gauge behind the door."

"Um," Suzanne said, "that's not a good idea. Not with Taylor here. No loaded guns where she can just pick them up."

"Damn," Bart said, looking sheepish. He got up and walked out of the room, returning moments later.

"I put the shotgun in the chest freezer."

"That works."

"What about the booze?" Bobby Ray said.

"As of now, you're no longer a drunk," Bart said.

"Do what?" Bobby Ray said, eyes wide and weathered face more wrinkled than normal. "That can't be good," he muttered.

"That's how it's gonna be, old friend. Sorry. We've got a bunch of rum. But we may need that to trade, or if worst comes to worst, we might need it for medicine."

"Well," Bobby said, a wry smile, "I need my medicine."

"You're going to have to figure out another way to cope, I'm afraid," Bart said. "I don't like it either. But we can't have a member of our team passed out, not even once. If you fall off the wagon, people could get killed. If you don't want to do that, then you can go find some other folks to hole up with. We won't be offended. But I'd consider it a kindness if you'd stay here. We can use your help."

"Well, I guess," Bobby said.

*

In the wee hours of the morning, Suzanne heard voices outside the front door. She'd just taken over the watch from Bobby.

Bart had nailed a piece of plywood over the window on the door, so there was no way to look outside. They would have to do something about that. It sounded like two people, just outside.

Suzanne considered waking everyone up, but decided to wait. The Beretta in her hand felt solid, a reassuring heaviness to it. She'd learned to shoot as a child, one of the few things she did with her father on a regular basis when he was around. She walked up to the door and held her breath, straining to listen.

". . . other houses," she heard.

". . . saw her with . . ." Suzanne heard only bits and pieces, but it was enough to know that these guys were casing her home. She felt violated and indignant at the same time, and with that there was anger and a bit of recklessness. She recognized it, felt the adrenaline pumping in her.

One of the things she had learned from Henry was that if there was going to be a fight, it's best to hit first. You proceed with violence and do not stop until the threat has ended.

Beowulf stood behind her, looking intently at the door, but neither growling nor barking. Malamutes were not prone to barking.

Suzanne knocked back the dead bolt and flung the door open with her left hand, holding the Beretta in her right.

There were no streetlights, no house lights, but the stars and moon were bright under the clear winter sky and she saw the two young men standing surprised a few feet away from her. One of them held a crowbar in his hand and the other one had a baseball bat, bringing it up as if to swing.

"Whoa," one of the men said, taking a step back and dropping the crowbar. It clattered on the marble tile outside the front door.

"Get the hell off my property," Suzanne said. She kept her voice low, daggers in it.

"Hey, now," said the guy with the bat. He was short and wiry. He had not dropped the bat.

"Last chance," Suzanne said. She shifted her finger from the trigger guard to the trigger itself.

The bat fell to the ground and the two men ran away into the night and Suzanne stood in the threshold breathing hard. She wasn't shaking, exactly. It was more like she was vibrating, her whole body tingling and amped up. It was like the way she felt when she was swimming with sharks, but even more powerful, a kind of euphoria and the feeling of being completely alive.

What worried her, standing there in the cool night outside her home, was that she saw in herself the propensity to kill another human being. Worse, she knew that a part of her had *wanted* to kill that man with the bat.

"For the love of God, wake me up next time that happens," Bart said from behind her.

Suzanne jumped at the sound of his voice and turned to face him. She could not see his face, but she heard the smile and tension in his voice.

"There could have been more of them," Bart said. "They could've had guns. Don't do that again."

"Okay," Suzanne said. But still, she felt good. She felt like she had faced down fear and doubt within herself and come away knowing something vital. "You're right."

She finished her watch and then tossed and turned until dawn. She wondered where Henry was, whether he'd gotten the divorce papers. She prayed he hadn't, that he still loved her and would be coming home to her and Taylor.

The sound of jets tearing the sky kept her awake, and then Taylor was asking for breakfast and why she couldn't watch Elmo on TV, and Suzanne pushed herself out of the couch and decided sleep would have to wait.

HOUSTON, TEXAS

Reince Blackaby felt his confidence coming back. The Directors seemed to be willing to cut him some slack, or perhaps they merely wanted him to finish damage control; either way, he was still breathing, and that was a little surprising.

He had assured "Mr. Smith" that any incriminating information had been erased. Blackaby wiped his hard drives, shredded paper documents. The colonel that had become a security risk had been eliminated, along with the rest of that particular unit.

Blackaby issued the orders to commence operations himself. The two Wolf Pack units, Alpha and Bravo, were one of Blackaby's strokes of genius. The Directors had required a way to control certain things within the United States utilizing methods that exceeded blackmail and media persuasion and public policy. Sometimes, boots on the ground were a necessity.

Blackaby had exerted the full influence of the Directors to form the two units right under the noses of the NSA, the CIA, the FBI, and every branch of the military. The government itself did the hard work for him; the military provided recruiting, training, and physical assets, believing that the Wolves worked exclusively for them. It was a shell game of magnificent proportions, taking advantage of the cumbersome bureaucracy and convoluted chain of command. In fact, the majority of the operations conducted by the Wolves were legitimately ordered by the government. It was perfect. This was also part of the problem, though, because the dogs seemed to have turned on him. A little too smart for their own good.

Now, Blackaby could see through his satellite feeds, that the Directors were once again making money hand over fist in the international exchanges. His failure to contain the situation in the US had a potential silver lining. They would be dumping US dollars, buying Chinese yuan, and signing defense contracts for overseas production at a feverish pace. With zero oversight from Congress, there was no telling what the Directors could accomplish within a short amount of time. When the dust settled, they might net trillions of dollars. They would make money rebuilding the country. In a few months, they would start buying US currency again and make even more money when the dollar increased in value. He hoped his superiors would look at it that way. They'd taken a hit, but in the end, they'd make a killing.

Reince considered trying to contact his wife, who would be in Canada by now, but he decided against it. The cabin in Ontario contained a satellite phone for emergencies only. If the Directors were tracking Reince, one phone call could potentially give away her position, and he did not want to give them the leverage. His plan now was to disappear.

He'd stockpiled enough money in offshore accounts to last him and his children and his children's children. He was done playing Master of the Universe. He used his radio to contact his pilot, who was waiting on the roof with a helicopter.

He stood and swept his gaze around his office for the last time, bidding farewell to his life's work. The skyline was beautiful around him and the sun was golden and clear reflecting from the glass on the downtown skyscrapers. Reince Blackaby blinked one last time before everything went dark and he never heard the shot, never felt the round that spattered his brains across the window in a mist of pink and then there was the sound of the metal balls clicking back and forth in a perfect and predictable display of action, reaction, and the transference of energy.

Jack Stryker unscrewed the suppressor from his weapon and holstered the 9mm under his suit coat. The pompous windbag he had just terminated lay facedown behind the desk. Stryker walked around the desk and turned the man over with his boot. The round had entered at the base of his brain and exited through the jaw, leaving a mangled mess, then ricocheted from the bulletproof glass.

Stryker sat down and began to cull through Blackaby's computer files. *Wiped clean; no surprise there.* He rifled through Blackaby's suit coat and pockets, hoping to find a flash drive, but there was nothing. The leather briefcase contained a burner phone and a yellow legal pad with rows of handwritten numbers on a single page. He planted tiny charges on each of the computer drives. Stryker grunted and grabbed the briefcase in his left hand and made his way out of the office, headed toward the stairs and the rooftop.

Stryker felt nothing. He was neither satisfied nor remorseful, and he was self-aware enough to understand why. Jack Stryker knew he was a sociopath, and he was at peace with that. He did not go out of his way to inflict harm upon others, was not a sadist like some of the men he worked with. Taking a human life meant no more to him than stepping on an ant or closing a door. Stryker thought of himself as a survivor. He was a predator when he needed to be.

He had been an outstanding soldier, but had washed out of Delta Force selection when he failed a battery of psych tests. When a general contacted him out of the blue with the opportunity to work with the Bravo Pack, Stryker had been almost, but not quite, happy. He had been with the Bravo for five years; for the first three he was a squad leader and SAW gunner, carrying out missions primarily in the Northeast. He laughed and joked with the men, fought bravely and competently, and faked his way through in the way he always did. There were those on his team who considered him a brother, not knowing that Jack could not possibly reciprocate the feeling. He was a chameleon, adept at blending in while always being somehow apart. There was an essential stillness about him that some found unsettling. They had nicknamed him "Frost."

Jack Frost, Frosty. Iceman. That's me.

Jack Stryker had long ago given up on humanity, both within himself and the world as a whole. People were bags of meat walking around waiting to die. There was no purpose, no hope, no sadness. Existence was everything. His back bore the scars of an orphan who has been in scores of foster homes. There were cigarette burns on his arms and legs, craters on the surface of a smashed soul.

He'd realized he was broken after he killed an older foster kid, and at first he worried about it. For some reason, any time he did a job, he would think about that kid even now, a memory unbidden flashing before him. Paul Hewes, a name Jack Stryker would never forget, was a stocky seventeen-year-old, perverse and cruel and twisted. Jack was only twelve when he shoved his nemesis from the top of an abandoned rock quarry. Jack went back to the house, feigning tears and telling a tall tale, waiting to be discovered.

What happened after that, after Jack confessed to his priest, broke him irrevocably. There was blackmail and coercion and unspeakable pain and guilt. Jack could not smell incense without gagging even all these years later. The priest was the next person Jack Stryker killed; he was fifteen by then.

For two years now, Stryker had been an assassin, and he found this suited him. He worked alone, answered only to disembodied voices on the phone or computer.

Of late, the Directors were giving Stryker an increasing amount of authority and latitude. He was beginning to understand his employers, and with this knowledge came admiration. They were like him, albeit more influential.

He considered this mission a success. His primary objective was to eliminate Reince Blackaby. Stryker had been monitoring Blackaby's communications for a day, hoping to find some evidence that he had betrayed the Directors, but the man was careful and smart.

On the roof, Stryker nodded to the pilot and stepped into the waiting bird. Using his Integrated Infantry Combat System, he linked to command and control.

"It is finished," he sent. "Awaiting orders." He kept the notepad to himself. He had a feeling it would become important.

The helicopter lifted from the rooftop and Stryker headed east and a small part of him wished he could feel something other than the vibration of the aircraft.

NASHVILLE, TENNESSEE

Leon Smith hunkered down in his dark one-bedroom apartment all night, afraid for his family. The gunfire just beyond his doors continued all night long. He heard the boom of shotguns, the crack of pistols, and once, a burst from an automatic weapon. That these things were technically illegal had no effect on the gangs.

He'd slept in his easy chair facing the door, the revolver from his dead boss in his hand. Leon's children and his wife slept fitfully, all piled up into one bed. He could hear them tossing and turning.

Leon hadn't heard any police sirens. There were no rescue vehicles coming to help people. This part of Lower Antioch was a place that the cops avoided to begin with. It seemed they'd written it off entirely now. There were just screams and shouts and the sound of gunfire and things breaking and shattering.

A Laotian gang had taken over this sprawling apartment complex last year. The Blood Spiders, they called themselves. A bunch of teenagers and twenty-something kids with nothing to live for but drugs, violence, and the tenuous brotherhood of being a part of a pack.

The sun was coming up, and Leon knew he needed to get his family out. He had nowhere to go. His world was contained within these walls, everything and everyone who mattered. His wife had a sister in LA and a brother in Atlanta, but Leon had no intention of trying for either of those cities. He wanted to get out into the country. Maybe drive for the Rocky Mountains. The more he thought about it, the better the idea sounded to him.

He put the weapon in the waistband of his jeans and began to pack in the semidarkness of his meager apartment. He picked up a teddy bear, Little Eddie's favorite possession.

Leon felt the kind of shame a man cannot show, and the threadbare couch and bare walls and the gunfire outside accused him of being failure as a husband and father; in his most important job, to provide a safe place for his family, he had fallen miserably short.

Clutching the tattered bear he'd won at a fair for his boy, Leon knew he'd let everyone down. He raged against the poverty and the racism and the feeling of being stuck in quicksand from the time he got out of bed in the morning until the moment he shut off the lights. His children deserved better; they deserved a chance, and it seemed they would never get one. This complex was a shithole before the country started to kill itself, and he hadn't been able to find a way to extricate himself from it. There was never enough money. There were not enough jobs. He had been living hand-to-mouth since he'd gotten out of the army, and they'd all been drowning in slow motion, gasping for air and hope.

From the unit next store came a sudden burst of shouts and the sound of a door being kicked in. A woman was screaming. Leon knew the matriarch in passing; a kind, churchgoing lady raising her grandkids. The two older boys had dropped out of school. The young girl, Leisha, played with Leon's boys. He heard the child howling through the thin walls, the grandmother yelling for intruders to get out. Leon guessed it was some kind of gang-related thing. Retaliation or a drug grab or guns. The kind of thing that went on with frequency in poverty-stricken areas all over the country and got ignored by the media because it was not sexy violence. *If a pretty white woman kills her husband, that's national news, and the trial will become a media circus. But when poor minority kids kill each other, no one cares beyond the grieving families.*

Leon put the teddy bear on the easy chair, checked the .357, and went outside.

"Where they at?" one punk was saying. He was small, wearing a red bandana on his head. Pants sagging halfway down his butt. He and another kid, maybe fifteen, maybe twenty-five, were standing just inside the doorway to Leon's neighbor's apartment.

"I don't know. They ain't here. Now you get on outta my house. Go on GIT! Both of ya." Leisha was screaming in the background.

That might have been the end of it. Maybe they would have left on their own without hurting anyone.

One of the gang members held a sawed-off shotgun. He turned to face Leon.

"Mind you business, old man," said the young man. His mouth curled into a sneer. He pointed the shotgun at Leon's chest. "Unless you want some of this."

"Put a cap in his ass," said the other punk. Eager. It was all a joke. A video game.

Leon stepped forward until the shotgun was almost touching his chest. He looked down at the dark-skinned man-boy in front of him. One of the Spiders.

"I'll blow a hole through you, Army. You don't scare me. Now give me your piece. I know you strapped." He laughed, a high-pitched, girlish laugh. Leon wondered if he always laughed like that.

"You leave that man alone!" said Grandmother.

"Go on outta here," Leon said. The gun in his waistband. He hadn't come out the door holding it because he was afraid of what the gun would do in his hands.

"Shoot him! He crazy!"

"Leave. Now." Leon bored into the kid with his eyes. He'd do it. Right here, shoot this damn kid in his big, mean mouth.

"You see this gun? Right?" The stubby barrel touched Leon's chest.

Maybe it was because he had already killed a man, or maybe it was the feeling of failure that was in him. But Leon, at that moment, did not care much about anything. Maybe that's how the punks felt too.

Leon moved with unhurried fluidity, drawing the revolver from his waistband and placing the barrel of the nickel-plated .357 against the punk's forehead. He put his left hand on the stock of the shotgun and pointed its muzzle away from his body. The punk stood staring at him in surprise and fear.

"That's what I thought," Leon said, taking possession of the shotgun. "If I see you again, I'll drop you on the spot. I don't give a damn if your momma was a crackhead and your daddy whipped your ass with coat hangers. You got no excuse being the punk-assed bitch you are."

Leon pressed the barrel against the boy who claimed to be a man's temple. "You mess with me or anyone around here again, I'll find you. You send your 'posse' or your 'crew' or your 'spiders' or whatever the fuck you call yourselves because you're too much of a pussy to do it yourself, you'd best hope they kill me. 'Cause I'll find you. You get me?"

"That dude's crazy," one of them muttered as they scurried down the hall, grabbing sagging pants so they didn't fall down completely, trying not to trip over themselves as they slunk away.

"You shouldn't have done that," Grandmother said. "But thank you."

"You should leave," Leon said. "We're getting out of here."

"Where is there to go?"

"To the mountains."

CHAPTER TEN

Smoke and Shadow

COLORADO

There are dreams which become nightmares, and nightmares are often born in places that once seemed heavenly. Colorado was a twisted hell, the sharp scent of pines and mountain air, forever mingled in Henry's mind with the burning and dying in the way that haunts a man for as long as he dreams. Henry, Carlos, and Martinez trudged across much of the state because of the roadblocks, abandoned vehicles, and seemingly random airstrikes against civilians on the road.

They had climbed into a four-wheel-drive truck on the side of a state highway. On the outskirts of a small, nameless town, a missile tore apart a minivan half a mile in front of them. They had been following the van for about twenty miles, at times closely enough to wave at the children in the backseat.

The missile, fired from a drone or a jet, smashed into the white van, too fast for the eye to follow. Henry had been driving. He floored the accelerator and when they arrived at the van, it was already too late. The vehicle was an inferno, twisted and on its side.

From then on, they traveled on foot, staying close to the trees lining the roads, moving steadily south.

The next afternoon a column at least ten miles long rumbled past. There were Abrams tanks, infantry piled into armored personnel carriers, and support vehicles at the end of the column. Supply trucks, medics, and engineers. An army. At the tip of the column were heavy vehicles with oversized wheels and shovel blades shaped like a cowcatcher on a train. These behemoths cleared the road of burned-out husks of cars and trucks that had been left to the winter.

Helicopters flew overhead, circling like buzzards to provide air cover for the column. Far above the helicopters and the mountains, fighter jets ripped the day.

The Wolves retreated into the woods and watched the army pass. American flags had been replaced by colors Henry had never seen before.

Jets screamed through the sky. Before the rebel column appeared, Henry heard the terrifying sound of an AC-130 Spectre gunship unleashing holy hell. He could not see the aircraft, which was beyond the next low mountain. The heavy minigun made a distinct sound, a vibration deep in the chest even from that distance. Its 105mm cannons whumped and rained fire. He knew the sounds, had once welcomed them, because it meant that some jihadis were getting blown to shit. Terrible in a good way, then. Now, just terrible.

There were thuds from artillery and mortar rounds and bombs dropped from the jets. By the time the first vehicles churned up the frozen road, an oily smoke hung in the sky seven or eight miles away, hugging the mountain and drifting down into the valley.

Henry was burrowed into the snow and covered with spruce branches, and still he felt naked and very small. The force moving past was an entire division, ten to fifteen thousand troops.

"This is bad," Carlos said.

"This is *murder*," Martinez said. Good God."

"Those are rebels," Carlos said. "But who are they?"

"It's a mix," Martinez said. "I saw some Texas flags. I think units out of Texas linked up with some of the Colorado National Guard. They're pounding the hell out of whatever is in front of them."

"I'd like to find the commander and rip his nuts off," Carlos said. "Treason. Evil, that's what this is."

"Too late for that," Martinez said. "This goes beyond some renegade general. We're looking at something that's been in the works for a while. Somebody was planning this. They were ready for it. From the politicians on down to the brass."

"All these infantry guys, though," Henry said. "I don't get it. They aren't a part of some grand conspiracy."

"Of course not," Martinez said. "They are loyal to their squad first, then their platoon. If their squad is going to fight, most of these men are going to stand by their brothers."

"I wouldn't," Henry said.

"But you would. You did."

"What's that mean, Sarn't Major?"

"Look at us. We're not part of the regular army. So we're not marching along with the rest. But here we are, holed up in Colorado in the suck together. What's left of our unit. The last squad. And we've got blood on our hands, like it or not. We've been part of whatever this is. We didn't know it, but we were."

A deep boom rolled over the valley.

"You'd have shot a cop, Wilkins."

"Well—"

"You would have. We both know it. You'd have done it to protect your brothers. I would, and so would Carlos. That's how it is."

Henry knew Martinez was right, although he was not comfortable about it. He was ready to die for his fellow teammates, and willing to kill for them as well. It was the emotional glue which made combat possible, the thing that made men charge into a hail of lead and fall on grenades. The idea that you knew the guy on your left was willing to die for you. This brotherhood was more powerful than fear, more deadly than rage.

Dangerous in the way of a weapon which is neither good nor evil but can be used for either.

In the real world, or a normal one, Henry would never think about harming a civilian, let alone a police officer. The lines were blurred now. Combat could happen at any moment, and issues of right and wrong could be subverted by the loyalty to the pack. Morality was not something that mattered when rounds were buzzing around and there were split-second decisions to make.

As Henry thought about what Martinez said, he was simultaneously chilled and sad. That brotherhood was being used against the very men who formed it. Men trained to kill, conditioned to be ferociously loyal at the squad level, had been unleashed on the country. Men like him, who would kill as a reflex.

The politicians and extremists who had been calling for a coup for years had no real idea what it meant. Henry did. He was looking at the reality, listening to the sound of bombs falling on American soil. He had seen a family incinerated in front of him. He'd had an HK aimed at a local sheriff. One second away from committing outright murder.

In this fight, there were no good sides; there was just the hope that he could protect his family and his brothers and make it home. Civilians were dying by the thousands. Men in uniform were killing each other and the country itself was broken. Henry had never voted for a Democrat, but he paid little attention to politics in general. He wished that both sides had found a way to work together. He knew Carlos and Martinez were registered Democrats. First and foremost, they were Americans.

And there was Operation Snowshoe. He hadn't murdered a sleeping child, hadn't pulled the trigger. He'd been there, shooting and killing, a weapon perhaps, though not a mindless one. A rifle does not mourn, the knife does not remember, a bullet cannot grieve. Steel has no soul, and the dead do not dream. Henry had nightmares.

The Wolves skirted the battlefield, sticking to the wooded hills. They steered clear of vacation homes and pockets of civilization. From a distance, Henry looked upon the devastation.

An entire town had been obliterated. Houses were not houses anymore, but toothpicks on streets littered with charred husbands, fathers, and mothers and children. Henry could see the difference through his scope, and it shattered him in a way he would not have believed possible. He had seen children bleeding in Afghanistan, along with American medics braving gunfire to save those kids. What he saw now went beyond anything he had prepared himself to see.

There were swing sets and church towers smashed and lying crooked, and houses that were not houses anymore but were tombs. All of it black and consumed by fire and death, and Henry hated it.

Henry Wilkins was not the kind of man to hate. It came unnaturally. He felt it now, as if it were under pressure, bottled up and fierce. He needed to unleash it. He yearned to bleed off the violence in him in the way of a man that punches a brick wall even though he knows he will break his hand. Sometimes he waits and thinks about what he's going to do, and sometimes he doesn't.

The wind shifted and brought smoke and the smell of burning meat and diesel fuel. There were destroyed military vehicles littered throughout the town's streets. It looked like a small loyalist force had attempted to make a stand against overwhelming firepower.

On the south side of the town, at the edge of the devastation, a brick school blazed. Henry looked through binoculars and saw a knot of people milling about in the parking lot. He could see mothers on their knees in the snow. The smoke was black and malevolent and Henry thought he could hear the wailing of bereaved parents, even though he knew it was impossible.

"Sarn't Major," Henry said.

"I know," Martinez replied. "I see it. We'll head that way. Shit."

"We'd better hope the drones are gone," Carlos said. "They'll smoke us."

"We gotta try to help," Martinez said. "Damn."

Henry followed Carlos through deep snow, moving down hills through second-growth forest. The air was still, and there was no sign of any aircraft circling.

It was a hard mile, and Henry was sweating despite the cold by the time they arrived at the parking lot. A fire truck manned by a few firemen had pulled up while the Wolves crossed through the woods. A few firefighters manned a tanker truck, spraying the blaze from a hundred feet away. People were shouting and crying.

"How can we help?" Martinez asked one of the firemen. The man was leaning against the truck, his face blackened by soot and smoke. He looked exhausted.

"Nothing to be done," the man said. "There's people trapped inside but we can't get to them."

"Why not?"

"They were in the center of the school, in the gym. The fire's too intense. We tried. I lost a man." The fireman gestured with his head. There was a pair of boots sticking out from underneath a blanket. "Smoke," he said.

"Have you got a ladder truck?"

"Had one. The bastards hit the firehouse with a bomb. We're just volunteers. I've never seen anything like this."

Henry looked up at the school. The building was two stories, and what he assumed was the gymnasium was taller.

"We tried going in from every entrance. There's no way."

"Ropes," Martinez said. "Do you have anything we can use to scale the building? We can go in through a window."

"Yeah," the fireman said. "But the roof itself is on fire. Look for yourself. There's smoke coming up through it. That means it's not only hot, but also that it could collapse any second."

"Get the ropes," Martinez said. "Find ladders."

*

Henry gripped the nylon cord in his hands and began to climb up the face of the brick school. His boots found toeholds and he used his upper body strength to hoist himself hand over hand toward the rooftop.

Martinez was ahead of him, already almost to the top. Someone had found ropes and a grappling hook, taking precious minutes. Then there were the frustrating attempts to get the hook to bite on the roof. All the while, a keening sound rose over the whoosh and roar of the fire.

He pulled himself onto the roof.

The rooftop was gravel, and it was slanted because there were holes in it. Gouts of flame licked the air and smoke seemed to come from everywhere. Henry could feel the heat on his legs and face and hands. The building itself seemed to shift as something inside gave way, and Henry fell forward, catching himself with his hands. The rooftop was as hot as a burning stove. He pushed himself to his feet and ran to follow Martinez, who was already smashing a window next to the gym. Carlos was right behind.

"Carlos, you're the anchor," Martinez said.

"Copy that."

"I'll go first, then Wilkins."

Henry helped Carlos hold the line while Martinez slipped through the window. Smoke drifted out. The crying and screaming was louder now.

Henry followed Martinez into hell. Visibility was poor.

On wooden bleachers, thirty or more men, women, and children cowered, trying to escape the flames spreading into the gym.

Once he made it to the top steps, Henry slipped the rope from beneath his armpits. It was chaos. A man was begging him to take his child, screaming in Henry's face. The acoustics of the room served to amplify the roar of the fire and the squeals of people afraid to die. There were bodies on the wooden floor.

Henry took the child, a boy of maybe seven or eight, and put the rope under his arms. The boy was not crying. His eyes were scrunched shut like he was trying to wake up from what he knew was a nightmare. Like when he opened them again, the world would go back to normal.

Two hard pulls on the rope, and the boy began to slide up toward the window.

They tried to get people to form a line. The civilians were panicked and out of their heads with fear for themselves and for their kids. Henry had to subdue a father and a mother who were clawing at him while he was trying to help someone else. As a father, he understood.

During the bedlam, Henry was relieved to see several firemen coming down ropes. The crowd of trapped people calmed somewhat and the evacuation proceeded.

They got everyone who was still on their feet out, as the fire grew unbearable and the smoke in the gym too thick to see through. Henry tried not to think about the people on the floor, the ones who weren't moving anymore. There was not enough time to pull them out. It damn sure wasn't fair.

Henry was the last man off the roof. Carlos, shaking from exhaustion, went just ahead. Much of the roof was gone, and Henry had to step around gaping holes, burning timbers, and blasts of searing ash.

He staggered to the fire truck and accepted an oxygen mask someone put on his face. His eyes burned and teared and his nose was running. Beside him, Martinez nodded, a mask obscuring much of his face, which was covered in soot.

A pretty redhead in a business suit shoved a handheld camera in Henry's face and started asking questions.

"They say you're heroes," she was saying. "Tell our viewers what made you do it?"

"Get lost," Henry growled.

"Come on, give me something here," she said. She was trying to be soothing. It sounded to Henry like she was trying to coax a small child into doing something he didn't want to do. "With all the tragedy happening, this is a great story."

"You want something? Here it is. Go get fucked."

"Well—"

"You've got one second to get that thing out of my face before I do it for you."

It hurt to talk. Henry's throat felt like someone had dumped a bucket of scalding coffee down his gullet. The woman walked away, looking offended. Henry learned later that more than five hundred people from the town had perished in that fire. They had gone there seeking shelter from the war. But there was no safe place. It was *not* a good story.

KEY WEST, FLORIDA

Suzanne squinted against the glare of the sun on the water, waiting for her father to arrive. In the marina beyond the bar, sailboats and yachts bobbed on gentle waves. The rigging on the sailboats rang against metal masts, a sound Suzanne had always loved. It was a hopeful sound. She did not feel that way now.

A tight-lipped young sailor had delivered an envelope to her, a message from the old man. "*Losers, noon,*" it said. The tavern was a hangout for locals, mostly service industry people and charter boat hands. She sat at a wooden table stained with bird guano near the dock. Behind her, the bar counter was lined with crusty locals downing warm, flat beer and shots of liquor. A gas generator droned from somewhere inside.

She saw her father then, wearing a straw hat, dark sunglasses, a polo shirt, and khaki shorts, making his way toward her. He looked ridiculous.

He grinned at her as he stepped up to her table, opening his arms. "Hey, Suzy-Q," he said.

She hugged him. "Hey, Dad."

"What? Not glad to see me?"

"Of course I am. I've been worried. Why are you dressed like that?"

"We'll get to that," he said, sitting down. "How are you? How is Taylor? I thought you'd be on base."

"We're all right, I guess. We've got Bart and Mary with us. Ginnie, too. We're managing."

"Good. Good. I'm glad you've been safe. I don't know how to say this, so I'm going to come right out with it."

"That's a change."

"Henry's been killed in action. I'm sorry, baby."

"What? *No*. That's not true. What are you talking about?"

"It's true. There's no way to make it better. If there were—"

"No. I'd *know*. He's not dead."

"I only found out yesterday. His whole unit was wiped out."

"I don't believe it."

Suzanne had battled nightmares about this moment. She'd tried to come to grips, knowing the danger her husband was in on an ongoing basis. She'd ultimately gotten through those moments of terror in the middle of the night by deciding Henry was too durable to die. It would not happen. Now, confronted by the fact, she retreated into denial. He could not be dead because she still felt him. Like an invisible thread connected to her soul.

"He is gone. And we've got to leave," Suzanne's father said.

"No."

Her father looked exasperated. "What do you mean no? We've got to get out of Key West. Today. Now."

"I'm not leaving."

"You don't understand the danger you're in. Think about Taylor. You don't want to put her in harm's way."

"I am. We're staying here. It's home. It's where Henry will try to get to."

"Look," her father said. He leaned forward and rested his chin on his hands, took off the sunglasses, and lowered his voice. "There are a lot of things you don't know. And there's not much time."

"Enlighten me."

"I've been working with some people. I've been helping you and Henry in your careers. That's why I did what I did."

"I don't understand."

"There's not enough time to explain properly. Let's just say, I've made some friends in high places. People that have a great deal of influence. They've moved things along for you and for Henry."

"So, what? You helped me land an agent? You helped me somehow get my first book deal? With your cronies in the Pentagon? I don't think so."

"Well, actually, it's something like that. A phone call to some helpful people."

"Crap."

"Whatever you say. The thing is, these people are dangerous. They're tying up loose ends right now. I'm probably one of those loose ends. They might come for you to get to me. They might have gotten to Henry. I don't know."

"What does he have to do with this?"

"His unit. Please, Suzanne. Trust me."

"What have you done?"

"I did it all for you. For your mother. For Taylor. Because I love you."

"What did you do? Are you a traitor?"

"No, no. Of course not. Nothing so drastic. Every so often, I'd have to move some things around. That's all. Just a little bit of information occasionally. Nothing top secret. I made one bad choice, Suzie, and then, well, I wish you knew how hard it's been for me. Because since then, I haven't had options. I had to keep doing what I was doing to protect you."

"Oh, Dad. How could you?" She felt sick inside. It was like a door had opened, a door she'd kept barred and bolted against something dark and sinister she knew lurked beyond. A thing she'd known existed on a subliminal level. The lavish vacations, the expensive gifts. She'd sensed something amiss for years. The realization and horror flooded into her.

"Say something," he said.

"There's no excuse. I wish you weren't my father."

"I didn't make an excuse. I'm telling you why. I did it for you. All for you."

"Bullshit. You did things to make yourself feel better. That's not the same."

"You're wrong. I wanted to give you everything. A better life for you than the one I had. I sacrificed every—"

"Henry's life. My childhood. My future. How *dare* you?"

"Don't raise your voice at me, young lady." Like he believed it.

Suzanne stood, warming to the anger, welcoming it. A lifetime of broken promises erupting. "I didn't want money. I wanted *you*." She punctuated the statement with fists pounding on the table, the drinks shaking. People were looking at them. She didn't give a damn.

"It's not that simple."

"It is. It was."

"You're not being fair. I—"

"You were *gone*. That's what you were. All I wanted was for you to see me. To go to the park or fishing or read a book together and for you to listen to me. You never listened. And I went on believing in you. I clung to this image of you. I thought you were doing something that mattered so I made excuses for you. But you just kept on breaking my heart. God, what was I thinking. You've done it for the last time, Daddy. I don't want to see you again. Ever."

"Suzy-Q, don't say that. You don't mean it."

"Oh, but I do. I had this picture of you in shining dress whites with medals and strength and courage. You were my hero. And you never should have been."

"Come on—"

"You're still not listening. You let me down in every way that mattered to me. Because I believed, through the long deployments, the nannies, the *when's Daddy coming home*, that you were doing something good. It was a lie. You are a lie."

"You could die if you stay here. Things are getting worse. Taylor could die. Don't let your anger at me cloud your judgment. You and your mother—"

"Yeah, Dad, while we're at it, let's talk about Mom. She was the bee's knees for a mother. I was always an inconvenience, a disappointment. Never elegant enough, smart enough, to be seen in front of her friends. Give me a break."

"Well, you certainly inherited her temper."

"You think? How about this? Fuck you."

If Suzanne had hoped to provoke a reaction, she was wrong. Her father nodded and stood, there in the bar with the flies and the tourist outfit. He looked wounded as he extended his hand.

"Okay, then," he said. "You're hurt and angry. I understand."

Suzanne stared at him.

"You're going to shake my hand, you miserable son of a bitch? I'm telling you good-bye forever, your only child, your daughter, and you offer to *shake my hand*?"

"You hate me right now. I figured a hug was out of the question."

"Go hop on a plane. Or a sub or a helicopter or whatever your plan is!"

"Please come with me. Maybe I was a shitty father. I let you down, I'm sure. You don't need to even like me. But please trust me one last time. After you're safe, after Taylor is safe, you never have to see me again. At least let me do this for you."

"No. You've done enough. When you had the chance to do it right, you didn't. God. I should have seen this. You miserable, evil bastard."

"All right. I'm sorry for all of it. I love you, whether you believe it right now or not. I love Taylor, too. And Henry was a good man."

He turned heel and wound his way through the crowded bar and Suzanne watched him leave until he was lost in the shadows, which is where he had always been.

Good-bye is the hardest word. Even though you say it, it's not over with the word. Some good-byes take a lifetime. She'd been telling her father good-bye since she could remember him; her first vivid recollection she was certain was her own was of begging him not to go, as he stood tall in a shining white uniform in their driveway and he pried her from his legs and walked out the door for what seemed like forever. Now it really was forever.

She'd been saying good-bye to Henry, too, for years. The first years, parting was bittersweet, anguish and anticipation wrapped around each other, and each farewell held the promise of a glorious reunion.

For the last couple of years, though, a darkness had tainted these departures, and Suzanne had fantasized about a life without Henry even when he was home, at first in an innocent, rankled kind of way, and then in a more serious and corrosive and calculating fashion. She'd made up her mind to extricate him from her life, to divorce herself of him, and yet had not had the guts to tell him to his face. She'd begun the legal process of saying good-bye, started a thing she wished she hadn't, and now, it was too late. Henry was gone and she'd said good-bye with a lawyer and a paper and now she realized she hadn't meant it in the first place. She'd wanted to be seen and understood and heard. She'd needed to be valued and envision a future together in which she wouldn't feel like she had to fight tooth and nail for these things and then resent him for not meeting her needs. Perhaps, she reasoned, she'd merely wanted to get his attention.

Suzanne felt a kind of self-loathing and grief she'd never known before, the feeling of falling through a maelstrom of pain bereft of hope and she blinked back tears of regret.

"Good-bye," she whispered, choking on the word.

CHAPTER ELEVEN

Heroes

COLORADO

Henry sat up with a jolt. Two ideas formed almost simultaneously. He tore off the oxygen mask.

"Sarn't Major," he said.

Martinez screwed up his eyebrows, his own face obscured behind a mask misted with condensation. "What?"

"The reporter." It still hurt to talk. "SAT feed."

"Ugh," Martinez grunted, his face clouding.

"If—"

"Shit."

Henry and Martinez stood at the same time. Carlos remained with his back against the fire truck's front tire. "Now what?" said Carlos.

"We can use the satellite feed to upload this data," Martinez said. "Maybe. If they've got a truck with a dish. I should've thought of that before. Stay here and rest; Henry and I will go find her."

Henry and Martinez walked through the crowd of people who had gathered to watch the fire. Some of them were sitting in the cold and staring into space, others talking in small groups. There were cries and groans from tents that had materialized from somewhere. It was as if the town converged upon the school by some unspoken collective agreement.

Henry felt tears sting his eyes, not from the smoke now, but from the scenes of heartbreak and tragedy everywhere he looked.

A young couple clung to one another, sitting on the frozen ground, a small, unmoving bundle in their arms. They rocked back and forth, swaying to an unspeakable melody of pain and loss.

An old man, stooped and bent with years and anguish, murmured over a white-haired woman and he touched her face with trembling, bony hands.

A boy of nine or ten walked in circles, hands stuffed tight into his coat pockets, making drowning sounds and chanting "muh, muhm mamma."

Henry wanted to fall to his knees and weep.

"There," said Martinez, pointing. A white van with *Action News 4* painted on the side was parked near the edge of the throng of survivors. Martinez rapped on the door. A kid with curly hair and thick glasses poked his head out from the back of the van.

"Get lost," he said. He looked like he wasn't old enough to drive. Maybe a college intern. He tried to close the door. Martinez stopped him.

"Do you have a satellite feed?"

"Who the—"

"Wait," said a woman from somewhere behind the kid. "Travis, grab your camera. These are the heroes."

The interior of the van was crammed with electronics. Glowing screens displayed various scenes of carnage and destruction.

"You're famous," the woman said, beaming. "Four million hits in the last thirty minutes."

"So you have a feed," Martinez said.

"Obviously."

Travis was pulling out a handheld camera. Henry took it from him.

Martinez reached into a pocket in his jacket, a small black stick drive in his hand. "I want you to upload this. Right now."

"Give Travis his camera back, and we'll talk about it."

On one of the screens over her shoulder, Henry was carrying a child to a fireman. The camera zoomed in for a close-up shot of his sooty face. At the bottom of the screen, a headline scrolled in bold print highlighted in red, reading *Unknown heroes rescue school children in war-torn Colorado.*

"I don't have time to be nice," Martinez growled. He held out the tiny flash drive. "Upload this."

"For an interview? An exclusive?"

"Sure, lady."

She turned her head and said over her shoulder, "Travis, do it."

Travis took the drive and plugged it into a port, sitting in the cramped van. "It's encrypted," he said.

"Just do it," Martinez said.

"But it's gibberish. It won't make sense. It's just unreadable code at this point. I'd have to—"

"There's no time," Martinez said. "Put it out there raw."

"All right. Where do I send it?"

"Everywhere. Send it to everyone," Martinez said.

The kid was typing feverishly. "There's a ton of files," he said, peering at the glowing screen. "It's gonna take a few minutes."

"Huh," Travis said then, cocking his head. "The upload just stopped."

"Give me the drive," Martinez said.

"Hold on. It might be—"

Martinez climbed into the van and removed the drive from the computer. "You need to vanish," he said. "On foot, and right now."

"Wait!" the reporter said. "What about the interview?"

"Leave the van and go!" Henry said. "You're in danger."

Martinez had already walked away, and Henry turned to follow him back to the fire truck where they'd left Carlos. Martinez removed his jacket mid-stride and tossed it on the ground. Henry followed suit. They made it about a hundred yards.

Henry heard the hiss of the rocket a fraction of a second before the blast knocked him forward. He pushed himself back to his feet and saw an inferno where the news van had been. People were screaming again, running to nowhere in particular. Henry hoped the reporter and Travis had listened.

Carlos was on his feet next to the truck, a duffel full of gear over each shoulder. He handed Henry his own bag. They grabbed helmets from the fire truck and put them on.

"Evasive action," Martinez said. Let's split up. The church with the big steeple on the south side of town. Let's meet there in fifteen minutes. Go!"

Henry walked at a brisk pace, not quite, but almost a jog. He moved at an oblique angle to his destination, cutting through backyards and staying beneath the cover of trees as much as he could. Many houses bore wounds. Some burned, others had holes torn through them. It looked like a war zone, which, of course, it was. He cut through an empty house, grabbed an olive green parka from the coat closet, and put that on, along with a knitted cap. He walked out onto the sidewalk, slowed his gait, and limped just for effect.

He reasoned that somehow, the upload had been intercepted and stopped. Whoever had done that had ordered the air strike, and there were probing eyes in the sky scouring the town. Maybe drones, maybe satellites, or both. As he neared the church, he was aware of the thrum of the shattered town, straining to filter out the many sounds. There was the sound of sirens and car alarms and a wailing that seemed to emanate from the trees, which he was not certain was real. He strained to listen for aircraft, knowing that if a drone had him, he would be dead before he could react.

One of the things he had been trained to do was to think like the enemy. *I don't know who my enemy is, but I'm learning. If I were trying to silence an enemy in an American town, I wouldn't rely on drones and air power. I'd want people on the ground. If I were evil, I'd wipe the whole town off the map. I'd want to see the bodies.*

He forced himself to walk slowly, crossing the street to the church. The traffic light was dead and hanging in the middle of the road at just above head height. This part of the quaint town had seen heavy fighting. There were military vehicles smashed and smoking in the middle of the road, and uniformed bodies lying in motionless clumps. Blood stained the snow.

The thump of rotors, multiple birds inbound, which was a sound Henry had once loved, now chilled him more than the icy wind.

"Wilkins!" From off to his right. "Over here."

Henry turned on the sidewalk, catching movement from the corner of his eye. Martinez waved from inside a blown-out storefront. Henry jogged in that direction while the sound of approaching helicopters grew louder.

It was a hardware store, the kind of mom and pop place Henry remembered from his childhood but rarely saw anymore. Martinez and Carlos were inside, along with other soldiers.

"What took you so long?" Martinez said. "Nice hat."

"I'm right on time," Henry said, pointing at his watch. "Who are these guys?"

"These guys," said a square-jawed man in fatigues and a helmet, "have just had the shit kicked out of them. And now we're about to save your ass. Or maybe we're all just gonna die." He sounded like he'd walked out of a New York mafia movie. *Deese guys*.

"This is Captain Canella," Sergeant Major Martinez said.

"Colorado National Guard," Captain Canella interjected. "Of the *United* States of America."

"Sir," Henry said, saluting.

"Are you fucking kiddin' me?" Captain Canella snorted. "Kit up. It's about to get interesting again."

"Yes, sir."

Henry tore into his ruck. He pulled on his vest, strapped his sidearm to his thigh, and assembled his submachine gun. The helicopters closed in, and the pitch of the rumble changed as they swept past.

"Two birds. Chinooks, five hundred feet," said a middle-aged soldier, peering out the shattered window of the store.

The rumble shifted again, growing louder.

"Uh-oh. One is coming back. They're about to drop troops on our heads."

Henry noticed Carlos had picked up a SAW equipped with an ACOG scope, an extra belt of ammunition draped around his shoulders. There were maybe twenty other soldiers, some standing, some sitting or kneeling in the store. Many were bleeding. Toward the shadowy rear of the store, Henry could see some who were horizontal.

"We've got men across the street in some of the stores, and a fifty in the church," Captain Canella said. "I hope it's worth it. 'Cause they're all gonna die."

"I gave him the thirty-second version," Martinez said, edging his head from the door. "Captain Canella figures we should exfil now while he and his men engage." Henry knew that tone.

"They're inserting," said the weekend warrior with an M4 carbine slung over his chest and a desperate look on his face. The rotor wash from the Chinook sent snow and dust swirling down the street and through the quaint hardware store. Henry's heart rate accelerated and his chest was tight and his throat was raw. Soldiers rattled out the back door.

"We're going to do this," Martinez said. "I told the captain he could respectfully go fuck himself."

"Yeah, and I told him that was—"

A bomb hit the church, and whatever it was Captain Canella was about to say ended in flying glass and smoke and a shrinking of the lungs and balls and ringing of the ears.

"Taking contact!" someone shouted.

"Engage!" Urgent and close and sounding far away. Maybe it was Canella, or perhaps it was Martinez that gave the order.

Henry left the safety of the store. Carlos hunkered down behind the passenger side of a snow-encrusted car parked on the side of the road, and as Henry took up a position by the driver's rear tire of the old

Subaru, he saw the futility in the fight. The Chinook opened up, strafing the church and then the rooftops with heavy-caliber rounds.

The enemy soldiers fast-roped from the helicopter. Henry fired at them as they landed, placing his crosshairs at chest height. He used his elbows to form a bipod and fired short bursts. He focused on a group of three ropes, and cut down every man who landed. He went through two magazines in less than a minute, rolling slightly as he thumbed the release.

"Reloading!" he yelled.

From across the street, muzzle flashes sparked from doorways and windows.

The Chinook walked tracers up the street and through the vehicle Henry and Carlos were taking cover behind, and rounds slammed through the metal and whined from the road. Henry smelled gasoline.

"Los! Move! Gas!"

"Moving! Give me covering fire."

Henry continued to fire, now at flashes and movement, aware of the fuel spilling onto the road, the sparks all around him as rounds hit the pavement, the Subaru, and the buildings. The second helicopter, the one that had gone further north over town, came closer, and the door gunner let loose.

The attacking ground troops were nowhere to be seen. They had not marched up the road like untrained militia men who had seen too many movies. They'd taken cover, and were undoubtedly advancing, while the two helicopters pounded away.

The building across the street exploded, sending debris hurtling through the air and small pellets of angry glass into Henry's face. Hot ash and flaming pieces of building came drifting down.

Henry ran, slipping on the snow and ice. He could feel the rounds seeking his flesh as they cracked and slapped and zipped around him.

The Subaru he'd been taking cover behind exploded, and the blast threw him face forward. He lost his weapon and smashed his chin and felt his teeth clang together. Half blind, and with his brain in a vise, he clawed for his weapon, the snow and ice digging beneath his fingernails while he groped on knees and elbows.

Hungry hands found the stock, pulled it close. The machine guns continued to rain down. They fired and fired from above and everything was broken and ripped apart. The belly of one of the birds was less than a hundred meters overhead.

Henry rolled onto his back and fired, and there was a screaming in him as he expended one magazine and then switched to another. His was the rage of a bullied child at the moment he doesn't care if he gets his ass kicked and has to hit back because that's all there is left and even if he gets pulverized, then he did that one thing, he punched that son of a bitch square on the nose and made him bleed. Henry screamed out loud then, a death song which mingled with the chatter of the SAW and the sirens and alarms and thudding Chinooks, a primal howl amid the smell of propellant and taste of death on his lips, which was his and theirs and he took pleasure in it. No hope, only retribution and recoil and death.

Expended cartridges pinged to the ground with a music all their own. Cursing, Henry half crawled, half ran back into the shelter of the store, slipping and swearing, angry and afraid.

Rounds ripped through the ceiling and walls. Cans of paint spewed red and white and blue on the floor, explosions of color through air thick with smoke. There were many screams and some of them belonged to Henry.

He switched magazines, his head just below where the window had been. Carlos was next to the doorway, switching out barrels for the SAW.

Henry popped up long enough to see hostiles running into the ruins across the street. He sat up again and squeezed off a burst. The tile floor inside was littered with cartridges and pieces of drywall.

"Pull back to the rear door!" Martinez shouted from behind Henry.

Carlos abandoned the SAW and was firing his assault rifle instead through the door, lying prone and exposed. Henry popped up again, acquired a target. Squeezed. Ducked back down. Enemy troops were consolidating just across the street for an assault. Probably more on each side. The Chinooks kept hammering.

"Frag out!" Henry said, lobbing a grenade across the street.

"Smoke out!" Carlos said. "Move it, Wilkins!"

Henry tried to come to a crouch, but he slipped. Blood covered the floor, and his hand was warm and slick with it. Captain Canella lay on his back, some of his face gone and his shoulder separated from the rest of his body. Rounds from the Chinook had rained down from directly overhead, tearing him apart. Henry crawled toward the rear of the store, climbing over bodies while the store came apart around him. Toward the far left corner, something exploded, perhaps a propane tank or a fire extinguisher or paint thinner. The fire spread with amazing speed, devouring the rear wall and spilling out onto the floor. There was no way he could make it to the rear exit.

He crawled back to the door glad of the unpolluted air, trying to make himself small, and readying himself for a last charge into the light.

KEY WEST, FLORIDA

In Key West, Suzanne heard a different rumor every day. One day, the war was over and the United States was a single nation again. Later that afternoon, or the next day, people would be shouting that Miami had been hit with a nuclear weapon and troops were on the way to reclaim the Keys, to force them to join with the rest of Florida at gunpoint. Suzanne and Bart spoke to a boater who swore he'd seen a Russian armada thirty miles offshore.

Radio operators communicated with people from around the nation and the world, a new kind of coconut telegraph, and a fragmented picture of the state of the nation emerged. The country was broken and fighting continued. The president was still alive, and appealing to the international community for help.

Russia had thousands of troops massed on its borders, along with divisions of armor and attack helicopters. Western Europe was panicked, China wrung its hands. The United States was alone.

The bases were not letting anyone on post without proof they were active duty. The troops stationed around town vanished. A fire broke out in Old Town and consumed hotels and bars and tourist shops. No one knew how it started, but almost a hundred people died.

One of Suzanne's neighbors, an attorney named David Greenburg with a thriving practice in Miami, arrived by boat and banged on the door late in the afternoon.

Bart let him inside, and David collapsed on the couch, shaking, dehydrated, and hungry.

"Miami's gone insane," he said. His eyes were bloodshot and twitching. "They're animals."

"Have some fish, David," Suzanne said. "Calm down. You're safe."

"I didn't think I'd make it," he whispered. "They broke into my house. They took Jill and made her open the safe. She said no and they shot her. Just like that they shot my wife."

"I'm sorry," Suzanne said.

"Who? Who did that?" Bart asked.

"I don't know. People. Guys with guns and crowbars. I didn't know them."

"How did you get here?"

"They let me go after I gave them my car, my money, my wife's—" he choked. "Her engagement ring. Her jewelry. They laughed about it. They were in my house for less than half an hour and they took everything. They shot her in the back of the head like it was a joke. I walked to the marina in Coconut Grove where I keep the boat. Some of the other boats were smashed, some sunk. For no reason. I don't understand. Anything. I don't understand all of it." He was shaking.

"Is your husband here?" David asked, looking up with a glimmer of hope in his eyes.

"No. They say he's been killed," Suzanne replied. It was the second time she'd had to say that. She'd told Bart, although not her daughter. She could say it without breaking into small pieces because she was certain it was not true.

"Suzanne, I'm sorry for your loss," David said. "It is too much to bear."

"Thank you, David. I'll believe it when I see his dog tags. That man is too damn stubborn to die."

She knew the Greenburgs better than she knew most of her neighbors. David and Jill came down south at least once every month, more in the wintertime. They'd shared dinners and bottles of wine together, and David and Henry actually got along pretty well. She knew David was a veteran, and that undoubtedly helped to overcome Henry's innate resentment of wealthy people.

Bart came back into the room with some bottled water and grouper fresh from the grill. David ate with his hands and chugged the water.

"Have you heard any news?" Bart asked.

"Probably nothing you haven't heard. We've been without power since this thing started. You know about DC and San Fran, right?"

"Yeah."

"Well, that's true, I guess. Honestly, I was hoping you'd know what was going on, 'cause I sure don't."

"We're all in the dark," Suzanne said.

"Looks like at least you've got a generator," David said. "I don't suppose you'd be willing to let me—"

"The answer is yes," Suzanne said.

Bart cut his eyes at her, but she ignored him. David was out of shape and over the hill, and he would be drinking their water and eating their food. Still, he was smart, and he was a good man. In her mind, that was enough. If they could stick together, they could make one another stronger. The more people to stand watch, the better.

Bart had set up rain traps all over the property, and he was almost finished constructing an elaborate desalinization system, which would allow them to use seawater by evaporating the salt. That would help, though it would not be enough. Water would be a problem in the coming months, the dry season.

Already, a black market had sprung up in town, and Suzanne knew people were hoarding water.

David Greenburg wept into his hands. "Thank you," he said. "I'm sorry. I have nothing. No money, no guns. I can't really do much." He laughed, a bitter sound. "If you want me to sue someone or write a contract for you, you'll have free legal services for life."

"My friend," Suzanne said with a smile, "you have a deal."

*

That night the whole group dined together and Suzanne felt hope as she ate and drank with her friends. Even Mary seemed to be in better spirits, and Suzanne saw her old friend had lost a considerable amount of weight in only a few weeks, seemed less lethargic and more engaged. Bobby was clear eyed and his hands no longer shook, and he'd shed at least ten years, still wiry and ornery as ever, and proud of himself for the mangrove snapper and grunt he'd caught and put on the table. Ginnie was a flurry of activity, cooking and cleaning and seldom standing still. She, more than any of the others, seemed wounded down deep, and Suzanne understood. Taylor flitted from person to person and lit up the room by being herself.

Bart laughed and joked and he was relaxed for the first time in a long time. He flirted with his wife more than he did with Ginnie or Suzanne, which was a marked change. Suzanne had felt uncomfortable more than once with the way Bart employed lascivious innuendo followed by innocent looks. Sometimes the phrase was directed at Ginnie, and sometimes it came at Suzanne. Ginnie did not seem to mind, though she might have been oblivious; Suzanne did not like it. It felt like a betrayal.

"You put the rod into the hole," he'd said the previous day while explaining how to use the rod holders on the stern of his boat to Ginnie. "Just be careful with the rod. It's fragile, especially the tip."

"Ugh," Suzanne had said from the bow.

"Hey, she's probably never held a rod this big before. This ain't one of those flimsy ones. This is the real deal."

Suzanne, who had been pulling in the anchor, gave Bart a scathing stare. He grinned back at her with that guiltless expression. The *what did I do*? Look. And yet beneath it, Suzanne saw the thing, the underlying defiant truth which was as much an accusation as an admission.

They were friends, and that's all they would ever be. But that's not quite all they'd ever been.

So now, on this night, she was glad to feel an easing of tension, happy to see Bart flirting with his own wife.

Suzanne was on watch in the dark hours of the night, alone with a shotgun while most of the house slept. Bart and Mary were not sleeping, though, and Mary's cries were piercing and urgent one room away, defiant perhaps.

Suzanne had many regrets. Bart topped the list. She'd been young and reckless and bulletproof. That was the story she told herself. There had been rum runners involved.

"Ya know," Bart said years ago. Mary and Henry were crashed out in the hotel room, in the suite Henry had sprung for in Islamorada. Suzanne hadn't had enough reggae music or rum or stupidity to fill her soul, so she'd decided to keep on partying. "After you two, you know, call it quits, the two of us have to hook up. At least once. 'Cause it would be epic."

"Oh really? Is that what you think?"

"Yeah. Except I don't think. I know for a fact. And so do you."

"I thought he was your best friend?"

"Of course he is. He'd do the same to me, though. I'm saying, after."

"After what?"

"After he breaks your heart. Or you break his. That part's an even bet. Somebody's gonna get their heart broke, though. You ain't his first rodeo, let's put it like that."

"So you're saying, what?" Maybe she'd slurred her words. She didn't remember it that way, but she probably had. She was cool and unfettered. "It's not his first rodeo but it's mine?"

"I know it's not your first go-round, Suzy-Q. You're more woman than that country boy can handle."

The band played "Is This Love" by Bob Marley and the Wailers and she was tan and twenty and the air throbbed with reggae and freedom and youth. When he asked her to dance, she'd said yes. When he'd suggested they go in the water after that, when the band was done and the night was still and the stars were out, she'd agreed.

It was spring break. I was stupid that time in Holiday Isle and maybe Henry would have forgiven me and maybe he would have forgiven Bart but then things changed and the truth would have been undermined by the lies we had to tell ourselves. Next thing I knew, I was head over heels and Henry was falling for me and it was real and if I'd said anything, he would have lost his best friend and I'd have lost him. And that's the truth. I loved Henry, and I didn't want to lose him. I didn't want to wound him and I loved him and I still do and he's not really dead.

Mary howled from one room away, unabashed and echoing from the tiled floors in the dark house in Key West, an accusatory orgasm. *Your man is dead and mine is right here, bitch!* Mary quit moaning then, and there were a few punctuating gunshots in the distance, and Suzanne forced herself to smile.

"I'd give that a 9.5," Suzanne said. Loud enough to be heard, but in a way that might have been to herself, even though everyone knew otherwise.

"That was a ten," old Bobby crowed from the couch. "And everybody shut the hell up so I can get some sleep."

Mary giggled. A college girl hanging out in the Keys. "You wish you knew what ten was!"

"Now we can all get some rest," Suzanne said, feeling the edge in her voice which was tension and guilt mixed with resentment, and not liking herself much for sounding that way.

Suzanne patrolled her house for the next two hours, padding from room to room in bare feet and aware of the senses of the night, lost in part in her own mind, yet connected by history and sensation and love to those around her. The shotgun was cool and heavy and reassuring in her hands. The tile floors beneath her toes were cool, too, hard and quiet and with cracks in them, an uneven surface because Suzanne had insisted upon that particular porous flooring. Henry hadn't cared one way or the other. Without ceiling fans or air conditioning, the air was close and tinged with death and smoke and garbage and corruption that overwhelmed the salty breezes. Gunshots spattered the night and Bobby snored on the couch like a hibernating bear with nightmares.

The sensations were off. The wrongness was pervasive and almost a thing in and of itself, a separate sense the body and soul seem to recognize without being able to explain to the mind. There was the lack of boat traffic along the canal, a song Suzanne had come to regard as comforting as the rain in the way people who live next to trains, airports, or sirens do. Without the background noise, there was an inescapable thrum no amount of laughter could deny.

She wanted to go to sleep and wake up and have things be normal again, face a world she could understand, and even better, wake up when she was younger and hadn't made the mistakes she had.

Suzanne yearned to breathe a morning with promise and light and hope without the scent of disdain and destruction on her lungs and the feeling of an anvil crushing her chest. She wanted to make things right, and knowing she could not, wished to go back in time and undo everything gone wrong. The night was dark and oily and shimmering with the lingering wrath of bad decisions; the promise of a rising sun was broken. It would not cleanse her or banish the past. She mourned at that dying of the light, the spark in her that was extinguished before but which was apparent because of the void. She raged against it, helpless and hating her helplessness.

She saw herself from a sober distance and she flinched at what she beheld. She'd imagined herself to be the hero of her own life, strong and virtuous. Selfless. She recognized now the arrogance in that delusion. The characters in her novels, the *real* heroines, would despise her if they knew her. And even her writing, something which she had clung to and wrapped her soul around until it had become an essential part of her, accused her. While she'd built her life and dreams around words and books, she'd been losing the things which were deeply important, and in the end, her literary career was a fraud, a success engineered by her father and whoever he did favors for.

When Beowulf growled, a deep, vibrating rumble Suzanne could feel in her toes even though the sound was subtle and not loud, and the dog would never bark unless he was confronted with another dog, there was menace and danger in it and Suzanne was almost glad.

"Stay," she whispered to the dog. She went to go wake the others.

CHAPTER TWELVE

Scream of Battle

COLORADO

The fire spread and things exploded inside the hardware store while Henry crawled outside surrounded by billowing black smoke. The heavy machine guns on the helicopters pounded the rear of the building.

He targeted the nearest gunner and fired. He expended one magazine and switched, lying on his back. The bird was moving and he knew it was hopeless. One of his rounds must have come close, though, because the gunner started walking tracers his way. Henry felt the hum in his chest as the bright orange rain approached him. He kept firing.

He felt anger and fear and regret. There was nowhere to hide.

He was screaming at the helicopters when they burst into flames. A missile from an aircraft punched through one of them without detonating; a second later, another missile followed, and that one did the job.

As flaming debris rained down upon the street, the attacking Chinooks spiraled around each other until they disappeared beyond below the row of stores. Henry heard the crash and watched the columns of smoke.

He fought the urge to laugh.

He rolled over and crawled further down the sidewalk, and a pair of F-35 jets swept overhead like avenging angels.

A four-man squad, some of those who had descended from the attacking helicopters, darted from one building to another directly across the road. Henry lobbed a frag through a blown-out window.

The *whump* from inside sent glass and wood shards needling through the air, and two men staggered out onto the road screaming and clawing at their eyes.

Henry peppered them with rounds and they spun to the ground.

He jogged to the alley and cut around to see how his friends had fared in the fight. The rear of the building was on fire, and several of the National Guard troops were bleeding out. Carlos and Sergeant Martinez were huddled over a man, trying to save his life.

Small arms fire continued from the rubble of the church around the corner. Apparently there were more commandos headed toward the hardware store.

"Sergeant," Henry said. "We gotta go. The longer we stay here, the more people will get killed."

"I know, damn it!"

Carlos looked up at Henry and shook his head slightly. The guy on the ground was burned on his face and hands, the skin bubbled and charred. He was crying for his mother.

Martinez stuck the wounded warrior with morphine, a heavy dose, and the man went still.

"Fuck," Martinez said, standing with his hands on his hips and shaking his head in disgust.

The small arms fire continued, some of it closer now.

"On me," Martinez said. "The church."

Henry took up the rear, moving sideways so he could watch for enemies trying to come from behind. Henry was aware of the smell of burned flesh and hair, some of it his own. He decided he'd had enough of fire to last a lifetime.

They entered the church from what had been the rear; there was no easy way to tell the difference now, for the ceiling had collapsed and the front and back were open. Henry stepped past the pulpit, where a large cross had been blown onto the floor. The pews in the sanctuary were askew and torn.

Four Guardsmen were crouched down behind a smashed wall, and one of them was firing a light machine gun down the street. Spent cartridges clattered against the concrete.

"Friendlies!" Martinez said. The men turned their heads.

"Did the captain make it?"

"No," Martinez replied.

"Motherfuckers. There's more infantry. And I think I hear armor."

"Yeah, there's a Bradley, at least one, heading up the road," said another man.

"Get out of here," Martinez said. "Go home."

"Home is gone," said the machine gunner. "You go. I'm done." He leaned into the scope and fired a burst. "That's right!" he screamed. "Get some, you cocksuckers!" He fired again.

"Where is the rest of your unit?" Martinez said. "Did any of you fall back?"

The gunner laughed without humor. "You're looking at us."

"What about communications? Have you got a SAT phone? A radio linked to your brigade? Anything?"

"Captain Canella had a radio," said the gunner. He fired again. "They're trying to flank us," he said calmly. "I'd strongly suggest you get the fuck out of here."

"Good luck. And thanks," Martinez said. He turned and Henry followed him out through the back of the church. Behind him, the machine gun resumed and pounded away.

They cut through more yards and side roads until they were beyond the town and into the hills and woods. Henry contemplated the drones that might be searching for them, the satellites and surveillance aircraft, and he had the feeling of being a seal on the surface of an ocean of great white sharks, wondering when he'd be ripped to pieces, and knowing there was nothing he could do about it.

He hoped that he was not a priority. There was a war going on, and within that war were many stories. There would be command and control issues, communication glitches and lags. And there were only so many assets in the area that an enemy could bring to bear. Federalist forces were still engaging; the F-35s had proven that. Maybe they could slip away.

The sun edged below the mountains and the sky was golden and pink and the air was sharp in Henry's lungs. The woods were silent and still and brooding.

They slept for a few hours in a ramshackle cabin, probably a poacher's lodge. They were in the middle of some kind of national forest or park. The tallest peaks were behind them now, and the plains would be ahead. They decided to travel mostly by night, and the overall plan changed.

In front of a pathetic fire crackling in a stone fireplace, Martinez stared at the flash drive in his hands.

"Whatever this is, it's more important than we know. It's more important than any of *us*, anyhow. We've got an oath to uphold."

"What do you mean?" Carlos said.

"I mean, the information that is on this thing has gotten a lot of people killed. Not just our boys, either. I think maybe the reason for this war is on this thing. Maybe the people behind it. They're scared."

"If that's true," Henry said, "they'll never stop coming."

"Right," Martinez said. "They'll come for us, for our families, and they'll never quit. I'm guessing they know exactly who each of us is by now. They could have pulled down that footage the idiot reporter put up on the net and run us through facial recognition software. They have tremendous power and influence to have pulled off what they have. They stopped an upload. That means they either had control of that satellite, or the whole damn Internet. I don't know. And they had to know what they were looking for. That kid Travis said the upload stopped after only a few *seconds*. The airstrike, and I'm thinking it was a drone, was . . . what? Maybe two minutes after that? Whoever these guys are, they saw us on the Internet, knew we were a part of Alpha Pack, tasked a drone to that shithole town, and then waited for us to show our faces again."

"You really know how to inspire," Carlos said. "I feel all warm and fuzzy now."

"We're still alive, though," Martinez said. "So we managed to lose them for now. Those jets might have engaged some of their drones, saving our asses twice. So now we stay off the grid completely. They are powerful, but they're not God. They've got an Achilles' heel, and I'm holding it right here in my hands."

"But how are we going to use that?" Henry said.

"I haven't figured that part out yet," Martinez admitted. "But let me ask you something. How did you feel when you saw those kids? Those little children and their grieving parents?"

"Sad," Carlos said. "Angry too. *Really* angry."

"Yeah," Henry agreed. He'd been enraged and broken inside. It hurt to remember.

"Well, these guys don't care," Martinez said. "They don't care about taking innocent lives. They don't give a damn about leveling a town or killing a family in a van or hitting our capital with a nuclear weapon. They just don't care. So I've been thinking. What do they care about?"

"Power," Henry said.

"Money," Carlos added.

"Exactly. Power and money. And that's it. They don't care about anything else, because if they did, I don't think any of this would have happened."

"I don't follow," Henry said.

"Work backwards," Martinez said. "Who thinks like that? Who just doesn't give a fuck about anything but money and power?"

"Well, that's a pretty long list. Wall Street. Politicians. China, maybe. The Russians."

You're spot on," Martinez said. "I'm just a dumb grunt from LA with a little bit of community college, but I know *people*. I see patterns. Work with me here. For the last, what? Fifteen years, the global economy has been crap."

"Yep," Henry said.

"Europe and the US hit a major recession. The recovery we keep hearing about, well, we all know how that's been. China's real estate bubble popped and that made things even worse. Everybody is poorer than they were."

"Mostly," Henry said.

"Right. *Mostly*. Who's not? Who is better off now than fifteen years ago? The people at the very top, that's who. The clowns who have the system rigged in their favor. The guys with private islands and more than one jet. They've managed to turn tremendous profits while everyone else got poorer. I wonder how they did that?"

"They're smart," Carlos said. "And they work harder than everyone else." He chuckled.

"That's the campaign poster, right? That's what they want us to believe. And I'm sure some of them are for real. Some of those people are brilliant and earned every penny, and more power to them. Some of them, though, just don't give a damn. That's who we're fighting right now. The people who ordered the wholesale slaughter of innocents. You guys know anything about the Civil War?"

"You mean the first one?" Carlos said. "Yeah, man. I love Lincoln. Emancipation Proclamation. Gettysburg Address. Freed the slaves."

"Uh-huh," Martinez said. "Any idea how many people died?"

"Let's see," Carlos said. He smiled, his dark face getting darker in the flickering firelight, teeth white and shining. His voice changed, slightly lower in pitch, and his inflection altered. He sounded like a documentary voice-over narrator on the History Channel.

"The Civil War was the bloodiest war in American history. More than 650,000 Americans died. The bloodiest single day for America was at Antietam. We lost more men in a day than in ten years of fighting in Afghanistan and Iraq combined."

"This war is already worse," Martinez said. "And it's only been a few weeks."

"I'm lost," Henry said.

"What the sergeant major is saying is two things," Carlos said. "Number one, this war is going to become exponentially worse than the first Civil War because of the increased lethality of our weapons and training and the fact that the people pulling the strings don't give a fuck about killing everyone. Finally, it's our job to stop them. That about right, Sar'n?"

Martinez gave Carlos an odd, appraising look. "Yes, Carlos, that's about right."

"The Civil War was not about slavery or morality, not really," Carlos said. "It was about money and power. The men on the ground, the guys pointing the rifles at each other, they were caught up in it. Most Confederate soldiers were never even related to someone who owned a slave, and still they fought. Maybe they listened to the wrong sermon, or maybe because their brothers were all fighting, too, and that was the honorable thing to do. A bunch of dirt farmers and sharecroppers who fought like hell because they had been manipulated into believing in a system which benefitted the gentry at a disproportionate rate to the general populace."

"Where the hell did that come from, and who the hell are you?" Martinez said with a grin.

"I like history," Carlos said. "I love to read. But in the army, it doesn't pay to be *too* smart."

All three of them laughed then, and they told stories about foolish and dangerous officers they'd all served under. In the stories, the lieutenants, captains, and majors were buffoons. Henry rejoiced in the laughter and shared reminiscing, for the stories were similar. There were cowards, bullies, and grossly inept officers they'd all had the displeasure of serving under. It wasn't all funny, though; soldiers had died because of these fools. The conversation became serious.

"That's what this is, you know," Carlos said.

"What?" Martinez asked.

"The same kind of thinking, similar manipulation, but on a broader scale now, that compelled the South to really go to war the first time. Fear, misinformation, dehumanization, misplaced loyalty. Brotherhood. Money and power. But the money and power now, worse than then, is centralized in the hands of a few. And the economy is global. I'm guessing our real enemies have estates in Europe, Asia, all over the world. They're loyal to the dollar and the yuan and the ruble. They don't want to lose what they've got, and they've managed to get people to fight for them. And now we have a new 'bloodiest day in American history.'"

"I'm sorry," Henry said, "but it's not quite that simple. The government has gone nuts. They're in our personal business and no one is stopping them. They want to take our guns, hand out money to people who lay around all day and expect us to pay for it. Welfare, entitlements. Spending money the government doesn't have to spend. And you're wrong about the Civil War. The first one, I mean. It wasn't just about—"

"All right, Johnny Reb," Carlos said. "You tell that to the motherfucker with the private island who's trying to kill you. The team that comes for your wife and kid. We can debate the *Federalist Papers* and the theory of nullification then. Right now, there is an enemy that needs some killing."

"Amen, brother," Martinez said. "Now shut up and get some sleep. I've got the first watch."

KEY WEST, FLORIDA

Suzanne peered through the hole Bart had cut in the front door while the others took up positions around the house. Bart, carrying an AR-15 from Henry's gun safe, padded from room to room, checking the windows and doors. Outside, the gang of looters whooped and hollered as they pillaged the home across the street. Suzanne knew no one lived there at the moment.

The looters, at least thirty of them, loaded pickup trucks, trailers, and vans. Suzanne could hear them laughing and joking. These were the kind of people that longed for a breakdown of society. For them, this was an extended holiday, a chance to be free of the law and constraints of morality. A window of opportunity afforded by a lack of consequences.

Maybe they'll leave us alone. There are plenty of other houses around here.

More of them came, their ranks swelling through some invisible cockroach network, an announcement floating through the air that the light was out and it was time to swarm.

Ginnie took Taylor into the guest bathroom, the safest room in the house. They hunkered down in the bathtub with some blankets over them. They'd gone over this plan more than once, and even drilled on it. The tub might protect them from rounds tearing through the house. Although the walls were concrete, the hurricane shudders over the abundant windows would do nothing to stop a bullet.

Mary sat in the living room holding a .22 pistol in her hands and looking at it as though it were a poisonous snake.

Greenburg looked morose and tense and he had a baseball bat over his knees.

"They're coming this way," Suzanne said. The sun was coming up. She'd hoped these clowns would lose interest, but they seemed to be enjoying themselves. They'd set one of the houses down the street on fire.

The looters carried pieces of rebar, bats, crowbars, and guns. They were mostly young men, but Suzanne could see some who looked to be in their forties, bearded and crusty. A group of them stood in the road looking at her home, hands on their hips, apparently sizing things up.

There was more shouting and gesturing and the group of thugs formed up and started walking up the driveway.

"Get ready," Suzanne said.

"It's clear in the backyard," Bobby said.

"I'm not playing with these assholes," Bart said. "Suzanne, aim for the chest."

Bart stood next to the front door, the assault rifle in both hands. He had extra magazines stuffed into his pockets and a sidearm holstered at his hip. He paused for a moment, and Suzanne saw him nod to himself, as though he were counting down in his head.

He threw the door open, moving to his right.

Suzanne fired the first shot, at a man less than thirty feet away. He was carrying a black revolver in one hand, sauntering forward with a grin.

When the door opened, he started to raise his weapon, his grin fading into surprise while Suzanne pulled the trigger.

The blast knocked him two steps back, and he pivoted on one foot while his knees buckled beneath him, sitting down, then falling at an angle that would have been painful and awkward for a man who was still alive. The recoil from the shotgun slammed into Suzanne's shoulder and rocked her on her feet; she was already chambering another shell, racking the weapon and shifting the barrel slightly.

Bart was firing and moving off to the right. Single shots like firecrackers.

Suzanne fired again, feeling outside of herself, and surprised at how calm she was. She tingled all over, and her ears were humming.

The second guy was trying to run, but instead of turning away, he'd come straight at her. He was about twenty feet away when she shot him in the face. His head was transformed into pink mist and meat and his body twisted to the ground, arms and legs twitching.

There were other shots from further away, and Suzanne heard the crack of rounds hitting the metal shudders covering the windows only a few feet away. From inside, she could hear Mary screaming. It sounded like Bobby was shooting at someone in the rear of the house.

The knot of men who'd initially approached the house scattered and they were running for cover. Bart kept firing, and two more of them fell mid-stride.

The smell of propellant mixed with the salty air and sewage and smoke from the burning house down the road.

Bart cut down the driveway, crouching next to Suzanne's Mercedes, firing through another magazine.

Suzanne turned back into her house to check on Bobby, who was shouting with his wrecked voice.

"Go on, now!" he screamed. There were several shots. "Git!"

"Where are they?" Suzanne asked him.

"Down by the canal," Bobby said. "I can't get a clean shot. I think they're trying for the boat."

"Damn. Okay, you stay here. Greenburg, hold that door and open it for Bart!"

She went back out the front door and cut around the side of the house. The crushed coral crunched beneath her feet and the palms and flowers were lush and inviting. There was no time for remorse or thought beyond what had to be done. She had to protect her child.

At the canal, one man was stepping onto the *Mistress* while another crouched down to remove the lines from the cleats; the one on the dock had his back to her, and Suzanne shot him from forty feet away as she skirted the pool. The buckshot somersaulted him into the water.

The other man slipped and fell, perhaps surprised by the sight of Suzanne pointing the shotgun at him, or startled by the sight of his accomplice having a hole blown through his back. He cried out and vanished from sight, down on the deck of the boat. Suzanne came forward slowly, knees bent, another shell in the chamber.

"Come on," she heard the man say. "Don't shoot! I'm unarmed. We was just trying to get off the island!"

He stood up then, both hands in the air. Suzanne saw he was young, maybe under twenty, and his eyes were rolling and white and terrified.

I should shoot him. He might come back. They came to my house, trying to hurt me and my child. She hesitated, the gun leveled at the man's chest.

"Please," he begged. "I wasn't going to hurt anyone."

"In the water," Suzanne said. "If I see you again, I'll shoot you. I don't care if it's on Duval Street five years from now. I swear, I'll put a hole in you."

He sat back on the side of the boat and let himself fall over backwards, one hand pinching his nose. Suzanne watched him swim toward the opposite side of the canal and she turned back toward her house. The gunfire had ceased.

She walked the perimeter of her property, past orchids and sago palms, and palmettos along the edge of her land swished against her bare legs. Lizards scampered out of her way, and a snowy egret took flight from the walkway.

Bodies and blood stained the white coral driveway. So much blood. There were pools of it seeping into the ground and splashes of crimson against the rocks and on her car. Two old pickup trucks loaded full of loot smoked in the middle of the road pockmarked by bullet holes, windows shot out. She saw an arm draped over one of the doors, hanging lifeless. Thick blood dripped down onto the vehicle's door.

Sweet Jesus. What did we do? What did I do?

A shot that seemed louder somehow than all the other shots that came before it rang out and echoed from the other houses and the street; Suzanne jumped. One last parting shot from the looters.

Bart came around the mailbox holding the assault rifle in his right hand. His left arm was bloody, his short-sleeved shirt soaked, and his face was tight and grim.

"I'm okay," he said. "You?"

"Yeah, but you don't look okay."

"Through and through. Just a graze. Have you checked on everyone?"

"No."

"All right, then."

There was a clenching feeling in her, a choking, constricting sensation. She pushed the door open, dreading what she would find inside. Someone was screaming. She could take a lot, but losing Taylor wasn't one of those things.

*

Suzanne had never envisioned herself being a mother. She'd been driven and a little reckless and selfish, and she'd privately scoffed at the women she'd known who went from being smart, successful, and fun, to dowdy and dumb in less than a year. She'd resolved never to join that particular *settling* tribe of minivans and bake sales and PTA queen bees and passive-aggressive judo she heard about and saw from former members of her own tribe, the *let's do something with our lives* women she'd largely surrounded herself with.

She met Taylor, and her world changed.

It wasn't the sonogram that did it and it wasn't the initial shock of the test. Feeling the child growing inside her, she still felt reckless and even resentful sometimes. She loved Henry, and she knew he wanted to have a child, but sometimes late at night, she would scream at the loss of her youth and freedom and the idea that something had been taken from her.

The nurse put baby Taylor on Suzanne's chest. Swaddled and crying and with a little pink cap on her head, and hands so small they could hardly wrap around Suzanne's little finger, the child suckled at her breast, and everything Suzanne thought was so important before mattered less. The baby was purpose, future, and everything good and right. Taylor was perfect, unblemished by the world, and Suzanne felt an outpouring of love that was electric and true. She cried, something she never did, from the joy and promise of the moment, for what it meant for the rest of her life. Her child mattered more than anything else in the world.

Suzanne believed she'd lived her life with Taylor's best interest in mind; she'd sacrificed gladly for her baby girl, and hadn't become cow-eyed and torpid. The idea that a woman must give up sensuality, intelligence, freedom, and grace because she has a child seemed absurd, in retrospect. There was no dichotomy between motherhood and living a full life unless it was by choice.

Doing something with her life, though, meant raising a child, that little baby with the hand wrapped around her finger. That *was* doing something, the most important thing, at the end of the day. She'd thought about that when she signed the divorce papers with the heavy Montblanc pen in her attorney's office after weighing the pros and cons and deciding Taylor would be better off in the long run.

*

Bart paused for a moment at the door, his face a mask of pain and rage and an almost pleading look, a fear of the unknown, perhaps, which Suzanne understood. She wanted to open the door but she also didn't. Pain waited on the other side. Once she opened it, she would never be able to close that door again. There are nightmares and things which wake you up screaming and thrashing and sweaty, and then there is seeing that worst fear face-to-face and being powerless against dripping, hungry fangs, when everything that mattered before has fled and there is that one thing left.

Suzanne flung the door open and stepped inside.

Mary was screaming, lying sideways on the couch, her hands pressed to her belly in the way of a pregnant woman. Mary's hands were covered with blood. She howled and yelped and her legs kicked and shook.

Suzanne sat the shotgun against the wall and ran for the med kit while Bart went to his wife.

"Bobby, go out back and keep an eye out. Greenburg, you go out front. Take the shotgun."

Suzanne handed Bart the kit, and he tore into it, removing gauze, gloves, antibiotics, and painkillers. He gave Mary an injection, and within seconds she relaxed enough that she stopped screaming. Her eyes rolled back in her head.

Bart cut away Mary's white nightgown, which was now crimson and soaked.

"Water," Bart said.

Suzanne came back with a pitcher of clean water, and Bart poured it over Mary's bloody belly.

More blood oozed to the surface from a hole in her abdomen.

"There's no exit wound, so the bullet is still inside her," Bart said. Go see if you can find a doctor at the hospital. Take Greenburg with you, and the AR." He was packing the wound.

Suzanne grabbed her keys and jogged out to her car. She and Greenburg drove into town. She feared when she returned Mary would already be gone.

More than anything, she was glad Taylor had not been harmed; she was glad it had been Mary and not Taylor, and there was only a small part of her that felt guilty for it.

CHAPTER THIRTEEN

Heaven and Hell Are Relative

AMARILLO, TEXAS

Tony decided war was even better than sex, although his experience with both was limited. He loved the beautiful explosions, the raw power and destruction, and the feeling of being the hunter of game that shot back. It was better than *Call of Duty* because it was real. It was majestic.

He was nineteen and overweight six months before the war began, spending most of his time gaming in the basement of his mom's house, lost in virtual worlds, immersed in team death matches where he could be a hero. His friend Buzz, a guy Tony had known online for years, invited him to go to the shooting range one day, a real one, and it was glorious.

Buzz was part of a militia group because his parents had founded that group. Real hard-core people. Tony got to shoot an old .50-caliber Browning, shredding targets from a hundred yards away. It was like a dream come true.

Tony started borrowing his mom's car on weekends to make the forty-mile trek out into the desert, surprised at his good fortune. He learned how to shoot, and was amazed to discover that he had a gift. He was, according to Buzz's daddy, the "best shot in Texas." Tony warmed to the praise, and within a month, he told his mother he was moving out. She was not sad to see him go. When Buzz showed up with his jacked-up truck to load Tony's clothes and electronics, she didn't bother to ask where he was going. Just sat there on the front porch with her gross, sagging boobs squished into a bikini top, swatting flies and drinking her wine in a box. If Dad had been around, maybe things would have been different, but he was dead and gone, and so was Tony. Gone.

Once he moved into "the Ranch," the weight melted away. He stopped playing video games and started living. He was up before dawn, milking cows, cleaning chicken coops, tending the hogs, dirt under his nails and the sun on his back. In the afternoons, he and Buzz would take horses out to check the fences and cameras and make sure the motion sensors were working. Tony transformed, and he knew it, embraced it. He was no longer a chubby, pasty teenager with no real friends or family; he was a sun-bronzed man who finally belonged.

He learned firearms, discipline, and a great deal of history. He'd never cared much for history or current events before, but now he saw the connections. He saw how Texas and the rest of the country was being taken advantage of. Texas was its own country before it joined the Union, and there was nothing to say it couldn't be again. Folks in other parts of the US didn't know what it was like to have illegal immigrants wandering through their backyards, with the drug cartels and the gangs taking over. Tony didn't have anything against Mexicans; he just wished they'd stay in Mexico.

When word came down that it was really happening, Tony couldn't sleep. He would be attached to an expeditionary force of Texas National Guard infantry, supported by air cavalry and armor. "Contact," which is what the real soldiers said, was even better than he'd hoped. He'd gotten out of his bed at four in the morning and driven in a convoy of pickup trucks for hundreds of miles, until they linked up with the actual army guys. They pushed north, mopping up resistance when there was any, which didn't happen enough. It was a week before Tony got to fire his weapon.

Now that his first engagement was finished, Tony couldn't wait to hit the next target. The waiting was killing him. He could see the enemy soldiers, some on rooftops, some clustered behind circles of sandbags, tanks and armored vehicles at angles in the sprawling suburbs. He'd heard that negotiations were under way, but he hoped, down deep, that they'd fail. He didn't want this dream to end.

There were rumors that it was about to go down, but every time there was more waiting. Tony and Buzz played poker, weapons within easy reach, while they told lies and joked with other soldiers and insulted each other in creative ways. Tony tried not to think too much about his big brother. When those thoughts came, he pushed them away.

The memories came back, though, and threatened to pierce Tony's euphoria. His brother James was always smarter, cooler, five years older, and had gotten all the breaks. Tony loved his brother, but he damn sure didn't like him much. Not after the way he'd run off on his family after Daddy died. At least James got to know Daddy. They'd gone fishing and hunting together, and Tony heard all about it for years. Campfires and practical jokes. Tony'd never been there for that. He was always too little. And then it was too late.

The idea that his big brother might be in that town made him shiver. It was a thrill. A comeuppance long overdue. The ultimate competition. The Big Army Big Brother against little Tony. It was like a video game, except better. His brother always won, but maybe this time would be different. Tony was part of an army now, too.

The rifle felt cool and heavy and real, not like in a game, and he stripped it down and reassembled it again because he could, and this made him smile.

*

It was dark when the shelling started. The most beautiful thing he'd ever seen. Fireworks on steroids. The sky burst into color, orange, yellow, white, and red, and the sound was a crescendo of destruction and power and glory. A thing he felt in his bones, in is teeth, in his soul. The reality of it was like seeing the Grand Canyon in real life for the first time, even though he'd looked at pictures before. War was breathtaking like that, in a way the best game could never be. He felt the earth shudder, smelled the fires and the sharp scent of propellant, his heart hammering and his mouth dry, a surging, triumphant song in his chest as he charged when the platoon leader gave the order.

He felt light, as though he was in a dream where he was meant to fly, racing up the interstate behind armor, the sound of boots smacking the road and the rolling thunder of artillery and bombs detonating and rounds zipping and snapping through the dark. His commanding officer gave the order to hold west of the city.

Jets ripped through the sky, and Tony wished he could see the aerial battles. There were flashes and explosions, and some AA fire from the city. Probably on the air force base, which he'd heard was home to a bomber wing.

The suburbs burned bright, and as the fires joined and turned into one enormous firestorm, there was a wind that came rushing toward the town, the fire sucking in oxygen. It was like a work of art on a canvas the size of the Texas sky.

What he wasn't ready for was the counterattack.

Bombers dropped cluster bombs behind Tony's position, devastating huge swaths of infantry and supply vehicles. Less than a minute later, shells were exploding all around him.

"They're hitting us with UAVs," someone shouted. "Fucking drones!"

For the first time, Tony was afraid. Men were running, abandoning their positions. His platoon leader was nowhere to be seen. Vehicles were on fire, and every so often, rounds would cook off, adding to the general frenzy.

"Let's bail," Buzz said, his face inches from Tony's. Tony's hearing was pretty much gone at that point, but he got the message.

He was fleeing, his weapon forgotten on the road behind him, eyes rolling with panic, when Buzz went down face-first. Tony thought he caught a fast-moving shadow right before it happened, a dark blur the size of a bee that streaked into his friend's head.

He knelt down to check on his friend, and then there was another dark blur and this one came for him. He died on the interstate on the outskirts of Amarillo without time to reflect upon his sad, lonely life.

CHAPTER FOURTEEN

Everybody Dies Sometime

THE PLAINS

It took weeks to cross Nebraska, Kansas, and Missouri. Traveling in a Titan quad-cab truck, they took state highways over the snow-swept plains and open spaces. The small farming towns they stopped in seemed to be faring better than most of the country. When they ran out of fuel, they walked.

The people they encountered were mostly generous and kind.

In Elwood, Nebraska, they spent an evening with an entire extended family. The patriarch was an eighty-year-old man named Abraham with a flowing beard and penetrating blue eyes. They'd encountered him at a feed store outside of the town, and he'd invited them to dinner.

Hungry for more than just food, Henry had swayed his companions. There was something about Abraham, something true and good that tugged at Henry, drew him toward the man. A kind of moral gravity.

At a long oak table, the adults dined by candlelight on roasted chicken and potatoes, and Henry ate voraciously. The children sat at two smaller tables, and the atmosphere was like a family Christmas dinner Henry had only imagined as a child, where generations laughed together and were bound by stories, time, tears, and blood.

Abraham's children and their children lived on adjoining land that had been in the family for a hundred and fifty years. Abraham had served in Vietnam, and two of his grandchildren were active duty, one in the navy, the other in the army.

"Lord, we thank you for this bounty thou hast provided. Please watch over our young men and women," Abraham prayed before they broke bread. "Give them strength and wisdom. And Father God, please heal our great nation."

They did not talk about politics, and they did not talk about the war. There was no mention of race, and Carlos and Martinez loosened up within minutes of being inside the farmhouse with the white wooden porch, the sound of children laughing, and the smell of fresh bread in the oven.

Henry was enthralled by the family and he wondered what it would have been like to be raised in a family like this, surrounded by love and a kind of unity and acceptance more rare than diamonds, more precious than gold.

"Remember that time Daddy went out to the lake too early in the season and fell through the ice in that old Ford . . ."

"What about Harold and that wasp nest up in the barn . . ."

They were stories everyone had heard before, and there was continuity in them, a shared love and history and commonality. Henry laughed so hard he cried, seeing the old man plunging through the ice, but pulling the fish he'd sought for years out of the sinking car with him, trudging back home through the cold, only to have his wife give him a tongue-lashing when he walked through the front door for his stupidity. That fish hung over the fireplace.

"Was it worth it?" Henry had asked Abraham.

"Well of course it was. Look at that fish. He's beautiful!"

Abraham said it like it was the most obvious thing in the world, and everyone laughed. His children and grandchildren knew the story, and they hadn't forgotten it. Some things are worth fighting for and some things are worth living for, and they're not necessarily the same things. Abraham knew the difference, laughing and wise with his family and the fish mounted on the wall.

Henry slept on the floor next to the fireplace, and it was the best rest he'd had in months. When they said good-bye the next morning, Henry was sorry to leave. Abraham handed Henry the keys to his truck.

"You boys need this more than I do," he said. "I've got another one." Abraham was that kind of man.

*

As they traveled across the plains, they saw evidence of the war. Fighter jets screeched overhead on a regular basis, but there were no columns of troops, no towns on fire. From what they heard from townspeople in various places, the most intense fighting was still in Colorado and Tennessee, where federal forces were engaging rebel troops.

This was not good news for the Wolves, because they were now heading toward Nashville.

Sergeant Martinez reasoned that if they could make it to Nashville, they could find more men to help them, men they knew and trusted. They had a clear sense of mission now, and the only way they could accomplish it was with additional information and assets.

"It'll be a trap," Carlos said when Martinez finally told them where they were actually going.

"Yes."

"Why would we do that?"

"Because we have to have more information."

"Couldn't we go about it another way?"

"They're going to find us one way or another. Maybe we can find them first. I know we can get to the Air Guard base, get word to some of our people. They'll come through for us. I'm certain of it."

"Then what?"

"Then it's a trap. Only it's ours, not theirs."

"I don't know, Sarn't Major," Henry said.

"We're going on the offensive," Martinez said. "We've been reacting so far, and we're losing, and the country is going to hell. I'm sick of it." He was quiet, intense, and persuasive. "We've got to get the word out that some really evil people are pulling the strings. And then we're going to hunt those fuckers down and kill them."

"These guys are smart."

"They're not as smart as they think they are. Look at this war. They couldn't have wanted this. Not the guys at the top. It's bad for business. We've got to know exactly what's on this drive, but we need more than that. We need to have a chat with one of their operators who knows something."

"How are we going to do that, sir?" Henry said.

"I'm still working on that part," Martinez said with a rueful grin. "Something will present itself. We'll recon the base. If we can make contact with one of our guys, we'll try to slip in. If it looks like we're burned, then we'll move on to plan B.

"I'm all warm and fuzzy inside again, Sarn't," Carlos said. "You really know how to motivate."

*

They cut through the rolling hills of Kentucky, where patches of snow lay on brown fields and the trees were gray and leafless, and finally entered Tennessee, staying well west of Fort Campbell.

They traded the pickup truck for a battered panel van and three Tennessee driver's licenses, which they altered enough that they might pass a casual inspection at a checkpoint.

In Tennessee, the military presence was obvious. Even in small towns, men and women in uniform stood at street corners beside armored vehicles.

Helicopters churned through the sky, drones buzzed close to the deck, and at night, there were flashes far to the north like a distant lightning storm.

The people were tense and suspicious, and had a feral look about them. Food was scarce, gasoline next to impossible to come by. Civilians armed with hunting rifles stood watch at crossroads over makeshift barricades and signs reading "No entrance," or "Go away," or "If you're not from here, you'll get shot."

Henry drove slowly through a tiny community of tobacco farmers, an African-American hamlet of old wooden farmhouses dotting the hills, and a mom-and-pop feed store that doubled as a gas station. Henry had been through the town once, and had eaten a fried baloney sandwich at the old store; he remembered the floor being a bit slanted and that the sandwich was so good he'd ordered another. Everything was burned. The homes, the store, the gas station, and the bodies.

"What the hell?" Carlos said. "Pull over."

Henry stopped in front of the remains of a farmhouse. The barn and home were still smoldering.

Carlos bolted from the truck and walked toward the ashes. Henry kept the truck idling while Carlos paced around the dead farmstead with his hands on his hips.

When Carlos came back to the truck, Henry saw tears in the big man's eyes.

"Go," Carlos said. His voice was almost a whisper.

*

They never talked about it. Henry would never know exactly what happened in that hamlet. Growing up in the South, Henry had run into plenty of racist bastards, secret racists who assumed he was one of them because he was white, and they'd launch into a casual discussion which had nothing to do with race, and then they'd use a word Henry despised and somehow make a conversation about pickup trucks or lawnmowers or beer out of it. Thinking about it now, seeing his friend hurt in a way Henry could never understand, he wished he'd knocked a few more fools who'd used that despicable word off barstools.

Henry and Carlos were like brothers, yet there was no way Henry could really know what it was like to be a black man, judged and weighed and deemed lacking by an ignorant and pervasive few, based merely on the color of his skin.

*

Coming at Nashville from the west, they waited at a checkpoint on the outside of Bellevue, an affluent suburb of brick homes and rolling hills. Traffic in both directions was at a standstill, and there was nothing to do but wait. They'd learned from other travelers that there was no good way into town, so they'd settled on the most direct route.

Some vehicles overheated, some ran out of gas. Civilians helped each other out, pushing cars to the side of the road. Whoever was making the logistical decisions clearly either did not give a damn, or they were blatantly inept. While Henry drove in the eastbound lane, he passed the checkpoint going the other way. There were two separate checkpoints. It made no sense.

"They don't want people coming or going," Martinez observed. "They don't want to stop traffic entirely because then it'll look like they're the bad guys. Maybe that's what this is. Either way, they're strongly discouraging travel in or out."

The rain was cold, misting, and gray. It was the kind of winter day in Nashville Henry had come to loathe. He longed for the sun on his face, Suzanne at his side, and a band playing reggae music by the ocean.

The people leaving Nashville carried their lives with them. There were cars and trucks and vans loaded with children, mattresses, grills, boxes, bags, toys, and hope, and the people had a way of shaking their heads at Henry, as if to say *"What are you thinking? You're going the wrong way!"*

It was almost midnight when the crash happened, although the collision itself was hardly a wreck, a slight smack between a van and a pickup truck going the other way. What happened afterward wrecked lives.

KEY WEST, FLORIDA

Mary's death cast a pall over the group. Suzanne felt guilty, sweaty, sticky, despondent, angry, claustrophobic, and frightened. Her friends were worse off than she was.

Bart retreated into a gloomy fortress of silence and stone. He seemed to never sleep, and paced the house and grounds like a wolf in a zoo, until he wore a path around the perimeter of the grounds. His communication was a monosyllabic, a word or two at best.

Bobby found a bottle of rum, and then another.

Ginnie smoked a whole lot of weed, but she did not get the giggles or the munchies. She was lethargic, weepy, and cracked. She talked about her parents and her childhood, and sometimes she would follow Suzanne around until Suzanne would snap at her.

"Ginnie," Suzanne said, "shut up."

"What? I'm sorry; it's just that I keep thinking about, you know, my folks, and whether they're okay, and Miami without power for so long and stuff."

"I know. Now leave me alone."

"All right, dude."

"Don't call me dude again. Ever."

"Well, damn."

"Get a grip, Ginnie. I need you. But I need you to be *you*. Not this vapid dingbat you've decided to turn into. You're smart and capable. Be that girl. No, be that *woman*."

"Okay," Ginnie said. And then went off to smoke a bowl somewhere. There was no water, food, or electricity, but somehow, there was still plenty of marijuana.

Greenburg thought trying to make a run for Cuba was a good idea.

"We can all go on either my boat or Bart's. We've got the fuel."

"Nobody is stopping you," Suzanne told him. "If you want to try, go for it. You might be better off. It's a day trip. I'm not leaving. I'm not leaving my home for someone to burn. I'm not leaving because this is where Henry is going to try to go. I'm not risking the pirates that are out there preying on people, and we've all heard the stories now, and I'm not going to take my child out there with them."

"Henry's dead, Suzanne," Greenburg said. "Face it. We can get off the island and go to Cuba and be there tomorrow. Hot showers, electricity, no bands of thugs shooting at us."

"Have at it, Greenburg," Suzanne said. "You should go."

"I meant only we should all go—"

"Got that. Not happening. If you want to make the run, by all means, go for it. I'm not going."

"You'll get your ass shot off," Bobby said from the couch, curled up with a bottle of Jamaican rum. "And even if you don't, you'll be in Cuba." He snorted.

Greenburg left the next morning, just before sunrise, and Suzanne never saw him again. She hoped he made it to Cuba, and that he was welcomed there by salsa and ceviche and cigars.

*

Taylor was the perpetual optimist, the sweetness and light that kept Suzanne going.

"When's Daddy coming home?"

"Soon," Suzanne said more times than she could count. Sometimes they were fishing at the dock, other times Taylor was going to sleep with her softie-soft, and other times just eating a piece of grilled fish.

"And he'll bring me a present. 'Cause he does when he comes home and maybe he'll get me some ice cream. With sprinkles."

"Yes, baby."

"Is Miss Mary in heaven now?"

"Yes."

"Is she happy there? Are there unicorns and ice cream? Miss Mary liked them. She's happy, right? You'll see her again and you'll still be friends in heaven?"

"Yeah, honey. We'll still be friends in heaven."

"What if *you* die?"

"What do you mean, child? You know we all die. Just not for a long, long time."

"But Miss Mary wasn't old. You said she died. She's in heaven."

"Right."

"So what if you die. What if Daddy dies? Will we be friends up in heaven?"

"We won't die. Not now."

"But you said everybody dies."

"Yes."

"But you wouldn't leave me, right?"

"Well," Suzanne said, feeling overwhelmed and underprepared and inadequate and untrue, "someday, I'll die. And someday, so will Daddy, because that's how it is. But not for a long time, okay? Don't worry about it."

"But you can't die! You can't be in heaven and leave me here by myself!"

"Baby, not for a long time. Please, don't get all upset."

"Promise!"

Suzanne gazed into the eyes of trust and earnestness and faith absolute and she did what any parent would do. She made the promise and felt like a traitor.

What do I really believe? I do believe in heaven, and a God that cares about us. It's hard to remember that sometimes. But look at this child. She's my leap of faith, my proof in a higher power.

"Yay!" Taylor said, and then scurried out of the room, the problem solved. That Taylor believed in Suzanne so much that a mother's love could defeat death with a single word made Suzanne want to smile and weep at the same time.

*

By the time Suzanne had made it back home that morning, Mary was already cold. A hollow-eyed doctor at the hospital looked at Suzanne like she'd lost her mind while she begged him to come with her.

"Are you nuts?" he'd said.

"No. I'll give you anything. A car, money, whatever. Please help us. This woman is going to die."

"She's already dead," the young doctor in green scrubs stained with blood said. "I've got to go." And he'd turned and left Suzanne in the hallway of the hospital, one crammed with sick and dying people and the stench of corruption and death. "I'm sorry," the doctor said as he pushed Suzanne away with a lack of bedside manner he'd had to practice over the last month.

The doctor had been right; by the time Suzanne got home, Mary was dead.

*

Suzanne chaffed at her inability to control and contain the violence and death around her, and she felt burdened by her responsibility to her friends, her child, and herself in the face of this hopelessness. She struggled to put on a smile and brave face, yet the weight pushed down on her and made her want to sink to her knees. It was too much to bear alone, and even though she knew her friends were fighting to survive, struggling to cope, Suzanne felt the burden was more upon her.

When there was a question about food or water, everyone looked at her. When she insisted that they dispose of corpses, Bart, Ginnie, and Bobby acted like resentful employees. They wanted to postpone it, but there could be no procrastination, and they should have known that. There is no putting off the moving of a dead body outside your door, inside your home. It must be done, and someone has to do it, and if it's just you, then you do it.

Bart abandoned the projects he'd been working on and became obsessed with attackers. He constructed a miniature fortress on the roof, made of concrete blocks and palm-fronds and plywood, and he started spending nights up there. During the day, he'd walk the perimeter, shirtless, wearing flip-flops or boat shoes, with the AR in his hands, a knife strapped to his belt, and at least one sidearm on his hip or thigh.

They needed security, along with food, water, and hope. Bart was on overwatch with an assault rifle, and he neglected everything else, leaving it to Suzanne.

When Bart told her they were being watched, she dismissed it as paranoia at first.

"There are at least two teams," Bart said. "Across the canal, there are two operators, and they've been in four different houses on different days. The same guys, different places, tourist clothes, never seeming to look our way, but they're the same guys, and the homes are vacant, or should be. And the water guy? The guy selling water from a cart? Nope. He's not an entrepreneur. There's a corn-fed man with a beard always somewhere thirty yards behind him. The thing is, the guy with the beard has changed his clothes and his hair. But it's the same guy, I promise you."

"I'm listening. What are they doing?"

"Watching. The better question is why."

"The hell if I know."

"Bullshit."

"Bart," Suzanne said in a dismissive, exasperated tone she realized she'd been using too often of late, "Why would—"

"Right. Now, look, Suzanne, I know what Henry did. Does. He's black ops, and we can stop pretending now. I've known all along. Henry and I are friends. Brothers. There's some shit you can't talk about and some that you *pretend* you *didn't* talk about, and that's how it is. Some vodka and some rum, and then you know things, stuff maybe you didn't want to know. So, yeah, I've known about that, and it doesn't take a genius to figure out there's a connection now, in light of the civil war and whatnot, and these spooks watching us. There's a thing, and I know that much, I just don't know *why*. But we're being watched by professionals, your husband is some kind of a spook, there is a war happening outside your front door, and you know more than you're saying. Now's the time. Spill it."

"You're right."

"Never thought I'd hear you say those words. Go."

"My father told me some things. Said he'd done some favors for some powerful people. Bad people, maybe that's what he said. I should've told you, but I didn't want to believe it, not like it mattered. I should have said something, but I didn't want to besmirch—"

"What the hell?"

"I didn't want to stain things. Life. I didn't want to say the words. Because they hurt too much. That my father is a traitor, and his choices are still screwing me over. I didn't want to say the truth. I didn't want to speak it because then it might be right, and I've been dealing with everything else and I'm sorry."

Because sometimes you can know a thing is true and still lie to yourself. She'd done it, and denied it, perhaps an even worse sort of lie. Lies are easy at first. It's later that they come back to betray you. Lies we tell ourselves with the best of intentions are the ones which wreak the worst havoc.

"The admiral is a traitor? Your father? What the hell?"

"He admitted he'd done some things he shouldn't have. He warned me I was in danger. He wanted me to leave the country with him. I couldn't go with him. I just couldn't. When Henry comes home, he'll come *home*. I couldn't abandon you and Mary—"

"You could have told me about this! Suzanne! What were you thinking?"

"I'm sorry."

"They're watching us for a reason, Suzanne. These kinds of people don't do that unless they're planning something. We've got to leave. Lose them."

"I don't want to leave."

"I don't care! That's the right move now. Don't you get it? If we were targets, and there's no reason we should be, then we would have been dead a long time ago. You're bait. They want something or someone, and it's got to involve either Henry or your father. Do you have any idea how dangerous these kinds of people are? They are not in the business of failing. We've got to go."

"You're running around in flip-flops and not sleeping, and you're saying we should leave? Come on, Bart. You're not exactly the voice of reason."

"I'm right and you know it. We leave now. Stop arguing and start paying attention. You're proud, you're scared shitless, and you're stubborn. I'm a bit frayed. Doesn't make me wrong. This also means you might well be right about Henry being alive."

"All right, Bart. I get it. I don't want to, but I get it. We can't risk staying. Damn. How do we do this?"

"Good. I've been thinking. Do you remember Coyote McCloud?"

"Oh God. The hermit in the Glades?"

"Yep. Now, he's got a little fish camp, completely off the grid. Henry knows about it 'cause he's been there with me a few times. If we can leave word for Henry, he'll know how to get there."

"McCloud is insane."

"Yeah, no arguments there. But right now, he's our best bet. We've got to hole up somewhere and ride out the storm, away from prying eyes."

"Maybe we should have gone to Cuba."

"They would have captured us before we got out of the channel."

"They could just pick us up now."

"I'm guessing they will, anytime. Use us for leverage. I don't know what they want, why they want it. If they think we're going to make a run, you can be sure they'll stop us. We've got to keep this between us, load the boat over the course of the day. Maybe load two boats. One they don't know about. In the middle of the night, we'll make a try."

"I'll have Bobby leave a message at Captain Tony's for Henry. He might stop there if he knows we're at risk. Bobby going there won't look unusual," Suzanne said.

"Right. Just make the message 'Coyote.' Henry will know what that means. I can maybe carve that into the dock, too, in case he does something dumb like try to come straight here."

She thought about the maze of islands, sandbars, shifting channels, and mangroves that surrounded McCloud's shack. If they wanted to get off the grid, the Everglades was the place to do it. Getting there without being seen was going to be hard. Putting up with Coyote McCloud, Bobby, Bart, and Ginnie might be even harder. She'd never been to the shack north of Hells Bay, but she'd heard plenty of stories. McCloud was a former operator who was convinced the government had him on a kill list. He claimed to be ex-CIA. Bart and Henry believed him.

Suzanne felt a sense of relief. At least they were going to do something other than sit around in this house. And Henry was alive, she was more sure now than ever. She spent the rest of the day putting on a show for the surveillance teams; she sunbathed topless by the pool, strutted around the front of the house in a bikini picking oranges and grapefruit from her trees. Bobby went off to find a second boat.

Maybe, we'll all get a second chance.

CHAPTER FIFTEEN

Second Chances

NASHVILLE, TENNESSEE

Jack Stryker was a patient man, and right now he was intrigued more than annoyed by the fact that his quarry had eluded him again. He watched the video feeds from his new command post.

The images from the drones were black and white, and poor quality, but the video the news crew had uploaded was in living color.

The best drone feed came from a Reaper he'd tasked to the town. He'd gotten that directive from one of the Mr. Smiths. He watched it in slow motion again.

The news van locked on in red, a box around the target. A flash, which looked white to the camera. Targets fleeing into a crowd. The people get closer, as the Reaper descends, the camera zooming in to track two men, red boxes around them as they move through the crowd. Separating. Heading toward a store.

Stryker switched to a different view, this one from one of the helicopters he'd ordered into the town.

Tracers tearing apart the buildings, return fire coming from multiple locations. The original targets lost.

He'd requested more assets, but was denied.

The strike team gets cut down, then the feed goes dead. Damn jets.

Stryker watched the video the doomed news team had uploaded for the world to see, zoomed in on the faces of the men he had been ordered to hunt down and kill. The men appeared exhausted, frayed, yet determined. Emerging from a burning building carrying kids. Dangerous men because he did not fully understand them. He knew one of them personally, and now knew all of them intimately, from their deepest fears to their hopes and dreams to what searches they'd performed on the Internet. He could not wrap his head around what they'd done. Taking a calculated risk, with some benefit, that he could grasp. Simply rushing headlong into death for no reason other than to save some kid or fat housewife with no hope of gain? No. That did not compute. He knew people like that were everywhere; he felt uncomfortable because no matter how hard he tried, he grasped he would never understand them.

He had narrowed down their destination to several choices. He was patient. They had escaped, but he would complete his mission.

Jack Stryker switched to a live feed from Key West and toggled the comm. This image was in color. A pretty blonde woman picking fruit in a bathing suit. *Henry Wilkins has done well for himself. I might enjoy a taste of that fruit myself.*

"Status?" he said.

"Quiet. No change," came the reply.

"Copy that," he said, sighing.

Stryker was a realist. He knew his own life was forfeit once he'd done the Directors' dirty work. He had an insurance policy they did not know about, however, in the legal pad he'd taken from the man he'd assassinated, Reince Blackaby, and Stryker was pondering how best to go about utilizing this. He was a sociopath, but he had no intention of dying.

I'm a pawn, a cog in the wheel. What gets men in this line of work dead is when they think they're something more than that. Men like that Blackaby fool. They overestimate their value, and wind up shot in the back of the head. Not Iceman, though. Not Jack Frost. I'm going to see this through, and if I play my cards right, I end up with my own island. If I overplay my hand, well, I'm dead. God, I love it.

He realized he was grinning, not faking it in the way he'd grown accustomed, a genuine smile. His grin got bigger. *Wilkins is going to come for her for sure. Divorce papers or no divorce papers. A peach like that and a Boy Scout like Wilkins? He'll come.*

BELLEVUE, TENNESSEE

Jessie was tired of Nashville. He was hungry, thirsty, and surrounded by a bunch of Mexicans who refused to shut the hell up. Them with their generator and heaters and cooking food on the propane grill every night, just to show Jessie how much they had and how they were better than him. He had to go somewhere.

He'd waited long enough. Hung over, and out of beer and things to trade for more beer, he clutched his daddy's shotgun and stuck it in the gun rack of his truck along with an army bag he'd gotten from a surplus store, a sleeping bag, and some ripe clothing.

Everything smelled like shit. Without running water, the toilet was an open sewer. He'd cut a hole through the floor of his trailer and used that, and then the smell from underneath got to be bad. He couldn't take it anymore.

He took back roads getting to the west side of town, with a vague notion that he'd wind up somewhere in Kentucky, maybe head up toward Cadiz where he knew a guy from the bar had a little boat on a lake. They weren't friends, but they'd told some jokes together. He tried to remember the man's name, but he couldn't, then dismissed it. If the guy wouldn't let him stay there, there'd be somebody else who would, one way or another.

He cut through yards and sidewalks to get around vehicles that were burned, out of gas, or simply abandoned on the road. He'd gotten used to that. He stopped to siphon gas from a few, and came up empty.

His hands were trembling at the worn steering wheel while he waited in an endless line of traffic before the checkpoint. He'd been stuck in this line for hours.

Damn government. They want to control everything. I hate them. I hate all of them. I hate these niggers in front of me and behind me and all around me. I hate these Mexicans looking at me. I hate Big Brother and the news and the banks and Christians and Jews and Muslims and damn it I need a beer and a cigarette or somebody is going to die.

His mind was caught in a loop, a well-worn tape of all the injustices inflicted upon him by the world. No part of this inner diatribe of vitriol included any acceptance of responsibility, for in his black heart, he was a victim of circumstance. Life had dealt him a shitty hand, and he was sick and tired of acting like that was all right with him. There's only so much a man can take.

The line of cars and trucks inched ahead, and the red brake lights, streaked by the rain, dimmed, and Jessie, who wished fervently to be Marshall, hit the gas a bit harder than he'd intended to, and the car in front of him did not move forward as fast as he thought it should, and he smacked right into the rear bumper of that car. He twitched and swore, as the van behind him rear-ended him.

He looked over his shoulder. The guy was shaking his head at Jessie, hands on the wheel, looking angry, like he wanted to start something. The guy's dark face was shadowy and red through the muddy window.

You hit me, you motherfucker. Here we go. I'm tired of laying down for it. You run into me and then act like it's my fault? You disrespect me? I ain't getting pushed no more. I ain't getting hit again and not hitting back. And now you're hollering out the window at me? Watch this. I've got something for you.

Hands shaking, eyes bloodshot and bleary, stinking of his own feces and hate, Jessie got out of the truck with his daddy's shotgun in his hands. The rain was cold, and he felt it spitting in his face.

The gun felt good in his hands, made him feel strong. *I could have gone pro. Shake and bake, motherfucker. You're about to meet Marshall.*

NASHVILLE, TENNESSEE

She'd begged him not to go, and Leon listened because he loved his wife and because he didn't have a good plan anyway. She was conservative, sensible, and she demanded explanations of him, wanted answers he did not have. So he'd waited. The violence in the complex got worse. They ran out of water and food, until she figured out she could trade her medical services for it. She treated gunshot wounds and infections, and the community rallied around her and them, and for a while it was all right, and Leon was glad he'd listened to her. Maybe they could make it and things would get better and the war would end. He was proud of her, proud of his boys. They did not complain much, did not sulk or cry.

At night they told stories and sang songs, sometimes with other folks from the neighborhood. People helped each other out. They prayed a lot, and read from the Bible, and there was a kind of drawing together that made Leon smile. There were Asians sitting next to Haitians belting out hymns in a makeshift church that used to be an office, and sometimes the songs were in Spanish, sometimes in English or French or Korean. They were the same songs, and the language did not matter, for the people understood, the people felt the meaning and power and truth beneath the melody and lyric, and the chorus of "How Great Is Our God" or "Amazing Grace" would swell from the dark, candle-lit room sung in five languages at the same time, everyone understanding each other.

It was beautiful, hopeful, transcendent. When the voices lifted up to heaven, Leon would get chills on his arms and tears in his eyes, belting it out himself, and there was an energy in the air that connected each person in the room until Leon believed for the first time in God.

For the connection went beyond mere camaraderie. What unified them went beyond energy, science, or understanding, for it was too vast and powerful and perfect to be defined or explained in those terms. While Leon was no stranger to the church, growing up Baptist and knowing the hymns from the time he could walk, this was something new to him. He *yearned* to sing.

As resources dwindled, the violence worsened. People killed people for canned soup and dog food and powdered baby formula. Within a short time, Leon lost his voice. He grew angry again.

They'd waited too long, hoping for deliverance and the hand of God, he told her. It's time. She finally agreed, and they loaded the van with everything they could. The boys were ready for an adventure.

BELLEVUE, TENNESSEE

When Leon hit the truck in front of him, he was annoyed. The guy hadn't been paying attention. The airbags hadn't gone off, though, and no one was hurt. It looked like the old truck hit the car in front of it, and Leon hoped whoever was in that car would be okay.

Leon rolled down his window and put up his hands, in the universal *I'm sorry* gesture, and shouted, "My bad, man! You okay?"

The door to the truck opened, and out sprang a bearded hillbilly with a shotgun. His face was twisted and washed out with the headlights and rain, and there was murder in it.

Leon reached to his holster as the man stepped forward.

"Get down!" Leon shouted to his wife.

Leon opened the door fast, shoving it and pulling the handle at the same time. The windshield shattered, spraying glass on his face, and he felt something hot and wet on his cheeks. His wife screamed, and there was the boom of the shot with the sound of terror from his children and this redneck swearing at the top of his lungs.

Leon dropped to the wet pavement, extending his hands and weapon in front of him. Another shot, this one at the door, and then Leon couldn't see out of one eye. His face was on fire, sticky and burning, and he was having a hard time seeing out of his good eye.

He fired, aiming for a boot. He missed. *Damn. Five feet away. How'd I miss? Or maybe I didn't. Oh God. My kids. My wife. Oh Lord.* He couldn't move fast enough. Things were happening in slow motion and fast-forward at the same time, like a nightmare. The ones where his weapon ran out of bullets and the bad guys were always faster. The pavement was wet and cold against his cheek and he felt the scrape and sting, and the road seemed to shimmer, wet and red and mean.

The feet were on him then, and the barrel of the shotgun was swinging at his head. Leon fired again, in twisting, desperate agony. His nightmare continued, and he was aware of many things all at once and too late, which is the way of bad dreams and life.

He could hear his boys crying. He thought about how he'd let them down, how he should have been able to protect them and give them a better life than he had, and he wished he could do things over again.

He wanted to sing with his soul to them, to compress his love and hope for them into an instant so they would know. So maybe when they were older, they'd understand. They could open it up like a box and see him, hear him, even though he wasn't there anymore.

His voice was gone, and there was no more pain, yet still he sang into the night and far beyond, soaring with a multitude and it was joy eternal.

CHAPTER SIXTEEN

Fathers

BELLEVUE, TENNESSEE

The fender bender was unremarkable; they'd witnessed several in the last few hours, so when the wreck began, Henry was not alarmed. Carlos, however, was more observant and attuned. He later explained his reasoning.

"I'd been making goofy faces at those kids for half an hour. Meanwhile, that dick in the truck was so scrunched up on the wheel I could feel him from the other lane. Tight and mean-looking. Even in the dark, man, I could feel him there all bunched up, coiled up like a damn snake. And after that shit we saw earlier that day? I just knew this guy was like that."

Carlos was out the door at about the same time the guy in the truck decided to go crazy. It was quick, and Henry was opening his own door as the first shots cracked in the night.

Martinez, who'd been sleeping in the back, bolting forward, a step behind, coming out the passenger-side rear door while Carlos was already in front of the vehicle.

The guy in the truck blasted out the front windshield of the van before Henry knew violence was about to happen.

Carlos was shouting and moving. It happened too fast.

Henry scrambled around the rear of the van while Carlos came around the front. The kids were wailing, and then there were two quick shots right on top of each other.

The redneck with the shotgun was falling backwards, and the man on the ground was dead, shot in the face at point-blank range.

Henry shot the murderer once in the chest as the man tumbled. Carlos stood over the guy and stomped on his throat.

Martinez and Henry went to the children and tried to console them, shield them, and they clawed and squirmed and cried inconsolable tears. Carlos held the dead man's wife while spotlights illuminated the street from above, and a helicopter hovered a few hundred feet overhead.

"Go!" Martinez ordered. "Go! Go! Go!"

Henry left the children and the van and sprinted for the shelter of trees and homes up the slope. They were targets, and if they remained, more people would die. Henry hated it, running, slipping in the wet dark, the helicopters thudding overhead and the children crying, mourning the loss of their father. He wanted to fight.

He followed Martinez into the trees while loudspeakers demanded order. It might be a matter of minutes or seconds before the enemy analyzed video data and issued orders. Their gear abandoned, location known, the Wolves fled the scene of the crime.

Henry switched his night vision on. They sought the darkest places, the deepest shadows as they ran. They crouched, sprinted, crept, and lay still as stone. They moved through homes both abandoned and occupied, waiting for the buzz of a hunter-killer, which would be the last sound they would hear if the enemy had access to those particularly nasty drones.

They humped it all night and slept the next day in a basement at a day-care center, surrounded by children's toys. They were hungry and thirsty and hunted.

"If I'd been half a second faster, that man would be alive," Carlos said in the dark.

"I should have been there before you," Henry said. "I didn't see it coming. I should have."

"It's quick, man," Carlos said. His voice was thick with emotion. "Evil is. It's so fast you don't even see it strike and then it's already too late. Damn it. You try to stop it, but it moves so quick, like lightning. It's done before you even see it. By the time you hear the thunder, see the flash, somebody's dead."

"It's my fault," Henry said. "I was closer."

"No it's not," Martinez said. "Stop whining. You've seen men die. I don't mean to be harsh, but self-pity and philosophy don't save lives. You sound like a couple of cherries right now, and I'd like you to shut up. Get your shit together, get focused on what needs to be done instead of bitching about what happened, 'cause you can't change that."

"Copy that, sir," Henry said.

"Fuck you, Sarn't Major," Carlos said. "All respect."

"You want to change things? You want to win? *Be* the lightning," Martinez said.

Lightning craves a thing to strike. Henry yearned for a target. He'd witnessed a father murdered, a man simply trying to get his family someplace safe, killed in a traffic jam because he'd run into the wrong guy at the worst time. Now those children would grow up without a dad, and there wasn't any way to make sense of it. The chaos, the injustice, the essential roiling unfairness of it all.

"*Be the lightning*" was a hollow exhortation, the kind of thing a sergeant major was supposed to say, but which did not ring true at that moment. Martinez was probably barely keeping his own act together, worrying about his children back in Texas, not wanting to face his vulnerability or mortality in the wake of what they'd just witnessed.

Fathers die, even though they don't want to admit it or speak of it, as if by acknowledging the brutal truth a man gives death an undeserved power over him. It's a primitive, primal thing. The reason men avoid doctors, neglect wills, and hope for sons and daughters.

*

The next night, they set out again, ghosts moving silently through the shadows and darkest places. They saw houses lit with kerosene lamps and candles, and a few with generators. The city was mostly dark, though.

Packs of dogs roamed the streets looking for food, dogs released by owners who could no longer afford to feed them, hunting for cats and squirrels and garbage. The rain abated and the temperature dropped to below freezing, the roads slick now with ice.

Helicopters thudded overhead every half hour or so, and fighter jets screeched past in tight formations. The air was bitter and tasted like war.

In the suburb of Donelson, they slipped into a ransacked Walgreens and found a few cans of SpaghettiOs and dog food, which they ate with plastic spoons. The food was disgusting and cold, and Henry licked the can clean.

At a looted pawnshop, they searched for weapons, and came up dry. They did, however, find a battery-operated SAT phone in the back pocket of the bloated corpse of what was probably the shop's owner. The phone had a trickle of juice left in it.

"Make the call," Martinez told Henry.

"It'll be tracked," Henry said.

"Maybe. The bad guys already know we're here. At least you can let her know you're still alive. Your buddy might answer, or he might not."

"You sure about this?"

"Yeah. If I had somebody on the other end who would answer, I'd do it."

Henry called Bart's number from memory. It was part of a bug-out plan he'd put in place years ago. Three beeps, and then . . .

"Go," came Bart's voice on the other end.

"Barkis is willing," Henry said.

"Coyote," Bart replied, the signal clicking and breaking up.

"Out," Henry said, ending the call.

"You sure that was him?" Martinez asked.

"It was his voice. Doesn't mean it was him for sure, but I'm pretty certain, because he said 'Coyote.' I know what that means. Nobody else would."

"Well, all right," Martinez said. "Feel better?"

"Yes. Yes I do."

They waited another day and night, observing Berry Field, the Air National Guard base attached to Nashville International Airport, from a distance. There was not much activity. A pair of soldiers with German shepherds performed perimeter patrols. There appeared to be little security, and the base was no longer home to aircraft. The hangers were shut and the airstrips vacant.

"About oh three hundred," Martinez said. "That's when the body is at its worst, the most sluggish. We know that Corporal Simmons will let us on. He's good people. If he can convince whoever he's on patrol with we're okay, we might be able to get in to the op center undetected. The armory is bound to be empty, but Simmons might help us with that."

The plan was risky, and Henry could see a hundred different ways it was likely to fail. They had little choice, though.

Jets landed and took off from Nashville International Airport, which had clearly become a regional operations center.

Henry slept fitfully, waking up from the sound of the planes and from the drowning dreams that plagued him.

He dreamed of his father, dying hard in a hospital. He woke gasping, fighting for air. He knew what it was to lose a father. Those poor kids, they'd seen it happen in the street, seen their daddy get killed by some redneck tweaker. It was senseless, unfair.

He tried to go back to sleep, but sleep would not come. He thought about Taylor, that perfect baby girl, growing up without *her* father, and he felt shattered. He wondered what he'd been doing with his life. He spent another uncomfortable hour, and then it was time.

"Let's say hello," Martinez said.

*

Henry and Carlos cut across the street and approached the main gate, timing their advance to coincide with the patrol. Henry hoped Simmons was on post again tonight. Out of sight, Martinez would be creeping ahead from a position on the opposite side of the base.

The dogs started barking before Henry and Carlos made it to the fence. The patrolling soldiers sauntered toward the gate.

"Simmons," Henry hissed, feeling a bit ridiculous. He crouched in an open grassy area, waiting to be shot. His night vision optics, advanced as they were, did not reveal the details on the faces of the two oncoming men, but they did reveal the laser sights, a perfect straight line cutting across the green night, ending at his chest. Carlos received an identical deadly beam himself, dancing and moving as the perimeter guards drew closer.

The dogs stood growling, awaiting a command, and poised to attack.

"Simmons," Henry repeated. "It's Wilkins. We're what's left of the Wolves."

The lasers winked off. Henry stood, holding his breath.

"About time," Simmons said. "Welcome home. I was told to expect you last night."

"Great," Carlos muttered.

"Why the sarcasm? Welcome home, Wolves."

"Now what?"

"Debrief. You two could use a shower. I could smell you before I could see you."

"I'm a bit confused," Henry said, standing.

"War's over, brother," Simmons replied. "And you've got some friends in high places."

Corporal Simmons and the other soldier, whom Henry had never seen before, walked with him and Carlos to the fenced outbuilding Henry had been to hundreds of times, the nondescript concrete shack with a neatly stenciled sign over the front door which read simply "Maintenance."

They walked past rows of lawnmowers, shelves of tools, the smell of pesticide and rotting grass and mildew heavy in the air.

Henry waited while Simmons pressed a nail in what looked like a bare wall. The touch screen beneath it lit up.

"Wilkins, Henry. Whiskey Tango Foxtrot."

Carlos chuckled over Henry's shoulder.

"Confirmed," said a female voice through a tiny hidden speaker. He'd done this many times, but never at zero-dark-thirty, and never fearing for his life.

He watched while the panel on the floor slid back, revealing a steep metal staircase illuminated by harsh naked light bulbs.

Their footsteps clanged and echoed in the tight space, the concrete walls amplifying each step, and the air was close and smelled like another day of training ahead.

Simmons had his weapon slung over his shoulder. He appeared relaxed, grinning and joking over his shoulder.

"Damn war's over," he said. "Finally. That libtard of a commander in chief resigned. The VP was killed when the war started. So the Speaker of the House is our new president. They're reconvening Congress in Boston, if you can believe it. Symbolic, I guess."

They went down several stories and walked through another metal door, into the Wolf Den.

The underground facility was a Cold War relic, designed originally to house regional VIPs in the event of a nuclear war with the Soviets. It had been abandoned for decades, until the Wolf Pack was formed, and then money and technology flowed back into the sprawling underground labyrinth.

A gymnasium-sized room served as a live-fire exercise area. The Wolves rehearsed breaching and clearing rooms, using portable panels which they could easily configure to mimic the layout of a building or series of rooms. Sandbags formed a ring around the area. They called it the Rat Maze.

"Who's your friend," Carlos asked as they turned a corner, heading apparently for one of several briefing rooms.

"Oh, that's Wallace," Simmons said.

From the nonchalant tone Carlos used, Henry guessed he had noticed the same things about Wallace, who walked behind them.

"He doesn't say much," Simmons added.

At the first landing on the way down, Henry had made a point of getting a better look at Wallace. He was a large man, over six feet tall and at least 250 pounds, icy blue eyes and a rusty two-week beard, and a way of diminishing himself that set off alarm bells in Henry's head. There was a killer stalking Henry's six. Carlos knew it. And Wallace probably knew that *they* knew.

"Say hello," Simmons said.

"How ya doin'?" Wallace said from behind.

"He's another New York mick," Simmons said. "Don't say much, but he'll drink you under the table. Ain't that right, Wallace?"

"Damn straight. You still owe me a hundred bucks from the other night."

The bullet had not yet found his brain, but Henry was fairly certain where it would come from when the time came.

Simmons, leading the way still, opened the door to the briefing room. Henry walked through and froze.

Profound relief swept over Henry's soul.

Two men rose to their feet at the head of the wooden table, and Henry grinned.

It had been more than a year since he'd seen his father-in-law, and at the moment there were few people in the world he would rather have encountered. Admiral Bates, dignified as ever even in standard fatigues bereft the rows of ribbons which normally adorned his uniform, smiled back at Henry.

"Thank God, son."

"Sir!" Henry said.

"Shit," Carlos said.

"Have a seat," the unremarkable man standing beside the admiral said.

Henry was looking at his father-in-law, a man he trusted, watched football games with, carved Thanksgiving turkeys for, and Henry had never once seen the man defer to anyone.

"Iceman," Carlos whispered. "Jack fucking Stryker."

"I'm sorry, son," Admiral Bates said, his usual baritone grating with defeat, his face tight. "I had no choice."

Henry did not sit. He stared at the admiral in disbelief. It was worse than being sucker punched, worse than a cheap shot to the balls. He'd been stabbed in the soul.

"Please sit down," the admiral said.

Henry sat, feeling wooden, aware of the two armed men behind him. He did not understand.

"Weapons on the table," Stryker said. He wore black fatigues and a thin smile. He was an average-looking man, short dark hair and a lean build.

Henry prepared to attack, visualizing possible outcomes and responses, trying to come up with a plan of action that did not end in his own death. He came up empty.

Stryker tapped a screen built into the surface of the desk, and two monitors over his shoulder came alive. Each displayed a three-dimensional view of Henry's home in Key West. There was Suzanne, picking oranges and looking tanned and beautiful. On the other screen, Taylor played beside a pool choked with algae.

Henry tasted bile as he placed his sidearm on the table. The light inside him, the hope and joy and purpose, was gone, snuffed out in a moment.

"I'm so sorry," the admiral said.

Henry placed his palms on the table.

"Good dogs," Stryker said. "So, you have something I need. Something the Directors require. You will not live to see another day, but I can promise you that your family will not be harmed. You'll be buried in Arlington, full honors, and be remembered as heroes."

"Give him the drive, son," Admiral Bates said. He met Henry's gaze and flinched, looked back down at the table.

Stryker chuckled, and his lips curled into a humorless smile.

"They don't have it," Stryker said. He arched his eyebrows. "Martinez does. And he's where? Think hard."

"Fuck you," Carlos growled.

"On overwatch, perhaps?" Stryker went on, as though Carlos had not spoken. "Waiting. Maybe headed for the airport to try to hack the system? No, I don't think so. He's here."

Henry fixed his eyes on his family. A thousand miles away, but here in living color so real he could almost touch them.

Stryker pointed with his thumb at the screens. "When Martinez gets to the op center, he will be detained. If he does not willingly give us the drive, you're going to convince him it's the right thing to do."

"So," Stryker said, grinning again, making Henry think of a barracuda. The man was implacable, predatory, and possessed of an innate stillness, a cold and calculated conservation of movement, and the soulless eyes of a fish. "Confine them separately. We won't have to wait long."

"Hands on top of your head," Simmons said. "I'm sorry about this. Orders."

With his hands zip-tied behind his back, Henry walked into a chain-link cell, a temporary holding area he'd placed terrorists in. A concrete floor, nothing to sit on, four feet by four feet, a place targets would wait until men in suits from agencies with three letters would whisk them away to God knew where for enhanced interrogation. Henry never dreamed he would end up in one of these sad prisons.

Simmons placed a black hood over Henry's head, and Henry took it. At least they didn't gag him. His breath was hot and stale under the hood.

He was smashed. Betrayed by his country, shot through his Achille's heel by the man he'd respected and trusted more than most men he knew. Defeated by his ally. Henry sank to his knees.

The worst of it was the knowledge he'd let Suzanne down, put their lives at risk. He'd spent his entire adult life trying to defeat the bullies of the world, fighting against what he believed was injustice, and it was all for nothing.

It was like Carlos had said. The evil, the lightning, happened faster than the eye could follow. *It shouldn't be that way. It shouldn't be like this.*

He pushed himself against the rear of the enclosure and rubbed the plastic tie binding his hands against the metal fence, as he'd seen his former prisoners do. None had escaped, and he recognized the futility of it.

He pictured Taylor in the morning sunshine, hope and goodness, and he refused to surrender. His shoulders ached and his back burned as he moved his hands back and forth. Beaten, battered, yet still breathing, Henry struggled and raged against his bonds.

And something occurred to him, a detail he might have caught onto instantly under normal circumstances. It was after four in the morning in Nashville. Key West was an hour behind, still dark. But the video feed showed daytime. The feed wasn't live. It was still chilling, terrifying. He'd talked to Bart, though. Maybe. Maybe they were crossing the water right now. Maybe Suzanne would live to laugh and love again someday. And on down the line, perhaps Taylor would remember him, a small fragment perhaps, a sunny glimpse of a moment which fades too quickly of a day on the water, and she might smile, then, looking back.

Henry prayed for his wife and child, something he seldom did anymore. God had let him down before, and he placed more faith in brains and brawn and bullets than he did in the Lord. Still, he tried. He prayed for his family and for forgiveness and strength.

Help me, God. To defeat me, they must destroy me. I will fight for my tomorrows. Even if I die, if my life mattered, then I am undestroyed. My memory lives on, at least, and the things I did right hopefully overshadow the things I got all wrong, and a part of me remains. Didn't Daddy say something like that at the end? I didn't get it then. I do now. I understand. Cancer had destroyed the old man, who wasn't old when he'd died. Life knocked him down time and time again, yet Henry could hear his father's voice, steady and wise and indomitable, still alive. It is not an easy thing to destroy a good man.

CHAPTER SEVENTEEN

Rangers Lead the Way

KEY WEST, FLORIDA

"Are you sure about this?" Suzanne said.

"Yes. I'll be there," Bart replied. "And if I'm not, then keep going. The coordinates are loaded into the hard drive of the GPS on the other boat."

"Tell me this isn't a suicide mission for you."

"I want to live." The house was dark. A single candle burned on the coffee table. Bobby Ray, Ginnie, and Taylor were sitting on the couch, looking at the back door and at Suzanne like they were *not* ready.

"That's not an answer."

"It's not a suicide mission," Bart said. "I can do this. Just because the army says my knee makes me unfit for duty doesn't mean this old Ranger can't still kick some ass. This is my duty. Henry would do it for me and mine. It's time I repaid some old debts."

Suzanne leaned forward and kissed Bart on the cheek, lips brushing against his beard. Since they'd decided to make a run for it, he'd been revitalized, a spark in his eyes again. There was a grim determination about him, though, which made her cold.

"Thank you, Bart," Suzanne said. She touched Bart's cheek with her hand.

Bart stood. "I'm glad our boy is alive, Suzanne. I hope . . ."

"Me too."

"Time for a swim."

She watched him leave, a sinuous shadow against the night.

Lead the way, Ranger, Suzanne thought. What did Henry say once? "Rangers never die, they just regroup in hell."

She looked at her watch. Twenty minutes. It might be all she had left on this earth. The boats were ready. She wasn't sure she was, though.

Bart staggered up to the dock, wielding one of Bobby's rum bottles. He belched with vigor and urinated from the dock, thrusting his hips forward and arcing the stream six feet out into the water.

NVGs for sure. Hopefully not listening devices, 'cause if they're using those, then we're already fucked. Two-man team. Maybe one more, and that ain't good. These guys are trained and smart. But I'm not your average terrorist, either. Okay. Sell it. Underestimate me, you assholes.

He leaned against the piling, feeling the cool, wet wood on his face, then plunked down, letting his legs collapse beneath him. He'd seen Bobby do it enough times that he knew what it looked like.

He dangled his legs over the dock, the bottle of rum in his hand, and he took a long swig. The bottle contained only water.

Bart glanced at the glowing dial on his watch. Just a few more minutes.

I had a pretty good run, even though I screwed everything up. I've seen the sun set over the Kush in wintertime. I swam with dolphins and jumped from planes and shot and loved and fished. Never had kids, but that's for the best. I destroyed my own marriage and almost smashed my best friend's.

He let the bottle splash into the canal, and he slumped against the piling.

Time to reap what I've sown. And use what I've learned.

He toppled forward into the calm water. He kicked for bottom, only six feet down, and his hands found the knives he'd knocked over the dock earlier in the day.

He swam up the canal in the dark, letting the current propel him, feeling sponges and rocks and jellyfish graze his torso as he stroked. He angled toward the opposite side, a wall of coral dug from the remains of an ancient reef, spiny urchins and lobster lurking in the cracks and crevices.

He surfaced slowly, careful not to splash, and exhaled through his nose. The moon and stars were bright, and the water rippled with cheery indifference.

At a dock belonging to one of Suzanne's neighbors, he pulled himself from the water.

The knives were not the shiny kind. These were dark composite steel, designed not to reflect light in the dark places. Bart hefted them, one in each hand, as he cut through a fence, creeping through the yards of fabulous vacation homes. His feet were bare and his heart was pounding.

He cut the screen by the patio and slipped through, crouching. The sliding glass doors were all locked. He moved to the side patio door, probably a bathroom. He quietly worked the lock, prying back and forth with his knife until the wood came away and he could slide the inner mechanism with the blade. The lock snicked, and he opened the door.

Dripping and cold, Bart crept into the house. The floors were white tile, and his feet made no sound as he moved toward the stairway. From upstairs, he heard quiet laughter.

There was a faint light emanating from a room above.

He padded up the stairs, a knife in each hand.

He hesitated, pressed against the wall beside the open door.

". . . dumbest orders ever," someone beyond was saying. "These people are idiots. I want to shoot them just because."

"Yeah," said another man. "I'd like to have a go at the blonde, though."

"Yes, sir," the first man said, his voice altered and suddenly professional. "No change." There was a brief pause, several heartbeats which Bart felt in his temple. "Copy that."

"You think he drowned?" said an asshole.

"Who gives a—"

Bart was in the room then, knives blurring.

The two commandos were leaning against a desk they'd pushed against the wall of windows, elbows resting upon it. One of them had a scope pressed to an eye. The other guy turned as Bart rounded the doorway. That one had a wireless comm set on his head.

There was a computer resting on the table, a blank screen still glowing faintly. A suppressed sniper rifle leaned against the wall.

Bart did not howl, scream, or utter a word.

The man with the headset was first. Bart cut the man's throat, using his left arm to lock the soldier's head in place, while he slashed with the knife in his right hand.

There was blood, warm and slick and spouting onto the wall and the floor. Bart struck with his left hand at the face of the other man.

His blade missed, a faint hissing sound as it grazed a void. The guy was quick.

The soldier hit the ground as Bart's knife bit air, and he rolled to his feet, hands up in a defensive posture.

Bart was right-handed, though, and the blade in his right hand came fast and sharp. The enemy stepped back, light on the balls of his feet.

There was no shit-talking, no pleasant banter between foes.

Bart struck the man with the six-inch blade he held in his left hand, piercing him just below the armpit, thrusting and twisting, and then he stabbed with the knife in his right hand, just below the sternum, merciless, savage. The soldier was dead before he hit the floor.

He picked up the sniper rifle, then put it back down.

He needed to move.

He hit the stairway, forcing himself to stay alert, keeping his steps silent. His heart hammered in his chest and his mouth tasted like salt water and blood. He felt alive and terrible and fantastic. He headed for the patio, and the hole in the screen.

He did not hear the shots, but the sound of the television screen shattering over his shoulder was enough. Bart hit the ground, crawled forward.

Son of a bitch. Okay. Corn-fed is here. Stealthy bastard on perimeter security. Hopefully he doesn't have an uplink. Probably does, though. Where the hell is he?

He crawled ahead on his elbows. A burst from a submachine gun tore through the wall behind him. High rate of fire, suppressed. *And I don't know where he is. Somewhere by the dock. That's not good. If he calls the team on the other side of the canal, we're done.*

He had his knives, and there was the sniper rifle upstairs. Suzanne and Taylor had to make it. They just had to.

"Hey asshole," Bart yelled as he crawled toward the stairs. "Ever think that maybe you're on the wrong team?"

He sprinted for the stairway then, coming fast to his feet. Then slipping and falling as his knee betrayed him, refusing to obey.

Bart twisted, hearing more rounds smack the walls.

He crawled to the stairs, his knee angry and throbbing. The house was dark to his eyes, but corn-fed would be able to see him clear as day.

He waited at the landing for death to come inside.

Suzanne gave the boat a shove. The incoming tide was swift and strong and the boat drifted into it and lugged along. She and Bobby Ray stood at the bow, while Ginnie and Taylor crouched at the stern. Suzanne pushed off from the walls of the canal.

Beowulf whimpered on the floor, never a fan of boats. Taylor consoled the dog.

Each splash was a raging waterfall, every breath a hurricane, as they floated toward the bend. There was the sound of breaking glass across the canal, and shouts. A machine gun equipped with a suppressor. Suzanne jumped at the sound.

The bow got hung up as they turned the corner, the current pushing them into someone else's dock. Suzanne pushed, along with Bobby Ray and Ginnie, and the boat kept on sliding down the canal, picking up speed now. The boat turned sideways, and there was no way to turn it.

"Almost there," Bobby whispered.

"Everybody ready?" Suzanne asked. Nobody answered.

"Bobby? Ginnie? You got the bags?"

"Yep."

"Get ready to jump," Suzanne said.

"Taylor, baby? You hang onto momma, no matter what, okay? You can swim, and you can float with your vest. Okay?"

"Okay." Taylor's voice was brave.

"Here it is," Bobby said.

"Go!" Suzanne said.

The water was cold and dark. She felt Taylor beside her on the surface, and she grabbed the vest Taylor wore and pulled, swimming for the dock.

The second boat was there, as Bobby had said it would be.

Taylor sputtered and swam on her own, resentful of her mother's protectiveness. She knew how to swim.

Ginnie made it to the dock first, and she helped Taylor and Bobby, and then the dog, up onto the dock. Suzanne came last.

"Okay," Suzanne said, shivering, watching the *Mistress* head out into the open bay on the tide. "Let's dry off and hope Bart makes it." She looked at her watch.

"She don't look like much," Bobby said. "But this is a good boat. Draws nothing. Engine starts every time."

Suzanne looked at the boat Bobby had promised, there in the moonlight rocking on the wind. It was a sad, decrepit vessel. Twenty-five feet at the most, stinking of dead fish, a center-console craft built for catching fish, not Sunday jaunts. There were no extra seats beyond the coolers fore and aft. No canopy, no frills. It was the right boat.

The fuel tanks were full. The coolers contained water and MREs and weapons that belonged to Henry.

"You did good, Bobby. Thanks," Suzanne said.

"Pays to know people," he said.

They removed the lines from the cleats, and Suzanne looked at her watch again, straining to listen for shots, vehicles, splashing in the water.

"Climb aboard," Suzanne said. "Stay low, like we talked about."

She felt vulnerable and foolish, and the safety of the Everglades was as remote as another continent.

Something splashed in the water, and it wasn't a fish.

Bart grimaced at the radiating pain in his knee. He heard glass crunching beneath stealthy feet, patient steps. The enemy operator was in the living room, then at the foot of the stairway. Bart gripped his knives tightly, sitting at the landing, planning and hurting.

He could hear the man breathing.

When the bearded soldier's face appeared around the corner, a brief shadow against other shadows, Bart struck.

His blade found the man's eye. The soldier fell backwards and Bart rounded the corner, his knee shooting lines of brilliant, white-hot pain up his leg. The enemy toppled back down the stairs.

Bart gripped the railing and hobbled down. Corn-fed was wounded, rolling over, reaching for the weapon he'd dropped on the way down.

Using his good leg to propel him, Bart jumped the last few stairs. The enemy soldier grabbed the submachine gun.

Bart landed hard on the man, who brought up a knee.

They struggled on the floor, slick with warm blood. Corn-fed scissored Bart with his legs and let go of the weapon, pounding Bart in the ear.

Bart, the wind knocked from his lungs, fought for breath, and with one hand he pinned the soldier's right arm to the floor. The operative head-butted Bart, a sharp blow to the nose. Bart held on, though. He brought the blade he gripped in his right hand to the man's neck while corn-fed locked his wrist.

It was a life and death struggle of strength and will, their faces mere inches apart. Bart was losing. He was not as strong as the larger man. He hadn't been training every day. He felt a thumb bore into his wrist, stabbing at the tiny bones and tendons, and his hand screamed at him to drop the blade. He felt his arm being pressed back to the ground.

Bart returned the head-butt, hitting the man in the wounded eye. Bart bit the man's nose savagely, teeth locked down on whatever flesh he could find, tearing at him.

The man bucked and grunted and let go of Bart's wrist.

Bart plunged the blade to the hilt in the soldier's neck. Pulled it out, and struck again. The enemy went still.

Bart pushed himself to his feet, retrieved the submachine gun, and hobbled toward the bathroom door.

He felt a searing pain in his side, and there was the feeling of being punched. He thought he heard shots from across the canal. The other team had been alerted.

Bart fell, crawling toward the water.

Rounds smacked off the concrete patio and through the lush foliage around the pool. Kicking with his one good leg and using his elbows, he struggled into position behind a palm tree.

He lay still, listening. He heard muffled voices.

He brought up the scoped weapon and swept Suzanne's dock and patio. The scope was not equipped for night vision, and Bart could see nothing. The enemy probably had access to night vision contacts, giving them a distinct advantage.

The canal was about thirty feet away. Bart decided to go for it. The enemy crew might be trying to cross the canal at one of the bridges, or they might swim for it. There was no way to know. He kept the weapon out in front of him.

The moonlight revealed two men coming down the walkway across the water, headed toward the dock.

Bart fired.

The men hit the deck. Bart squeezed off another burst, still moving forward, and then the magazine was empty and he was at the water's edge. He tumbled in.

Rounds zipped through the water around him, and the water was sharp and cold, not welcoming in the way it was on sunny summer days. He let his weapon fall to the bottom and took a gasping breath before exhaling, emptying his lungs of air, feeling his buoyancy disappear. He sank into the darkness and let the current move him along.

CHAPTER EIGHTEEN

The Good Guys

Henry lost track of time while he tried to cut through the plastic ties binding his hands behind his back. All was dark, thanks to the hood over his head. There were no sounds beyond that of his own breathing and the steady chaff of plastic against metal as he wiggled his hands. It felt like he'd been there a long time. He heard a door open and footsteps on the concrete floor.

The cage door rattled open. Someone pulled the hood off. Simmons. He and Wallace stood over Henry looking down at him with something like sympathy.

"This isn't right," Henry said. "Simmons, you *know* me. I'm no traitor."

"It doesn't feel right to me," Simmons agreed. "Unfortunately, I follow orders. I'll make it quick."

"These people are evil, man. You're taking orders from Stryker?"

"From an admiral, actually. I'm sorry, Wilkins. Duty first. Hood on or off?"

"Look me in the eye when you do it," Henry growled. "I want you to remember my face."

"Fair enough."

Simmons reached for the holster strapped to his thigh.

Henry did not close his eyes. He straightened his back, knees burning, and thrust his jaw forward. Defiant.

It *was* quick.

Wallace, who hulked just behind Simmons, grabbed Simmons' wrist, twisting his arm into a hammerlock. There was the sound of twigs snapping and Simmons opened his mouth to scream.

Before he could make a sound, Wallace's right arm was around the man's neck, squeezing. His left hand came up and locked around the soldier's head in an unbreakable choke hold. Simmons lashed out with his feet as Wallace lifted him from the ground. Henry ducked.

Wallace released Simmons, who fell facedown, crashing into Henry.

"Bloody hell," Wallace said, hauling Henry to his feet.

"Who are you?"

"Turn around so I can cut you loose." Wallace had dropped the New York accent. He sounded foreign. Maybe Scottish. Henry complied.

"Take his weapon," Wallace said.

Henry took the dead man's pistol, a SIG Sauer.

"We've got to get to the surface," Wallace said. "It's about to get dodgy."

Henry shook blood into his arms and hands, stretched his aching legs, and followed his new friend out the door.

He heard shouts, shots, and screaming. The sprinkler system came on, and the lights went out.

Henry activated his ICS contacts.

Wallace must have done the same, for when a uniformed soldier burst through a briefing room door, Wallace shot him in the chest.

They skirted the Rat Maze and jogged for the stairway.

Wallace fired again on the move. Two-handed grip, steady, knees bent, the sound of the shots amplified by the close space. Henry bounded after Wallace up the stairs.

They cut through the maintenance shed, and Henry saw that it was already dawn outside when Wallace cracked the door of the building. Wallace said, "Cut behind this building and make for the fence. The extraction team should be there."

"Wait," Henry said.

"No time," Wallace grunted. He opened the door enough that Henry could squeeze through.

"Covering fire," Wallace said, leaning into the scope of his assault rifle.

Henry ran through the early morning rain.

He put the concrete building behind him, aware of the shots ringing out from various places around the base. Leaning forward, he crossed the open grassy field toward the fence. He darted between empty helicopters. Behind him, the rattle of machine guns increased in intensity.

He spotted the flare of a muzzle flash ahead. He prayed those were the good guys. He lengthened his stride, sprinting full out now, the need for speed greater than the idea of making himself small.

The heavy thump of rotors echoed from the buildings. Henry couldn't see it, but there was a helicopter inbound for sure.

A soldier in tan fatigues was waving him forward.

An MH-6 Little Bird swept overhead. Henry could see soldiers firing from the open side of the helicopter, feet dangling over the side. The bird landed on the other side of the fence.

He felt a round pass just over his head, close enough that his hair moved.

One of the men ahead pulled at the fence, revealing an opening. Henry threw himself down and went the rest of the way on his elbows, squirming through the hole.

"Where's Wallace?" said a commando who looked like another lumberjack. Bearded, bulky, wind-beaten, probably in his forties, hair down to his shoulders.

"I don't know," Henry said. "He told me to run."

"Fookin' bollix," the lumberjack said.

"McCoy, Riley. On me. You," he said, peering directly into Henry's face, "hop on that bird."

Henry ran to the waiting helicopter, and soldiers reached for him, pulling him onto the tiny flight deck as the bird lifted off.

He held onto a strap mounted to the side as the nimble aircraft banked and dipped. They flew for maybe a mile before landing in the middle of a high school football field.

There were several helicopters on the ground, along with about twenty soldiers.

An officer was shouting orders and gesturing with his hands while several men leaned in to listen. The man turned, and Henry saluted.

Henry walked forward and grasped the man's hand.

"Henry Wilkins," Colonel Bragg said. "Glad you made it."

"Sir," Henry said, "We thought you were dead."

"So did I, truth be told."

"How did you escape?"

"I doubled back into the bunker because May was taking her sweet time. When the bombs hit we were trapped in the tunnel. Took me a couple of days to dig us out. May made it. She'll hate me for the rest of my life." He chuckled.

"Who are these guys?"

"I'll brief you ASAP," the colonel said, turning away to men awaiting orders. "The situation is fluid. They're SAS."

Henry wondered what the hell was going on. He agonized about Carlos and Martinez. And he choked on the thought of Suzanne and Taylor a thousand miles away with an enemy team watching them through rifle scopes, and more than anything, he wanted to shoot the bastards. He wanted to find them and their families and hunt them down and kill them.

Henry reeled at the insidious effects of the venom of retribution choking his soul, clogging his veins in the way hatred does, slow and mean and consuming. His gratitude was overcome with anger. A terrible man, teeth barred in the way of a wolf at that last moment before the bear swipes his paw, the wolf snarling and snapping and dodging.

Henry was a warrior, and he wanted to fight.

"Get yourself squared away," Colonel Bragg said. "Change out of those civvies and kit up."

"Yes, sir."

"We're wheels up in ten."

"Copy that, sir."

Another helicopter lifted off while Henry changed into fatigues. He stripped down to his briefs in the chill rain, letting the water wash away some of the sweat, rank with fear and stress, clinging to his body.

A hard-eyed soldier with a pale complexion and square jaw handed Henry body armor and an M4 carbine with eight extra magazines.

Henry placed the mags in the webbing of his vest, examined his weapon, broke it down and cleaned it.

Someone gave him a few energy bars, and he consumed these without tasting them.

"On me, Wilkins," Colonel Bragg said.

Henry followed his commanding officer onto a bird, pulled on the headset that the colonel offered him as the helicopter took off, straight up, with the feeling of being in a fast elevator.

"There is an armistice right now," Colonel Bragg said without preamble. "We've got a limited window now to put an end to this business once and for all."

"How—"

"Don't talk. Listen."

"I managed to get a hold of some old friends, and now we're working directly with the Special Air Service guys. We're going to try to take down as many of these Directors as we can. They're running to ground."

"We tracked you the same way they did. You showed up on the web in Colorado, and then in Tennessee when you did what you did. I got here not long after you did. I wanted to catch Stryker. Also, I wasn't sure if I could trust you."

Henry kept his mouth shut.

"Sergeant Martinez managed to upload the data from the flash drive I'd given him. It's worldwide now. He died doing it. I couldn't get to him fast enough. Two problems. One, here in the US more than half of the population doesn't have electricity. Folks aren't connected. They don't know what the hell is going on. Two, the data is incomplete. It's damning, shows that there has been a massive conspiracy, but we need more information. We don't have the people at the top. The politicians, the CEOs. Those are the people that need to be taken to the mat. They probably didn't know what we had on them. They might even be relieved right about now."

"Congress is in session in Boston," the colonel went on. "There's talk of reunification, but some of the factions are stonewalling, from what I know. The cease-fire is tenuous at best. The international community is terrified of lost nukes and the economic collapse that has been happening around the world because of this damn war."

"My priority now is apprehending Stryker and your son of a bitch of a father-in-law. They are direct links to the command and control of the Directors. I have no idea where they might be headed, or whether they are even together. I suspect not. What that means for you is that you're going to go home to your wife. There's a remote chance Stryker will go after her because he's vindictive to a fault. I'm going to send you home, Wilkins, along with three of these operators, in the unlikely event Stryker does make a try for your wife."

"Sir, he already has. I saw the video feed."

"We know. We hacked their system. Suzanne is in the wind now, though. She made it away from your house. There's no reason Stryker ought to care one way or another about her now. She should be safe. Except he is a psychopath."

"I'm putting you on a C-130," the colonel said. "You leave in two hours for Homestead. I'm working on requisitioning either a helo or a Coast Guard vessel for you, but that's not a done deal. Things are changing from minute to minute. There is a whole lot of shit hitting the fan."

The helicopter landed on a runway at Nashville International Airport, which had been transformed into a military base. Commercial aircraft squatted in jumbled rows on fields and next to hangers, while fighter jets, transport planes, and attack helicopters occupied the runways. Henry had a sick feeling in his stomach, looking at a vital civilian hub taken over by the military.

Bart was dying, and there was nothing Suzanne could do to save him. The lightweight Boston Whaler skipped over the glassy water, up on a plane, the bow elevated and the engine humming along smoothly beneath a sky streaked with orange and pink as the sun rose in the Florida Keys. Their wake spread out behind them, foaming white and almost luminescent against the reflection of cloud and light.

She'd hauled Bart, who was barely conscious, into the boat and they let the tide take them for a few minutes before starting the engines and making the run through a maze of canals and then out into open water. They headed away from the channel and skimmed the flats, relying on Bobby's encyclopedic knowledge of the local waterways. The boat was designed to draw almost nothing. Bobby adjusted the engine, tilting it up so that it did not protrude far into the water. This reduced their speed, but it meant they could go places most boats could not.

They wound through mangrove channels in the darkness, heading north and east. Now Suzanne wondered whether Bart would see afternoon.

A bullet had torn through his side from front to back, a hollow-point by the size of the exit wound. She'd packed the wound, given him morphine, and cradled his head in her lap while Bobby steered the boat. Bart's breathing was shallow, and he was unconscious, his skin waxy and washed out.

The deck of the boat was awash in blood, as though they'd enjoyed a glorious day of fishing for dolphin or kingfish and were coming home with coolers loaded and bursting.

Taylor and Ginnie were curled up together in front of the center console, sleeping and no doubt cold. The blood gathered at the stern, mixing with seawater.

"We can make the turn west in another hour," Bobby said. "Cut Florida Bay. There's a lot of mangrove islands, places we can hide if we have to." They'd been staying close to the larger islands, hoping to throw pursuit off.

"Okay," Suzanne shouted back. The wind whipped around the boat and sea spray, salty and fresh, peppered her face.

"How's he doing?"

"Not good," Suzanne said.

"He gonna make it?"

"No. Maybe if he had a doctor and a hospital."

"He's a damn hero," Bobby said.

"Yeah," Suzanne said.

Two specks on the horizon behind them grew closer. Suzanne watched intently, shielding her eyes against the glare of the sun on the water.

"Bobby," Suzanne said. "Better make for one of these islands."

Bobby turned his head and looked back, squinting, his beard and shaggy hair blowing. The boat turned, a sweeping arc toward a nearby pair of islands. The aircraft kept getting closer.

Bobby cut the engine. They used poles to propel the boat over mere inches of water into a canopied channel between the two islands, a space of less than twenty feet, the current swift between them. Bobby tossed the anchor out to keep the boat in place, and the Boston Whaler swung on the current, winding up against a tangle of branches. A few birds twittered angrily at them.

Minutes later two helicopters grumbled a few hundred feet over the water, perhaps a mile distant, and then disappeared in the direction of the mainland.

Suzanne checked on Bart again. His eyes were open. He groaned.

"Hey," she said.

"Hey. Water. I'm parched."

"Okay," she said. She helped him drink some bottled water. He could not lift his head.

"I'm done," Bart said. He sounded far away. Like he could already see things Suzanne could not.

"You're gonna make it," she said. "You're a fighter. Come on, Ranger."

"No. Don't bother lying," he whispered. "It's all right."

"Thank you for what you did," she said, leaning close to his face, her wet hair brushing against his forehead.

"I'm sorry for everything," Bart said. "Tell him I'm sorry."

"You've got nothing to be sorry for."

"I want to be remembered as one of the good guys."

"You are. You saved us. You did that, Bart. You saved Taylor and me."

"I should've gone after *you*," Bart said. "A lifetime ago. Instead of her. Damn. Maybe things would've been better. What if I'd run you over instead of Mary? Don't you ever think about that?"

"Sure," she lied.

"I've always loved you," Bart said. His eyes lost focus and he smiled and was silent for a time. Gentle waves lapped against the hull. A great blue heron speared a fish in the shallows and took flight, graceful and beautiful. "Maybe I married her just to be close to you," Bart said. "I don't know. *If only . . .*"

His eyes stayed open, and a last breath escaped his lungs and his chest did not rise again.

Suzanne held him for a few minutes, and she shut his eyelids. Bart died with a wistful smile on his face.

They had nothing to weigh his body down with. Ginnie and Taylor kissed Bart's cold face, crying. It felt like a crime when they put him overboard. He floated into the shallows on his back under the shade of the mangroves. Soon the crabs would come for him, and the mangrove snapper and sharks.

"We'd better go," Suzanne said. "I'll take the helm for a while."

"All right," Bobby said. "I could use some sleep."

They poled the boat back out into deeper water and Suzanne turned the key. The boat surged forward and the sun was warm on her face. Taylor came around the console, and Suzanne held her on her lap and let Taylor help steer.

Taylor's face was pensive, her natural sunniness diminished and clouded by death. It was a day Suzanne knew her daughter would never forget. *She shouldn't have to see any of this. She doesn't understand. I'm not protecting her like I should. I can't shield her from this world, this crazy mean world.*

I'm not worthy of this child.

There was the feeling of desolation in her, mingled with soul-wrenching regret.

She could never be the person she wanted to be, for she was not the woman she believed she had been. The lies she told herself had formed their own kind of reality, and she'd built her life upon a kind of delusion, perceiving the world through glasses tinted to filter what she wanted to see, rather than truth. Suzanne had looked at herself in the mirror and liked the person smiling back. Proud, arrogant perhaps, and dishonest. She'd overlooked her flaws, excused her own bad decisions, blamed others, and never recognized the pattern of truth. Her life was marred by betrayal and selfishness. There was good in her she could acknowledge, potential that was real, and she knew she was decent at heart. She was never the heroine she imagined herself to be, though, self-sacrificing, long-suffering and devoted.

The apple didn't fall from the tree, I guess, after all.

There was a kind of freedom in recognizing the truth, and she inhaled a lung full of fresh, salty air, grateful for her daughter sitting on her lap at the wheel and the idea that perhaps she would get a second chance.

"What's that, Momma?" Taylor said, pointing.

"That's a storm, you know that."

"We're going toward it," Taylor said. "Maybe we should turn around. That's what Daddy does."

"I wish we could, baby," Suzanne said.

CHAPTER NINETEEN

Justice and Redemption

Jack Stryker was livid. Somebody cut the power while he was trying to decide on his endgame. Once he had Martinez and the flash drive, it would be time to vanish. It looked like he'd waited too long.

He activated his ICS system and paused in the dark. The admiral, that weak, sniveling asshole, stood at his elbow.

"We should—"

"Shut up," Stryker said.

"I can't see. Let's be calm and figure out what needs to happen next."

Stryker hit Admiral Bates, something he'd been wanting to do since he met the man. It was an almost casual blow to the officer's chest, which made him shut up.

"If you speak again, I'll kill you," Stryker said.

The admiral didn't have much to say. That was the idea.

Stryker examined the world before him in shades of green. He switched to thermal imaging, the heat signatures of running soldiers bright against a field of black, and then to a view from above. He was surprised to find no drones on station, and the best view he could obtain was from a satellite. It was enough.

He assumed his bosses were trying to kill him, and that was the reason for the sudden loss of power and the gunfire in the corridors of the compound. He waited for the telltale hiss of drones about to explode his skull, and he was surprised to find himself still alive while the shots echoed through the halls. He saw the helicopters, the soldiers running around the base.

Stryker was gifted at seeing patterns. He knew he was a liability now. He was trying to figure out why the Directors acted to kill him so quickly, though. He dragged the admiral by his collar and hunkered down behind a desk, sidearm in his hand.

What if it was the last op Alpha Pack went on? Operation Snowshoe. What if that's what this is about? They want every bit of evidence from Operation Snowshoe erased. Whatever in the hell these idiots saw is recorded. Maybe it was never only about the drive, it's about what they saw, and there are only a couple of them left, and me. I brought them the Wolves, and now I'm just another loose end. Think, Iceman. How can you beat them?

In the dark, hunted and cornered, Jack Stryker grinned, feeling invigorated in the way of a college kid with wind in the hair and the drop-top down and music blasting, alive in the moment in a way he seldom was.

He was broken and mean and deadly, and for him, this was a good thing. It was oxygen.

*

Hate is a black hole which consumes life and light, warping reality with ever-increasing ferocity until that which is good is crushed and destroyed.

Hatred begets evil. An evil man does not recognize the truth in the mirror, for his small acts of sin seem insignificant, compared to the crimes committed by others. There is always an excuse, a justification which prevents true conviction and remorse.

*

With the power of supercomputers connected directly to his cerebral cortex, he culled through files he'd viewed over the last two months.

He reexamined footage of Suzanne Wilkins' escape from Key West, seeking clues. She must have gotten in contact with her husband, somehow. And he probably got some information to her he shouldn't have. She could be the key to his survival, a final bargaining chip.

He thought about her means of escape, something tugging at him, and then he remembered. He'd hacked the boat's GPS system when he'd first set up surveillance. Now he accessed that file again, zipping through waypoints. He knew where *he* would go, if he were in Suzanne's position.

He waited in the dark for another hour, then walked through the underground maze, keeping the admiral in front of him, prodding the man to go left or right with a pistol pressed against his kidney.

He went to the cells where the Wolves had been detained, stepping over a lifeless Simmons. The cells were empty. This confirmed Stryker's hunch. *The Directors sent in another kill team to do a clean sweep.* They were hunting him now.

"Good-bye, Admiral," Stryker said, and placed the muzzle at the base of the man's brain.

"Wait," Admiral Bates said.

Stryker squeezed the trigger, the gun bucked, and the old man fell facedown on the floor.

Jack pulled out the piece of notebook paper covered with numbers and placed it on the admiral's back; then he sent an image of this to one of many cutouts reserved for one-time communication with his handlers. He included this brief message: "Call off your dogs. I have something you need."

He had no confidence it would work, but he had to try. There was no place he could hide where the Directors would not eventually find him.

Running from a fight was not in his nature, certainly not when it would mean his eventual demise. He was the kind of man who bided his time, chose his battles.

*

A cunning man, Stryker overestimated his own ability in the way that evil men often do, impressed by his ability to survive and thrive, and chalking this up to superior intellect rather than mere brutishness.

He'd killed more men than he could count, but some seemed more important than others. As he slipped out of the compound, he remembered some of them.

His childhood tormentor, of course. That pimple-faced sadist. That one always came to mind first. And the priest, even though Jack did not like to think about that time of his life. Those two murders taught him much about life, death, and himself. He understood that justice and revenge were the same thing, that redemption came from violence.

Sometimes, when he replayed murders over in his mind, he would find himself crying, and he did not understand this. Usually, the memories made him smile. One of the memories that made him smile most often was when he killed Lieutenant "Boy Scout."

It was a long time ago, back when Stryker was an eager, fresh-faced soldier, still trying to fit in and kick ass.

The lieutenant was some kind of a Baptist, who would pray with his men before patrols, levelheaded and brave, and his men loved him. Stryker tried to, but that feeling was not in him. There was a kind of admiration, at least in the beginning.

He had this way of looking at you like he knew he had a secret he wished you knew too. Like he was almost sad you didn't know it. But that changed over time when he looked at me. It became disappointment and then naked revulsion. It was as though the man had X-ray vision of the soul, and he judged me, decided I was beyond hope. Transferred me out of the platoon with no warning.

Stryker shot the man a year later with a suppressed sniper rifle somewhere in the mountains of Pakistan while his platoon was supposed to be providing security for Lieutenant Boy Scout.

*

Stryker believed in justice. He'd heard the Everglades were nice this time of year.

CHAPTER TWENTY

Sometimes . . .

The airplane bucked and jumped through turbulence and Henry ignored it, along with the other members of his team. They were no strangers to storms.

His team consisted of Scott Wallace, the burly, bearded lumberjack who'd saved him, Mark McCoy, and, as it turned out, Carlos. Wallace had gone back to save Carlos.

"This," Carlos said with a grin and thumb pointed toward Wallace, "is a bad motherfucker. Now I fully believe I'm the baddest man on the planet. But *this* sombitch is right behind me. No disrespect, Henry. You know I love you."

"I'm with you," Henry said.

"You should've seen him," Carlos said. "Quick and steady. Like one of us."

"I saw," Henry said. "He's good. Saved my ass."

"You know I'm sitting right in front of you," Wallace said.

"Did you say '*one of us*'?" McCoy snorted. He was stripping his sidearm for the third time. "One of *us*? I beg to differ."

"What's that supposed to mean," Carlos said.

"First off," McCoy said with an English lilt which made him sound smart, "the SAS has been around longer than any of your special forces outfits. You learned from us. Can we at least agree to that?"

"My mate's got a little package," Wallace said. "You'll 'ave to forgive him." He threw a bullet at McCoy's head and it plinked off the man's vest. Wallace guffawed.

"Think it's funny, do ya," McCoy said, "the yanks bashing around and fucking up the world and us with three dead mates back there? I don't think it's funny at all."

"Nobody thinks it's funny, McCoy," Carlos said. "Our entire unit was killed."

"I know. I'm just messing with you," McCoy said. "Mostly, at least. I'm a bit of a wanker and I can't help it. I had to say it. I'm sorry."

"It's 'cause he's got a compensation issue," Wallace interjected, snorting. "Really. Brilliant soldier. Just a bit of a package and insertion problem."

Henry listened to the insults that followed and smiled. There was a banter that had to occur, a busting of balls and posturing, among members of a team. It was inevitable. He abstained from this particular exchange while the plane tore through the clouds, preferring to listen and observe his new teammates. He knew it would not be long before they turned on him, testing.

They were professionals, and each of them knew it. Not professional in the way of the man in the business suit and Brooks Brothers tie and supple leather briefcase. It was a different kind of profession, with a code all its own. There is a thing that takes place which makes no sense to any human with a sane mind. It is a defining of the hierarchy, a sense of order that comes from physical combat, and wolves understand this and do not flee from it. It is their nature.

"So how's Jody treating your wife?" McCoy said, grinning through teeth which might have been seen to in the States.

Henry lunged across the plane, hurling his body at McCoy, shoulder dipped, head to the side, hands seeking a hold. They locked together,

Henry and McCoy, tumbling onto the flight deck and rolling around while Carlos and Wallace looked on.

The fight was not the protracted hand-to-hand battle of Hollywood.

Henry caught McCoy in the groin with his knee, as his opponent tried to snake away. It was enough. The blow slowed McCoy down. Henry was behind him then, arms around his neck and head, legs wrapped around his waist. Henry choked him out in less than a minute.

"Well," Carlos said, "I guess that's that."

"Right," Wallace said.

"I'd kick *your* ass, too," Carlos said.

"Cheers," Wallace replied.

"Good show," McCoy said when he regained consciousness, grinning. He thumped Henry on the head.

Like that, they were brothers. Maybe they were before, but now they knew it in a way they could all understand. The plane bumped and groaned and kept going south.

Wallace hailed from Edinburgh, Scotland. He possessed a bottomless well of ribald jokes, and Henry laughed until he could not breathe, as Wallace hit him with one punch line after another with Scottish burr and merry blue eyes. He was a curious man, Henry thought. He could have been anything. Why was he a Special Air Service soldier? Henry did not ask. Wallace might have kicked his ass and then made a joke about it.

McCoy and Wallace were old friends, and could not have been more different.

"You know what you are?" Carlos said to McCoy. "You're an English New Yorker, that's what you are. Right outta Brooklyn, except you've got that accent that makes you sound like a genius. But you've got the attitude." McCoy had grown up scrappy and poor in London. He despised the Royals, loved the Gunners, his favorite football team, and hated both American beer and politics. He was less than five foot ten, lean and wiry, with dark hair and cheeks that seemed to have been burned by the wind.

They talked about women and war and slept less than they should have. It was late afternoon when they arrived in Homestead.

The old air force base, smashed by Hurricane Andrew decades ago, was a shadow of what it had been. There were a few fighter jets on runways, some cargo planes and helicopters.

They wasted time trying to find the Coast Guard liaison, who never showed up. There was a slack, abandoned atmosphere at the base, and the officers and soldiers they spoke to were not eager to help; everyone seemed tired and vaguely resentful. Henry's orders came from a full-bird colonel, signed and authenticated, yet the airmen seemed to delight in giving him the runaround. It was the way of the military—too often, it seemed.

The armistice, at least, was holding. Waiting outside the first-floor office of a surly major, they watched a news feed.

A blizzard dumped snow in the Northeast, and people were freezing to death and starving. Riots continued, emergency responders were overwhelmed. Rolling blackouts plagued much of the country.

Henry saw clips of planes dropping supplies into cities, hundreds of crates descending by parachute. It reminded him of the black-and-white film he'd seen of the Berlin airlift after World War II, when the Allies flew food and supplies into West Berlin. It felt wrong, seeing this in America.

Mexico was on the brink of civil war. Refugees fled to America, where tens of thousands were rounded up and placed in camps. Why they thought they were better off in America at the moment, Henry did not understand.

China threatened to cut off the flow of money, demanding payment for interest on the loans it had made to the United States as the US defaulted on those loans. Wall Street had opened, and then shut down again, as stocks plummeted.

Russia was poised to invade Eastern Europe, with more than a hundred thousand troops massed along its borders. Armor streamed toward the front. Henry looked at the diagrams, the arrows in bright red, in dismay.

NATO scrambled to meet the threat, mostly with airpower and missile defenses systems, and the reporters and talking heads offered up opinions and dire predictions should a land war in Europe ensue.

"NATO does not have the capability to repel this attack," a retired, iron-haired general droned on. "There are not enough tanks, air assets, or infantry, should Russia proceed." There was talk of nuclear war, retaliatory strikes, the yield of missiles, and where to take shelter in the event that warheads were inbound. Megatons versus kilotons, fallout patterns and projected casualties.

From Damascus to the West Bank, there were burning American flags and crowds chanting in the streets, firing Kalashnikovs into the air with glee and burning hate.

"This is what I mean," McCoy said. He was quiet. Not angry, merely sad. "Do you see? You wanted to be a superpower. And now what? Your bloody war is killing the world."

"Easy, lad," Wallace said.

"Easy? Well ya, that sounds good, now doesn't it? I'll try 'an do that. Over-reaching, greedy bastards."

"You're right," Carlos said. "But it wasn't me or Henry or anyone I know that did this. We didn't cause it."

"Oh, I know that. With your McDonald's and Walmart and Wall Street. Wasn't you. It was them." McCoy was legitimately angry now, face darkened and nostrils flaring.

"It wasn't me," Carlos said. "It wasn't Henry. It wasn't most Americans that did this. It was a few people, and a lot of them probably aren't even Americans. So before you get to blaming us, think about that. You've got your share of rich assholes back over in the UK."

"It wasn't *our* bloody war that started this shit," McCoy said. "It was yours."

Henry fully expected Carlos to launch into a dissertation about the global economy, the evils of the information age, and the impact of the disparity in the distribution of wealth around the world.

"Copy that," was all Carlos said.

McCoy seemed to retreat into himself for a time, and Henry was glad of the reprieve.

Henry was close to home, and he wanted to be there. Wherever Suzanne and Taylor were, that was home.

Sweaty minutes ticked by in the office, and Henry felt his calm evaporating. He had heart-clenching fear and anticipation in him, and he was ready to strike out for a marina on his own when the major deigned to speak to them again.

"All right," the major said. "We've got you squared away with a boat."

"Outstanding," Henry said. He clenched his jaw and smiled. "Thank you, sir."

"I tried to get a bird for you, but I'm strapped here. My hands are tied. Not enough fuel."

"I understand sir," Henry said. The helicopter had been a fifty-fifty proposition at best. This officer seemed to have aligned himself with the separatists of his own accord, and resented the interference and intrusion Henry and his men presented.

"Best I can do is to put you in at Bayfront Park," he said, amusement flickering across his face.

"Sir, is this a Coast Guard vessel?" Henry asked, already knowing the answer.

"No. You will be in a civilian craft."

"Sir, all due respect, but this is a time-sensitive operation. It was my understanding that we would insert—"

"It is *my* understanding you are asking for my help," the major said. "Take it or leave it, because I don't feel like screwing around with you. My orders were to provide you with assistance. I don't give a damn what your CO wants."

"When can we leave?" Henry said.

This was the kind of guy that made him want to leave the military. *You can build a perfect, well-oiled machine, and then throw this wrench in there, and he single-handedly wrecks everything. This is the guy that gets heroes killed on the ground because he's worried about his next promotion. Never been out from behind his desk, petty and arrogant, and screwing around while people die between sips of coffee.*

"There's a car pulling up now, *Sergeant*," the major said.

"Go load our gear," Henry said.

Wallace held Henry's glance for a moment and nodded.

"Yes, sir," he said in his convincing New York accent, turning for the door.

"Is there something else, soldier?" the major said.

Henry stepped closer to the desk. "Yeah," Henry said. "I'm just curious. How'd you know my rank?"

"Are you fucking retarded?" the major shouted, standing. "It's on your orders, you moron. And you will address me as 'sir'!"

Henry struck the major in the throat, a lightning jab using his fingers.

The previously screaming officer crumpled to his knees, grabbing at his throat and opening his mouth in a silent howl.

Henry stepped around the desk, wrapped the major's head up in his arms, and choked him out.

"No, I won't call you 'sir,'" Henry whispered in the major's ear while he flopped and kicked and went still.

"Damn it, Wilkins," Carlos said from the door.

"Sorry," Henry said. "Got any zip ties?"

"Just when I think there's no hope for the world," McCoy said, striding back into the office with Wallace trailing behind him, "there's this." He was smiling and pulling duct tape from one of the pockets in his pants. "Brass fucking balls," he said, tearing the tape into strips. He bound the major's mouth, hands, and feet. "What?" he said. "Well we can't leave him here, can we? Find something to put him in, for fuck's sake."

"Here we go," Wallace said. He'd found a suit bag, a black nylon zippered case the pompous major likely once used for weekend excursions. Wallace bent the major's legs and forced him into the bag. He didn't fit.

"I'll see if I can get rid of the driver," McCoy said. "Shouldn't be too hard. Not like *that*," he added.

"What the hell?" Carlos said. Rain pelted the roof and windows.

The black bag began to writhe. Wallace kicked in the general vicinity of the thrashing head, and the movement ceased. He chuckled.

"Well now," Wallace said, "sometimes you 'ave no choice but ta punch a bastard in the throat."

CHAPTER TWENTY-ONE

Into the Storm

Cool wind whipped her face as Suzanne piloted the boat toward angry clouds ahead, flying across glass-calm water. Dark clouds loomed ahead with orange flashes within and chain lightning. The temperature had dropped more than ten degrees in the last thirty minutes, and cold air swept down ahead of the violent thunderstorm. White, jagged strikes, forked and terrible in their beauty, lanced the sky. There was the deeper rumble of thunder, distant and menacing over the whine of the Mercury and the slap of the hull on the water.

Earlier in the afternoon, she'd tried to refuel near Islamorada. Bud 'N' Mary's marina on Upper Matecumbe Key was burned. Deserted cars clogged the Overseas Highway.

There were boats stuck on the flats, but other scavengers had already come by, and every tank was bone-dry. They *might* be able to make it with the extra fuel tanks already aboard.

She piloted the boat north and east. The route was circuitous by design. The hull of the craft was not a deep "V," which would have allowed them to cross the open Gulf of Mexico from Key West. The boat was made to skim over shallow water, not withstand waves. Anything more than a light chop would be uncomfortable. If they ran into six-foot waves, they'd get swamped.

She'd cut past Lignumvitae Key, then past the Dump Keys, and now the clear, light-blue welcoming water of Florida Bay was a memory.

They were in the backcountry now, winding through a maze of endless mangrove islands and channels, sandbars and turtle grass that poked through the surface of the water. At low tide, many of the channels themselves would be impassable to most boats. Under normal circumstances, she loved the wild beauty of it.

In the winter months, these waters and estuarine areas were home to thousands of migrating birds, and great flocks exploded into the air at the sound of the engine, a flurry of color and flapping wings. Suzanne saw great blue herons, egrets, cranes, and roseate spoonbills stalking prey in the shallows.

Flamingos, pink and awkward while they fed in the shallows, took flight and were graceful and admirable, swooping into the air with beauty and economy of motion.

An osprey raked the water with talons and hurtled into the sky with a fish in its grasp.

The air was rich with the scent of salt and death and rebirth emanating from the tidal marshes and snaking creeks. It was a smell Suzanne loved most of the time, the aroma of a relaxing day on the water and the promise of fresh fish and warm sunshine.

The boat jumped and bucked as she ran over another shark that couldn't get out of the way fast enough. The water was less than a foot deep for much of this run, and marked only by pathetic sticks. She could see the sharks, dusky shadows just below the surface, trying to swim away as the boat cut ahead. Usually the sharks made it, but sometimes they didn't. She'd hit three so far, and seen many more swish away in clouds of sediment and flashing tails, dorsal fins cutting the water in a lunge to escape.

There were many species of sharks inhabiting this area. The bay and shallows were a nursery for fish, and a buffet for larger predators. Bull sharks, tigers, black tips, and lemons cruising these channels hunting and feeding.

Pythons, alien invaders to these wilds, thrived and reproduced with astounding efficiency, along with saltwater crocs. It was, in every sense, wild.

There was something eternal about it, a reassuring sense of continuity in the cycle of life and death and rebirth being played out thousands of times over every day all around her. She breathed it in, she saw the evidence of it in the creeping and changing mangroves as they built islands from nothing.

A curtain of rain obscured the horizon less than a mile ahead. She pulled back on the throttle and came to full stop. The bow turned with the wind shear and downbursts, cool and threatening.

"We're gonna get wet again, okay?" she said.

Bobby didn't budge, curled up near the bow. Ginnie nodded, shivering. Beowulf raised his head from his paws and then sank down. Taylor, from the cooler in front of the center console, saluted and tried to smile.

Suzanne reasoned this was likely a cold front moving through. This time of year was generally dry, but when a front hit, the weather could be nasty for days. In the summer, thunderstorms popped up every day, and were violent for an hour, then gone as if they'd never happened. There was no way to know what they were in for.

"Bobby! Get up and help out. We need to secure our gear. This wind is gonna pick up."

"All right now," Bobby said. He scampered around the boat, tying down bags of supplies while Suzanne made sure their weapons were clear. They did not need a chambered gun slamming into something and going off on its own.

"Look here," she said. Bobby joined her at the console. "The last marker was about a quarter mile back. I can't see it now. But it was this one." She pointed at the laminated map they'd brought from the *Mistress*. "Where's the next marker? Can you see it?"

Ginnie and Taylor joined them, scanning the trackless wilds, looking for a pinpoint against the water. She couldn't see anything.

Small mangroves had a way of tricking her, appearing to be a marker, luring her off course. It had happened more than once already.

"Nothing," Bobby said. "We oughta be able to see it. That storm shouldn't be over it yet. Not unless you missed the last marker."

"I might have," Suzanne admitted. "I don't think so."

Whitecaps frothed the water. Not big waves by any means, but curling with the force of strong wind behind them, and building, even in this shallow water. The churning water made it harder to spot the markers.

"Well, we know the direction, anyhow." He pointed at the compass mounted onto the fiberglass console above the wheel. "Keep your bearing."

"Yeah," she said. "Okay, everybody get back behind me toward the stern, and hang on tight."

"I've got Taylor," Ginnie said.

"Bobby, keep looking for that marker."

"I am."

Suzanne pulled the throttle down, and the boat surged ahead. She gave it more gas until it was wide open, the bow up in the air. She adjusted the trim again.

The rain assaulted Suzanne, stinging her cheeks. Visibility dropped to less than thirty yards, and the air was cold.

Thunder boomed and crashed, as though a final war in heaven was raging right over their heads. Suzanne could feel the vibrations, and the hair on her arms stood up from the electricity in the air. The rain obscured the chain lighting, and the strobe-like flashes seemed to come from everywhere at once.

"Hard to starboard!" Bobby shouted in her ear, pointing at a mangrove island materializing through the sheets of rain.

Suzanne turned as hard as she dared. Boats do not turn on a dime, and if she cut it too sharply, there would be dire consequences. She swung the boat into an arc.

The boat shook with abrupt violence, banging against the sand flat spreading out ahead of the mangroves. The engine bucked in its mounting.

"Son of a bitch," Bobby said.

Suzanne pushed a tangle of hair from her eyes. She'd kept her hair pulled back behind her head for the last couple of months. The wind had set it free.

"You get up on the bow," Bobby said. "I'll put her in reverse."

Suzanne and the others moved forward to try to even out the weight on the boat. Although they were up on a plane, most of the weight and contact with the water belonged toward the stern. Now, they had a problem. Momentum had carried them well into the sand flats, and the boat was mired in the mud.

The engine grumbled and the prop tore into the muck.

"Ayaugh," Bobby grunted. "She's digging like a pig. I don't want to bust the prop."

"Ginnie," Suzanne said, "time to get your feet wet."

Suzanne stepped off the stern and into the water. Her feet sank into the rich mud. The water was less than a foot deep here, but the mud was almost as deep.

"Oh, this is disgusting," Ginnie said.

"Shut up and push." Suzanne was acutely aware of the sharks. They were juveniles, mostly. A bite from a five-foot shark could be fatal out here, though.

They struggled at the bow, putting their backs into it. The boat turned, inches at first, then gaining momentum as the wind helped them to turn it.

Suzanne felt crustaceans and shells against her bare legs, scraping amidst the primeval slime. She pushed so hard, her left foot got stuck, deep down in the muck. She fell facedown when the boat slipped away.

The unrelenting storm poured down thunder and lighting and sideways rain.

Suzanne pushed herself up with both hands and strained to pull her foot free. She managed to do it, but lost her sandal in the process.

"Eek!" Ginnie squealed. "Something just rubbed against me."

"Well, go!"

The water was up to Suzanne's knees now, and the boat was drifting away. She could hear Bobby cursing and then the engine caught, and the sound shifted when he put it into gear. Suzanne hustled, letting Ginnie climb aboard at the stern with a hand from Bobby.

She climbed aboard, breathing hard, and minus one shoe. "Damn," she said.

"Maybe I'll take the helm for a bit," Bobby said, a wry smile wrinkling his sun-battered face. "You did good. I've been resting. Your turn."

"No way I can sleep now," she said. "But you can take the helm. I'll help navigate."

"We're within a few miles of the channel to Flamingo," Suzanne said. "That's Snake Bight off to starboard."

"Yup," Bobby said. "We find our way there, then it's easy sailing for a little bit. Then, course, we got Whitewater Bay to cross. And Hells Bay. Ugh. I got no idea why that crazy old fool decided to hole up north of Hells Bay. Coyote's crazier than I ever thought about being."

"Let's hope we can find it," Suzanne said. "By that, I mean you."

"Oh, I'll find it," Bobby said. He tapped his head with a bony finger. "I know where it's at. I just don't like getting there much. Especially not in this mess. All right, hang on. I'm gonna take it slow until I can find the next marker for sure. We don't want to have to walk out of here."

The next few hours were maddening. They made little progress, continually running aground, then having to nurse the boat ahead. It was dusk when they spotted a red channel marker. They'd gone a mile off course. The rain tapered off to a drizzle and finally ceased.

By the time they made it to the entrance of the deep channel heading into Flamingo, the stars were strung out across the sky, brilliant and majestic.

"Momma," Taylor said. "Have you ever seen the sky like that?"

"Not with you, hon. It's beautiful, isn't it?"

"Yes. I wish I could take a picture. So I could show it to Daddy when he comes home."

Suzanne laughed and hugged her girl. Bobby pulled the boat beneath a canopy of mangroves, and they spent the night under the open air, curled up in the boat.

CHAPTER TWENTY-TWO

Hells Bay

Stryker flashed his ID badge to the MPs at the entrance to the Nashville airport, and drove past lines of military vehicles choking the road. He parked in the garage across from the terminal and went inside. He needed a plane.

His superiors had provided him with written orders and identification that gave him the authority to commandeer a jet if he chose to do so. The problem was, if an officer decided to authenticate those orders, Stryker would be apprehended at best, shot on sight at worst. He decided to take a different course of action.

He wandered onto the airfield, smiling and chatting with the soldiers who were going about their business. There was a sense of relief on the base, and soldiers who might have been baleful and resentful a week ago were eager to help. The bandage on his neck helped, a war wound, he told them, a piece of shrapnel he caught in Colorado.

Removing that damn ICS chip by myself was more dangerous than getting shot at. The Iceman could have been a surgeon.

He caught a ride on a civilian jet bound for Miami, loaded with supplies and a few airmen. He slept on the plane.

At the airport in Miami, he found a helicopter pilot conducting a preflight inspection of his aircraft. When the rotors began to turn, Stryker approached the bird with his weapon drawn.

Stryker convinced the pilot it was in his best interest to fly him into the backcountry. The pilot, a man in his early twenties who told Stryker he had a wife and baby at home, pleaded for his life.

"If you do as I say, you will live," Stryker said. "I just need a lift."

"We could get shot down," the man said.

"You'd better figure something out," Stryker said.

"I'm supposed to be headed north to Fort Lauderdale."

"Fly north and then drop down to the deck. Report engine trouble."

"All right. There is a bad storm headed this way."

"Perfect. Remember," Stryker said, "if you cross me, you're dead."

"Copy that."

The small aircraft took off and headed north, then due west. The smoking city below receded and gave way to the Everglades.

They flew just above the trees, the rain pounding the windshield and the wind buffeting the aircraft. The pilot gripped the stick tightly, working the levers with his feet and cursing under his breath. The engine was a roar and small vibrations rippled through Stryker's chest.

"Where are we going, exactly?"

Stryker produced the GPS coordinates he'd written down. "Here, he said. Just north of Hells Bay," he shouted.

"There's nowhere to land the aircraft. It's all water, from the looks of it."

"Don't worry about that," Stryker said. "I know how to swim."

With an airspeed of just over a hundred miles per hour, they arrived in the vicinity of the target in just over an hour.

Visibility was poor, and there was nothing to see but a tangled maze of mangroves. Stryker began to doubt the wisdom of this trip.

"Keep circling," he told the pilot.

"There's nothing here," he shouted. "What are you looking for?"

"We'll know it when we see it."

"We're right on top of these coordinates."

"Put us closer to the water. There in that pond."

"Roger that."

Something snapped against the windshield, and a spider web of cracks appeared. A second later came plinking sounds against the light metal skin of the helicopter, and the pilot pulled hard on the stick, the bird lurching and spinning.

"We're taking fire!"

The engine whined, sounding unhealthy, and Stryker saw black smoke through the rain. Deep booms of thunder crashed around the helicopter.

About thirty feet over the channel, with the helicopter struggling to right itself, Stryker grabbed his bag, opened the door, and jumped feet first, pulling his legs up close to his body.

The impact jarred him from his tailbone to his molars. He was lucky. The water here was deeper than he thought it would be, and he felt his feet slamming into the yielding silt below. He stood in brackish water up to his chest.

He ducked under the water and breaststroked for a tangle of mangroves, surfacing like an alligator, eyes just above the waterline.

The floundering helicopter righted itself and gained altitude. Smoke billowed from the engine behind the cockpit. Stryker watched the helicopter fall with the suddenness of a bird stripped of its wings, plunging into the swamp and exploding on impact.

Good. No time for a distress call. Whoever did the shooting just did me a favor.

Stryker scanned the trees for movement. The rain made dimples on the surface of the water and a fish jumped off to his right. He kept still, waiting.

Insects buzzed and bit his forehead. He ignored them.

A skiff, painted with camouflage, nosed into the channel. It edged into view, silent and slow like an animal emerging from its lair.

A man stood with legs spread apart and an assault rifle in his hands at the stern of the boat. Stryker smiled.

Less than thirty yards away, the boat glided on the current, swinging slightly. The man with the weapon was bearded and wild-looking. He wore a floppy green fishing hat on his head. He knew how to carry a weapon, though.

Stryker observed the way the swamp man scanned from left to right and back again, bending his legs to compensate for the motion of the boat, his aim steady and practiced.

The old man waited like that for thirty minutes before he put his rifle down and picked up a long pole, pushing the skiff in the direction of the downed helicopter.

Stryker held still until the skiff disappeared around a bend in the creek, and then he swam underwater in the direction it had come from. His lungs burned and he could see nothing in water darkened by tannins and silt.

He forced himself to exhale through his nose when he surfaced, careful not to splash. Cammie netting was strung over the tops of the mangroves here, and just ahead was a floating shack. The wood was gray and weather beaten, the roof tin. The entire structure floated on rusty drums. Wooden Appalachian chairs sat on a dock, and a few fishing rods rested in rod holders, lines out in the water.

He waded around the building. The open door and windows revealed a primitive, spartan interior. He could see no radio, television, computer, or anything requiring electricity. A wooden bed, neatly made with sheets tight on a skinny mattress, sat next to the main window. Stryker saw mosquito netting rolled up over the openings.

He waited in the water, shivering, and was glad when he heard the old man singing and splashing. The skiff came back toward the hidden creek.

He ducked under the water and lurked on the side of the shack while the old man docked his boat and tied it off to a cleat. The wizened man stood, hands on his hips, looking out at the channel.

"You just can't leave him alone, can you? But he's not going to let the FBI in his backyard, nope. No sir. Not Coyote McCloud." The old man giggled. "Maybe you're going to come out here looking for your G-man bird? Well, you're not gonna find *me*, you sumbitches. This is a big swamp."

Jack Stryker shot the man in the back twice from ten feet away.

Coyote McCloud toppled facefirst from his dock, and splashed into the water.

Stryker waded around to the body, just to make sure the man was dead. He pulled the corpse behind the shack, dragging the man by the arms, and pressed him into the shallows, half submerged in a tangle of roots. Stryker got out of the water then, found some rope in the shack, and tied the old man to the trees. It wasn't pretty, but it would keep the body from drifting out with the tide.

Inside, he found some fresh fish filets, and put them on the woodstove, humming as he cooked.

The interior was surprisingly neat, everything stowed away, from tackle, to scuba gear, to a few rifles on a rack above the stove.

The old man had rigged up a water collection drum on the roof, and Stryker saw iodine tablets he presumed McCloud used to purify water when his drum ran dry. Stryker almost admired the way this crazy coot had lived off the land, off the grid. The more Stryker thought about it, the more he liked the idea for himself. This might be his ticket. He could stay out here indefinitely. All he had to do was get rid of Suzanne Wilkins.

CHAPTER TWENTY-THREE

Gators and Sharks

Suzanne woke with the early morning sun warming her face. The sky was clear, a deep electric blue, and the air was crisp. She ignored the insect bites on her face and arms, and slipped over the stern to pee.

The water was warmer than the air, and goose bumps popped out on her skin when she got back into the boat. The others woke up when she pushed herself onto the boat. They were a sorry bunch.

Bobby's wispy hair stuck up at odd angles, crusty and stiff with the salt water. Ginnie's face was swollen and lopsided. Apparently, she was a bit allergic to something that fed on her during the night.

Welts covered Taylor's arms, and she seemed subdued. They ate some cold canned food, and Beowulf licked the cans, looking put-off and disappointed.

"How much further?" Suzanne asked Bobby.

"Depends. A few hours, if we don't get turned around and the tides cooperate." He sniffed the air and looked out at the water. "Low tide now. That's good. We'll run the channel quick. Get past the marina in case there are some undesirables around, if you know what I'm saying. From there, we cross Whitewater Bay, and then we scoot into Hells Bay and we're almost there."

He walked to the stern and checked the tanks. "We might even have enough gas." He cackled and coughed at the same time.

Bobby took the helm and the bow lifted. They wound through more channels, and then the Flamingo marina came into view.

Another boater passed them going the other way, and people waved.

They swept past the docks and boats in slips and canoes on the shore. Families sat around small fires in front of tents and recreational vehicles. Flamingo had fared well, it seemed, during the conflict.

"Maybe we should get some gas?" Suzanne shouted over the engine.

"Naw. We'll make it. The less people see us the better, right?"

He had a point.

Suzanne went forward to the bow and sprawled out, letting the sun warm her chilled bones, while Taylor curled up next to her. The dog moved enough to let them in, and Suzanne scratched him behind the ears.

Taylor clapped her hands with delight when she saw the first of many gators in the water. There were some big ones, nine and ten footers. Suzanne was as fascinated by the creatures as Taylor was. They were dinosaurs, scaled and toothy and explosive when they needed to be. They seemed slow and languid, but she knew that an alligator could outrun a horse over a short distance. She'd never seen one move like that on land.

*

A few years ago, she and Henry joined Bart and Mary on a houseboat adventure into this backcountry. They rented a boat at Flamingo, got hopelessly lost, and had a fantastic time.

That excursion had been in September, and the mosquitoes were thick. They ran into trouble when the battery connected to the operating systems died. The boat was dead in the water, and nothing worked. The toilets wouldn't flush, and the air conditioner wouldn't run. They had no radio, no phone service, and their water supplies were dwindling. For Suzanne, it was just enough danger to make the trip epic.

The first night, they'd sat out on the roof of the boat drinking sangria, gazing at the stars, and telling stories. Henry and Bart had rigged some heavy fishing rods using big catfish for live bait. They used empty five-gallon water containers as floats to keep the cats close to the surface.

One of the rods started screaming a few hours after the sun went down. Something big devoured the bait and was running.

Henry and Bart jumped down the ladder to the stern, howling and laughing. Henry fought the shark for an hour, and it put up a good fight.

When Henry pulled the fish close to the stern, Bart leaned over to cut the line. The shark was a juvenile bull, maybe four feet long, thick and thrashing in the water under the light of kerosene lamps.

Bart strained to pull the fish close so he could cut the line above the metal leader and get a better look at the shark, leaning down over the stern. "Right out of the Darwin Awards," Henry said later that night.

An alligator chomped down on the exhausted shark, skewering it between massive jaws. The gator thrashed its head furiously, shaking the fish like a rag doll.

"Shit!" Bart screamed, cutting the line.

"That was a big-ass alligator," Henry said.

Suzanne thought it was one of the coolest things she'd ever seen. An apex predator devoured by another predator. She had the feeling that night of moving down several notches in the food chain.

*

The boat bounced over the light chop of Whitewater Bay. They passed countless mangrove stands that all looked the same, squat trees with roots gnarled and curving into the water.

"Here, take the wheel," Bobby said. "You see that marker? Head for that. My hands are cramping up."

Suzanne obliged and Bobby stood next to her, opening and closing his arthritic hands. They flew past the marker, down more narrow corridors of water and leaves, and then crossed the muddy expanse of Hells Bay.

They'd only seen a few moving boats since leaving Flamingo, all of them far away.

For more than an hour, they cruised the northern side of the bay while Bobby tried to remember. They tried more than one channel, only to come upon a dead end and turn back the way they had come.

"It's a lot easier with a GPS," Bobby said. Suzanne dumped it over the side before they pulled out of the canal back in Key West.

Suzanne groaned. Everything looked the same.

It was late in the afternoon when Bobby started to get excited. "This is it for sure," he said. "I remember that stand right there. The branches are extra white, see? The sharp V shape in between."

She didn't see.

"This is goanna get tight, and then open up again. We're close."

"I hope you're right," she said.

"See. Like I said. Getting narrow. Looks like there's nothing ahead. Keep going. We're lucky, it's high tide. I swear I can smell it."

Suzanne had the engine barely above an idle. The branches reached down and pushed at her face and the boat, but there was enough clearance to get through. Minutes later, she saw an open area, like a pond surrounded by more mangroves.

"This is it," Bobby said. "I'm sure of it. You put on your best smiling face, 'cause Coyote don't care much for strangers. He's twitchy. He tolerates me, but he doesn't know you."

CHAPTER TWENTY-FOUR

River of Grass

The boat the officer had promised waited in the water at Bayfront Park, guarded by a bored-looking MP. Henry stepped out of the car and walked to the boat while his companions got their gear ready.

The boat would not do. It was a nice boat, a thirty-foot open fisherman that would have been ideal for trolling in the Gulf Stream for marlin.

Henry groaned.

"Look," he said to the young soldier. "This isn't what we asked for. It's an open-water boat."

The guy shrugged. "Best we could do," he said. "Look around. Do you see many boats? Everybody who could left already. You're lucky to have this one."

"It's not going to get me where I need to go," Henry said. "We're headed south to Lake Surprise. Card Sound." *A thin bit of misdirection.*

"Sorry, man."

"How did you get here?" Henry said.

"What do you mean?"

"Did you walk? Did you fly? Did you teleport?"

"A car. There's no need to be a jerk."

"How much fuel have you got?"

"Full tank," the man said.

"I'll be taking that," Henry replied. "You go on back to the base in our car."

"Whatever, man."

*

Henry drove west through the Redlands, past wide open fields where crops languished, brown and decaying. This would have been strawberry season. There was no one to work the fields and no water to irrigate them with.

The roads were mostly clear and ruler straight, and Henry kept the accelerator pegged. His chest was tight and he was frantic with worry. Carlos and Wallace tried to distract him with jokes and war stories, but Suzanne and Taylor filled his mind.

They entered Everglades National Park, blowing by the Anhinga ranger station at a hundred miles an hour.

The river of grass stretched for endless miles on all sides. It amazed Henry that an area as wild and huge could exist so close to the sprawling megatropolis of Miami. Brown and green saw grass danced in the gentle breeze, and hardwood hammocks rose in places like islands of green. Anhingas, curious-looking waterbirds with serpentine necks, perched at the edges of the water with wings stretched out, drying off in the winter sun. A few deer bounded through the tall grass. Alligators, looking like blown-out car tires, sunned themselves on the side of the road and sometimes in the middle of it, where Henry went around them.

Henry saw a few campers on the side of the road in different dry spots, tents bright and cheerful against the subdued tan and brown tones of the wilderness.

He prayed they could find a boat at Flamingo. If there were no boats, he would search for a canoe. It would be a long trip, but it was doable. He'd find a way.

"We'd better hope that major doesn't come in this direction," Carlos noted.

"He's got no idea where we're headed," Henry said.

"Well, he's not going to let it go, you can be sure of that."

"I know it. I shouldn't have done what I did."

"We'll be all right," Wallace said. "He'll wake up with a headache and a bad attitude. It'll shake out in the end."

Henry hoped Wallace was right. The major was the least of his worries.

*

They made excellent time. *Not having the right boat was a blessing in disguise. Let's see if our luck holds.*

There were hundreds of people there, camping, a spontaneous community of folks who'd escaped the suburbs.

Teenagers played a game of touch football in the parking lot. Kids ran around with squirt guns and bathing suits. There was the smell of cooking fish mixed with the scent of the water.

A uniformed park ranger who looked like he was on the verge of forced retirement ambled toward the vehicle, waving at them and smiling.

"Howdy," he said. "Military?"

"Yes sir," Henry replied.

Carlos, Wallace, and McCoy opened the trunk and pulled out rucksacks loaded down with weapons and ammo.

"There's nothing happening around here," the ranger said, looking worried. "Everybody here is kind of minding their own business. Helping each other. We don't need a bunch of shooting. Lot of kids, as you can see. Families."

"I see that," Henry replied. "We're not going to be staying. I need your help. We need a flats boat. It's very important."

"We're rationing fuel here," the ranger said. "Started to pool our resources right away."

"Like I said," Henry said, keeping his voice calm, "*Very* important."

"Where are you headed?"

"I'd prefer not to say. Please, we just need a boat."

The ranger gave Henry a quiet stare, then nodded his head. "All right. I can give you a lift."

"I appreciate that, but it's better if you just lend me your boat."

"Hmm."

"Safer for you," Henry said.

There was a crowd forming around them.

Henry lowered his voice. "People might get hurt. We need to be gone."

"All right," the ranger sighed. "I'm too old to put myself smack dab in the middle of whatever it is you've got yourselves into. I hope it's worth it."

"It is."

"Boat's got better than a half tank. That gonna be enough?"

"How far will that get me?"

"Fifty miles or so, give or take."

"That'll do. Thank you."

*

The boat was a well-maintained Fish and Game craft, ideal for crossing into Hells Bay. Henry pulled away from the dock with a final wave at the ranger and was up on a plane in seconds. He was almost home.

He grinned into the wind as it whipped through his hair, and the sun was warm and good on his face.

CHAPTER TWENTY-FIVE

There's Dying, and
Then There's Dying

Jack Stryker made himself at home. He sat in a comfortable chair at the dock and fished, letting the sun warm his face through the dappled shade of the mangrove canopy. He munched on dried venison jerky and dozed, torpid and satisfied, glad of his dry clothes and the AK-47 that Coyote McCloud had so generously left him.

The incision he'd made on his neck hurt, and was infected. Stryker was not concerned, though, and helped himself to the box of antibiotics McCloud had bequeathed him.

This was the life he should have made for himself to begin with, he decided. No people, no nonsense. He saw that he had been wronged by the world from his first breath. He'd been herded along every step of the way, prodded and poked and made to do things he would not have done. It wasn't his fault. The world was mean and evil, and the only way to live was to kill or be killed by it. This forgotten place was as close to paradise as he would ever get.

He was sure his propensity for violence stemmed from others, not from within himself. If he'd been left unmolested, he could have been anything. A surgeon, perhaps. Or just a quiet hermit minding his own business here in the middle of nowhere. But they'd hurt him until he couldn't hurt anymore, couldn't *feel* anymore. The blood was on their hands, not his.

Maybe now, he could feel alive in the way others seemed to. He could fish and hunt and kill alligators with his bare hands if that's what lit him up. He didn't really need the private island and the yacht.

He'd never been in the game for those things in the first place. It was all about finding a reason to draw the next breath. A flickering moment of interest to extinguish a lifetime of lassitude and pain and numbness. He'd been a survivor for this long, and he was confident in his ability to continue an existence characterized by a flat horizon. He was intrigued by the possibility of something better and more meaningful. A way of living on the fringes of death and society without going through the motions of fitting in.

He'd never cared about the Directors or their money. That he'd never been taught how to fish did not worry him. He was a Ranger. He'd learn.

He daydreamed through the afternoon, content and in no hurry for anything in particular.

Jack Stryker's eyes flashed open at the burble of an engine coming up the channel, and he grabbed the AK-47.

He'd never understood the expression "shooting ducks in a barrel," because he'd never hunted ducks, and even if he had, he wouldn't have thought to shoot them in a barrel. But he did anticipate killing Suzanne Wilkins and starting his life over again without anyone making him react or hurt again.

He put a knee to the dock and brought the solid wooden stock of the Kalashnikov to his shoulder, aiming down steel sights.

"McCloud," a wrecked voice shouted, "Friendlies inbound. Don't shoot! Ya hear? I've got some folks with me. So put that damn AK down."

He already did. He gave it to me.

Suzanne was elated by the glimpse of Coyote McCloud's fish camp through the tangle of branches swatting her face. The straight lines of order and humanity stood out in stark contrast to the twisted chaos of the swamp.

Bobby walked to the bow, shouting, while Suzanne slid over to the helm. She put the boat into neutral, allowing it to glide over the shallow water.

Beowulf stood and shimmied. The old dog was probably about to burst, since he'd steadfastly refused to urinate in the boat. Malamutes were not water dogs.

Taylor sat in Suzanne's lap, perched on the captain's chair with small hands tight on the wheel. *She's got to be exhausted. What a joy she is, a marvel. Through the bugs and the cold and the bullets, still smiling.*

Ginnie, with an uncharacteristic burst of energy, and perhaps the desire to be the first in line, stepped around the center console to join Bobby. Ginnie's face was streaked with mud and her hair caked with salt and silt, and she squeezed Suzanne's shoulder in the way of an old friend who had been through the mud and the crud. She smiled a faint smile, as if to say 'I can't believe we made it.'

There were rapid shots then, angry terrible things, but not as awful as the spatter of blood and brains on the deck of the boat. It happened so fast.

Bobby was shouting, Ginnie standing just behind his shoulder. Bobby coughed and pirouetted, bullets tearing through his chest. Ginnie didn't have time to swear. A round tore through her throat and she flew backwards onto the deck of the boat. There was blood on the deck and the snap of rounds around Suzanne's head. She reached for the .38 on the console and she swept her daughter up in her arms and tumbled backwards over the side of the vessel. She was sure she heard hysterical laughter.

Taylor was screaming when Suzanne took her over the side of the boat. There was no way to calm a four-year-old child being spattered with brain matter.

Bullets popped against the boat and swarmed through the air. Suzanne was terrified and enraged. She pulled Taylor into the mangroves stroking backwards.

"You stay right here," Suzanne told Taylor. "No matter what happens, right?"

Taylor nodded, blue eyes sad and grave in the way a child's eyes should never be, and Suzanne kissed her on the forehead, cradling her face.

"I'm your momma, and I'll always love you." There was no time for a proper good-bye.

Suzanne took a deep breath and swam under the black water toward the dock with the revolver in her hand.

There was a rage and fury in Suzanne as she stroked to her doom, terrible and scathing and powerful. Instinct to protect her child propelled her forward.

The assault rifle hammered again and Suzanne could hear rounds zipping through the water. She pressed her belly into to the silt at the bottom of the pond.

She didn't know who was shooting, but she was sure it wasn't McCloud. He would have recognized Bobby's voice.

She swam to the stern of the boat and surfaced. There was no sound other than her breathing and distant splashes.

She brought the revolver up in a two-handed grip and stepped around the boat. The shooter was nowhere to be seen. She crouched beside the transom.

Off to her right, she could see Taylor's face through the mangrove roots.

A burst of fire tore the water a few feet in front of her child. Taylor shrieked.

"Come on out," said a male voice. "Hands on your head."

Suzanne shook with fear and rage. Her fear was not for herself. How could she stop this man?

Another shot. "Last chance," he said. He sounded neither angry nor sad.

She stuck the gun into the waistband of her cutoffs and put her hands on her head. She stepped around the boat and waded through the water, waiting to die.

"Momma!" Taylor cried.

"It's going to be all right," Suzanne said, choking back a sob.

A man with dark hair stepped out onto the porch of the shack with an AK trained at Suzanne's head.

Suzanne kept walking. At least he was pointing the weapon at her now. The water was only up to her knees when she got to the dock. She thrust her chest out and put a swivel into her hips when she stepped onto the faded wooden dock.

But for the weapon pointed at her chest, this man was unremarkable. He was maybe five ten with a lean build and businessman haircut. In his thirties, she guessed. She caught him staring at her breasts. Her white shirt clung to her, and she was cold. *Good.*

"Turn around," he said. "Nice and slow."

"Let my baby live," Suzanne said.

"Maybe," the man replied. "Turn around."

She clenched her jaw and turned. He lifted the revolver from her shorts, then patted her down, hands lingering on her chest.

"Tell Taylor to get into the boat," he said.

How does he know her name? Oh, Lord.

"Honey, can you swim to the boat? Can you get in for Momma?"

She stood dripping on the dock, racking her brains for a way out, feeling the heat of a muzzle centimeters from her lower back.

Taylor climbed into the boat, which was drifting toward the dock on the gentle current.

"Tell her to wait there," the man said. Suzanne did.

He took a step backwards and told her to turn around. She faced him. His eyes were hungry and he smiled at her, a chilling, grotesque gesture. He stepped to the side, the assault rifle unwavering. "Walk inside," he said.

"Who are you?"

"Oh, we'll have time for that later," he said. He sounded pleased with himself.

The interior of the shack was dim. She saw the weapons on the walls, a filet knife on the table. She was going to have to act.

The blow to the back of her head sent her facedown on the floor. He'd cracked her over the head with the butt of his weapon.

Her vision blurred. He kicked her in the ribs. She tried to crawl under the table. Wood dug under her fingernails as she clawed ahead.

"If you behave yourself, I might think about letting the kid live. Maybe. Just to be sure, though, I'm going to have to tie you up. I hope you understand." He kicked her again and the air left her lungs.

She rolled over onto her back as he turned to the corner of the room. She had nothing left in her. She was no match for him physically. She could try to bite him in the throat, maybe.

He leaned the assault rifle against a wall.

Taylor deserved better.

The man rummaged around and came up with some heavy fishing line in his hands, grinning at her, leering and predatory, walking with casual indifference, taking his time.

She pushed herself farther under the table with her legs, gasping for air.

Directly over her head, under the far edge of the table, was a sawed-off shotgun, mounted there, no doubt by a paranoid Coyote McCloud. The weapon faced the door. *God bless him*.

Suzanne reached up and pulled the trigger. The sound was deafening and her ears rang. Over the whine in her head, she heard the man screaming as he fell backwards. Suzanne crawled out from beneath the table, adrenaline surging, heart thudding with wild abandon, and newfound hope in her.

The man was trying to kick himself backwards toward the assault rifle. The floor was slick with his blood.

Suzanne got to her feet, almost slipping, and caught herself on the wall. She picked up the Kalashnikov.

"Bitch," the man growled.

The blast had caught him in the crotch. Suzanne cracked him in the jaw with the wooden butt of the weapon. She stepped to the door. The boat, with Taylor perched at the bow, had drifted next to the dock.

"Taylor, can you come up here?"

"Okay."

Suzanne hugged Taylor tight, still holding the assault rifle.

"You sit in one of those chairs. Dry off. I'll be right back."

Taylor was crying silently, and she nodded her head.

Suzanne stepped back into the shack and stood over the man who lay bleeding on the wooden floor, his feet splayed, and hands on his crotch over a spreading stain on his trousers.

His eyes were closed.

She put her foot on his groin and put her weight on it. The man opened his eyes, screaming. She took two steps back.

She pointed the weapon at his face.

"Talk," she said. "Who are you? Why are you hunting us?"

"You know damn well," he snarled. "Whatever Henry told you. Whatever your dead father told you. They . . ." He groaned, eyes rolling in his head.

Suzanne heard the whine of an engine.

"They what?"

"They couldn't let you live. The Directors. You'll never be safe."

"How did you know we were here?"

"Water," he gasped.

She stepped on his mangled balls.

"How?"

After he finished screaming, he said, "Bart's GPS system."

"We didn't bring that boat. How did you track us?"

"Waypoints."

"Where is my husband?"

"The Directors eliminated him in Tennessee." The man smiled at her again.

Suzanne heard shouts outside. Someone hollering "McCloud? Suzanne?"

"Daddy!" Taylor said.

Suzanne smashed the killer in the face again and rushed outside to greet her husband.

Henry strode to his wife and child while his friends dealt with an unconscious Jack Stryker.

Henry held his family tight in his arms, shaking from gratitude and relief. For a time they did not speak. Taylor put her head on his shoulder, one arm around her father and the other around her mother, and they stood on the dock that way.

They were safe, and they were together, and that was the only thing mattered in the world.

"I'm so sorry," Suzanne said to him, her blue eyes filled with hurt. Her hair was matted to her cheeks and streaked with mud and blood.

Henry put a finger to her lips and then kissed her.

"I never meant to hurt you," she said.

"I'm just glad you're both okay."

"The papers I sent you," she said. "I didn't mean it."

"Good," Henry said.

"Can we start over again? Someplace far away?"

"Whatever you like," Henry said. "Anything."

There was a splash as the men tossed Stryker into the water.

"I need to talk with this jackass," Henry said. "And we need to get the hell out of here."

Death isn't so bad, after all, Stryker thought. He was floating. That was nice. Everything was dark and he felt disembodied.

Then pain began to permeate his calm. Just the edges of it at first, a diffuse thing, until it became sharp and jagged, centered in his groin and sending howling, rolling waves throughout his body. He opened his eyes.

He *was* floating. He was on his back. Henry Wilkins peered down at him from the dock. There were other soldiers behind Wilkins.

Stryker flailed, and found he could not move his arms or his legs properly. He was bound. An orange life jacket kept his head above the water.

"We're going to have a conversation," Henry said, "about your bosses."

"I don't know anything," Stryker said.

"Let me tell you something," Henry replied reasonably, as if he were discussing the weather. "Old Man McCloud was a friend of mine. He's an odd bird. Was. One of his eccentricities being his taste in pets."

"What are you talking about?"

"See, McCloud's been out here for about thirty years. He got lonely. He had one friend here, though, by the name of Rocky Balboa."

"I told you I don't know anything. They used cutouts. Encrypted comms. There's nothing I can say you don't already know."

"Rocky is a fourteen-foot alligator," Henry went on. "McCloud fed him. The gator kept the sharks out of the channel, kept other gators away. It was like they had some kind of unspoken agreement. I've never seen anything like it. I passed old Rocky on the way in."

"You're going to kill me either way," Stryker said.

"True," Henry said, nodding down at him. "But there's dying and then there's *dying*."

Stryker floated in the water, trying to think past the pain devouring him. He was done. "Screw you," he gasped.

"See, what gators do is they bite you and roll you under the water. Then they carry you around for a while until you get soft and ripe."

Stryker slow blinked and clenched his jaw. "You'll make it quick?"

"Yes."

"In my ruck," he said. "An envelope. Numbers. I don't know what they mean. I took 'em from that guy. Oh fuck this hurts. Blackaby. One of them. In Houston."

"Good dog," Henry said, turning away.

"Wait! Shoot me. One soldier to another. You gave your word."

"It *might* be quick," Henry said. "Depends on how hungry Rocky is."

CHAPTER TWENTY-SIX

A Deeper Kind of Darkness

"Got it," Wallace said from inside the shack, holding up an envelope. "A little water damage, but not much. A page full of random numbers. I'm uploading it now."

"Any way we can get through to Colonel Bragg?" Henry said.

"No. They're dark. We're on our own. That's all right."

"Let's move out, then," Henry said.

"Why the rush?" McCoy said, slapping a mosquito. "It's getting to be dark."

"Maybe," Henry said. "But if Stryker was able to hack my friend's GPS system and figure out where we were going, so could the Directors. They might be coming for *him*."

McCoy arched his eyebrows. "Ah."

"Let's get squared away."

Henry wanted to be able to talk to Suzanne and relax. To say things that needed to be said. There wasn't any time, and he had that hunted feeling in him he'd come to know well.

Henry took whatever fuel he could find from the skiff and the boat Suzanne had used to get to McCloud's camp.

The bodies of his friends were still sprawled on the deck of the boat, Beowulf too. He focused on the tanks, promising to come back to this spot when it was all over and say some words and prayers.

"We've got a lot of weight in the boat," Henry said, backing out of the inlet. "There's going to be some pushing."

Wallace smiled grimly. "Through the blood and the mud and the crud."

Henry was more concerned with a drone strike than anything else. With the armistice in place and the unraveling conspiracy public, he hoped the Directors would have limited resources now. If they came, knowing where to look, there would be no escape. Thermal imaging would reveal heat signatures through any canopy of leaves or cover of darkness.

When he heard the whine of boat motors, he was tense. Either help was on the way, or they were in for a hell of a fight.

*

"I hear it too," Carlos said. "What do you think?"

"Suzanne, take Taylor. Now. Head back to the shack. Grab that scuba gear and get under water, deep as you can. Stay down."

"They're coming right for us," Wallace said. "More than one boat."

"Let them come. Set up an ambush. I'm going to block this channel with the boat."

Suzanne and Taylor splashed over the side.

"You want me to set up the SAW at the shack?" McCoy said. "Direct line of fire. I can light them up when they push through."

"No. If they've got RPGs they'll hit the shack first. Let's stick to the mangroves and keep our heads down. We put them in a kill zone when they come all the way through. They can't know how many of us there are."

"Roger that," McCoy said.

"Were you serious about that alligator?" Wallace said.

241

"Yeah. I didn't really see him around, though."

"That doesn't make me feel better."

"Least of our worries. I'm thinking he'll snack on Frosty before he comes after one of us, though."

Henry pushed the boat so that it blocked the channel. The tide was slack, but it would turn soon. They split up, each soldier selecting a spot far underneath the hanging branches. Henry scooped up muck and smeared it over his face.

As he looked around the pond, he could not see his comrades. Suzanne and Taylor were out of sight as well.

The sound of the engines ceased.

*

The boat eased back from the narrow mouth, slowly enough that it might have been pushed by the wind. Henry knew otherwise.

Henry could see two commandos at the stern of the craft. More coming behind them.

The soldiers waded ahead, weapons above the water. Henry put his sights on the nearest one, waiting. He thumbed the firing selector to semiautomatic. *A fight, then.*

He counted six men.

They crossed the pond, communicating with hand signals. They were spreading out.

Squeeze.

The stock of the assault rifle bucked against his shoulder. He put two rounds into the head of a man less than fifty feet away. A cloud of pink mist in the air, and a wash of blood on the side of the boat.

Gunfire erupted from the perimeter as Carlos, McCoy, and Wallace found targets.

McCoy, on the M249, cut a swath through the mangroves, branches and leaves falling under the torrent of hot metal.

The gunfire ceased. Blue smoke hung over the water and there was the smell of battle. Henry saw three bodies floating facedown.

He headed into the deeper water of the channel until it became too shallow to swim. He eased forward, digging in with his knees. He was exposed. He crawled ahead through the slime, his movements slow and deliberate to reduce the splashes, his elbows deep in the mud.

He did not see the boats the attackers used right away. They'd stowed a pair of inflatable Zodiacs under the canopy.

Two boats. Four men to a boat, most likely.

He scanned the shadows for movement.

Behind him urgent gunfire erupted again. He focused on what was in front of him.

A brief flash of metal caught the sun. Henry zeroed in, firing three rapid shots.

Pain rippled through his right arm and he heard another shot, close and off to the side. A round punched through his bicep and slapped the stock of his weapon, tearing it from his grasp.

Henry pushed himself backwards, reaching for the assault rifle. Another round sent up a geyser of water inches from his face.

He wished he had a grenade. He kept backing up, searching the swamp for the enemy. His right arm was on fire and his hand and forearm were slick with blood. He sought his weapon with shaking, urgent hands. *There.*

Another round snapped over his head. He caught the muzzle flash.

He switched to full auto, brought the weapon up to his shoulder. His arm was shaking and his hands were clumsy.

He fired two bursts as he retreated. His weapon jammed. He tried to reach for his sidearm, but his arm was turning into a dead thing. He was faint from blood loss. The round might have nicked an artery.

Wallace hauled him backward with strong hands, pulling him into deeper water.

"He's hit," Wallace said. "McCoy, on me. Carlos, take Wilkins to the shack. Check on Suzanne."

"Copy that."

"Enemy at three o'clock," Henry mumbled, darkness pushing down at the edges of his vision.

Moments later, Henry heard the sound of explosions and the whump of an M203 grenade launcher, but that was the last thing he heard.

*

Suzanne, holding Taylor by the wrist, took the regulator from her own mouth and put it to Taylor's, their faces inches apart.

The water stung her eyes and even this close, Taylor was a blur.

Suzanne held her breath while Taylor breathed through the reg. Air bubbles burbled around them.

Gunfire rolled over the water, muffled, lethal, and angry, and she could hear the zip of rounds cutting through the water. A hissing thing.

She squeezed Taylor's arm to let her know it was time to let Suzanne breathe. Her chest burned. Taylor squeezed back.

Suzanne took the regulator from her child's mouth, hating herself for it. Taylor liked to use scuba gear in the pool, and she'd stay at the bottom using a SNUBA rig for half an hour. This was different.

Suzanne had taught Taylor how to buddy breathe in clear, clean water. Now it was life and death. Taylor had to stay calm. Panic would kill them both.

Something brushed against her foot. Suzanne froze, aware of the bubbles tickling her face. She could not see through the murk.

There was a lull in the gunfire. It had been going on an eternity, it seemed.

What just bumped my leg?

She put the reg back in Taylor's mouth, and still holding the child with her left hand, reached behind her to remove the .38 from her shorts.

She pulled Taylor slowly to the surface, gasping for air.

Five feet away, a soldier wearing jungle fatigues crept around the dock of the shack, a submachine gun in his hands. He spun to face her.

Suzanne shot him in the neck.

He toppled backward, dropping his weapon and reaching for his throat. Suzanne took two steps forward and pulled the trigger until it made clicking sounds. Lifeless eyes stared back at her, and the soldier slipped into the water.

She hauled Taylor onto the dock, leaving the tank in the water, and picked up the dead soldier's weapon.

Another wave of gunfire echoed over the water, and she crawled into the shack on her belly.

"Stay low to the floor," she whispered to Taylor. "Keep right in front of me."

They crawled under the table and Suzanne kept the weapon pointed at the front door. There were explosions and then there was no more fighting.

"Suzanne?" she heard Carlos say.

"In here."

"Let's get out of this shithole," he said.

"Henry?"

"He's hit. Lost a lot of blood."

The enemy attackers were all dead.

They piled into the Zodiacs the commandos used because the Fish and Game boat was riddled with bullet holes.

Henry was unconscious for the journey; Carlos applied a field dressing to the wound.

Suzanne put her husband's head in her lap. His face was an unnatural gray and his breathing was shallow. He moaned in his sleep sometimes. Taylor held his hand. It seemed unfair. Unjust. *He can't die now. Not after all of this.*

"Come on, Ranger," Suzanne whispered in his ear. "*Fight.*"

It was dark when they pulled into Flamingo.

Stryker faded in and out of consciousness. He thought he heard gunfire, but that might have been his imagination. Maybe it was thunder.

He floated. Sometimes the pain was worse than others, and he could retreat into a deeper kind of darkness.

Mosquitoes and sand fleas bit his face and crawled on his exposed skin. He opened his eyes again and saw the Milky Way. So many stars. He tried to count them to keep his mind from focusing on the agony he was in. He could feel fish nibbling away at his fingers. Something was crawling up is pant leg. Maybe a crab.

The night was alive with mysterious splashes, skittering sounds in the mangroves, and the call of insects. He was terrified.

His hands were bound behind his back. *Maybe,* he thought *I can push back to the dock and get a knife and cut loose.*

He tried to raise his head enough to look around. The dock was gone. The tide had taken him and he was floating somewhere in the middle of a channel. He kicked down with feet bound tight, trying to feel the bottom, waves of pain rolling through his body. The water was deep here.

Near dawn, he felt a sharp pain in his calf and something jerked him under water. He bobbed at the surface for a time. A black fin cut the water, just the tip visible.

Sharks fed on Jack Stryker. They were juveniles, three and four feet long. They took small pieces from his buttocks and legs, while he screamed and thrashed. He was weak with blood loss. The sharks let him go, though, and he was relieved for a moment.

The alligator glided through the glassy water leaving a soundless wake behind a sinuous tale, cold-blooded eyes locked on Stryker.

When the eyes slipped below the water, Stryker's blood was ice in his veins. He knew death was coming, and there was nothing he could do to stop it.

His legs in a toothy vise, he gulped air and water at the same time and went down into the black water, rolling and rolling until the pain and darkness were all one thing and it lasted for an eternity.

CHAPTER TWENTY-SEVEN

Redemption Song

The July sun slipped below the western bank of the St. Johns River. The glassy water shimmered orange and pink, and Bob Marley's "Redemption Song" floated down the dock from the patio speakers.

"I had a bite," Taylor said. Her bare feet dangled over the side of the wooden dock.

Henry grinned at Taylor. "Better check your line," he said.

She cranked her little blue rod, and the hook came up clean, bereft of the shrimp Taylor put there.

"He got me," she said.

Henry heard footsteps and felt the dock shudder. He glanced over his shoulder.

"Margarita?" Suzanne said, armed with a pair of glasses clinking with ice. Her hair was short now, and dyed red. She was beautiful and radiant, and Henry felt his heart swell when he saw her, a feeling of amazement and gratitude in him.

"You read my mind."

She sat down next to him and handed him a chilled glass. The lights of downtown Jacksonville winked beyond the Buckman Bridge.

"I like it here," she said, slipping an arm around his waist.

"Me too."

"Tell me honestly," she said. "Do you miss it?"

"Are you joking?"

"Come on, Henry, I *know* you, remember? Be honest."

"I miss the brotherhood," he admitted. "I'd rather be here with you and Taylor."

"I've seen you training," she said. "If you're thinking about going back, you can tell me. It's all right."

"I'm just trying not to get fat," Henry joked. "A little bit of PT is good for a man of my advancing years."

"Uh-huh."

"Seriously," Henry said. "I'm done. After what we've been through as a family? No. I'm content being a househusband." He chuckled.

The home they lived in was a gift, along with new identities, from Colonel Bragg. Henry did not ask how the colonel had pulled it off. He received a handsome check every month in the mail. Suzanne was halfway through with another novel, this one a serious piece of literature, written under a pen name.

"Is that who you really are, though?" Suzanne said. "A kept man?" She kissed him on the forehead.

"It is now," he replied. "It's not who I've been. But, a man can learn from his mistakes, can't he?"

"Sure," she mused. "I'm not sure you made that many mistakes, though. Maybe it only felt that way. Maybe that was the mistake. Feeling like that. I blamed you, you blamed yourself. You were doing what you thought was right. We lost each other along the way."

"I made plenty of mistakes. It would take an act of Congress to pry me off this dock, though."

They both laughed.

The war was over, but Congress was still a joke. Politicians squabbled and jockeyed for power and position as they always had. The American people had less tolerance for that now than before, though.

At the Constitutional Convention, a new group of leaders emerged, replacing many of the old guard. Healing was a slow process.

While the nation remained divided over many issues, the people recognized war was not the solution. Grassroots rallies and patriotic protests sprang up all over the country in the immediate aftermath of the fighting. A lasting peace was emerging, not because of the politicians, but because of the wisdom and strength of the American people. A nation built on compromise and values, remembering its roots.

"The world is still a dangerous place," Suzanne said. "When the Pack comes calling again, and they will, what are you going to do?"

"I'll say I've done my duty." He said it. He wanted to believe it.

War in Europe looked imminent. The news was depressing, and Henry generally avoided it. So far, it was angry rhetoric. The United States, reeling from self-inflicted losses, had little will to engage in another war. There were rumors that the nuclear blasts that leveled Washington and San Francisco were not the work of domestic terrorists. China and Russia denied any involvement. Henry felt safer knowing that people like Colonel Bragg were tracking down the perpetrators. Sometimes in the middle of the night, Henry would walk out onto the dock and wonder what his friends were doing at that moment, wishing that he was back in the fight.

The Directors were on the run, at least. Hounded by hackers, Interpol, the CIA and FBI, the shadowy group of criminals who had inflicted untold pain upon the world for personal gain faced the wrath of an angry world. Their names and faces were plastered over the news all around the globe. Two of them were tried, convicted, and after a speedy trial, executed.

*

A crisp, black, sport utility vehicle bounced down the long dirt driveway, sending up plumes of dust and pebbles as it came on.

Abraham saw it coming. He wished he didn't but there it was. A dull ache spread from his heart through his limbs while he rocked in his chair with a glass of lemon iced tea.

The glass was slick in his hand and threatened to fall. He stood up, aching. Bent with the yearning and the earning.

Two neatly folded flags. Damn them.

Abraham wept.

*

"Well," Suzanne said. "I'll enjoy you while I have you. Happy Fourth of July."

They sat on the dock together until the stars emerged and the air was sweet and smelled like hope.

Fireworks exploded across the river, red, white, and blue, stark and brilliant against the darkness.

ABOUT THE AUTHOR

Sean grew up in Miami and was blessed with parents who gave him a great love for reading. When he's not writing, he can be found fishing, hiking in the woods, or hanging out with his family in North Florida.